Insatiable

Books by Morgan Hawke

Kiss of the Wolf

Insatiable

Sexy Beast III
(with Kate Douglas and Lacy Danes)

Insatiable

Morgan Hawke

APHRODISIA

KENSINGTON BOOKS

http://www.kensingtonbooks.com

APHRODISIA BOOKS are published by

Kensington Publishing Corp.
119 West 40th Street
New York, NY 10018

All Kensington Titles, Imprints, and Distributed Lines are available at special quantity discounts for bulk purchases for sales promotions, premiums, fund-raising, and educational or institutional use.

Special book excerpts or customized printings can also be created to fit specific needs. For details, write or phone the office of the Kensington special sales manager: Kensington Publishing Corp., 119 West 40th Street, New York, NY 10018, attn: Special Sales Department, Phone: 1-800-221-2647.

Aphrodisia and the A logo Reg. U.S. Pat & TM Off.

ISBN-13: 978-0-7582-1547-5
ISBN-10: 0-7582-1547-9

First Kensington Trade Paperback Printing: December 2010

10 9 8 7 6 5 4 3 2 1

Printed in the United States of America

For Tina H.,
thank you for your guidance and generosity.
You will always be my very first.

1

The Orient Express—*en route to Prague from Vienna*
One hour after sunset

"Might I have your company for the night?"

"Huh?" Elaine glanced up from her belly-down sprawl across the private compartment's plush banquette sofa. The art deco lamp directly over her was on, but the polished cherry-wood walls made the rest of the antique Pullman car very dark. She blinked. *Where did he come from?*

A tall man, in a nearly floor-length black leather coat, stood just inside the deep shadow of her compartment's door. His hands hung loose at his sides. "Pardon the intrusion." His voice was soft, low, and velvety, with a touch of an exotic Eastern European lilt. He tilted his head toward the closed door. "I did knock, and your door was unlocked."

Elaine bit her lip. She hadn't heard the knock. Hell, she hadn't heard the door to her train compartment open, either. Damn it, she had to start remembering to lock that door. She sighed. *Too late now.* "I'm sorry, my best friend says a bomb could go off when I'm drawing and I'd miss it."

"An artist's concentration, I understand." He stepped into her pool of light. Blue highlights gleamed in the unrelieved blackness of his hair. He wore it combed straight back from the deep peak of his brow, hinting that his hair was long and tied back. Midnight-dark eyes peered at her from under straight black brows. Sharp cheekbones and a strong jawline defined his aggressively masculine face, but the lush fullness of his mouth and the pale ivory color of his skin belonged in a neoclassical painting.

Wow, GQ *magazine must be missing a model.* She had to close her mouth. The man's face was *that* freaking gorgeous. "I'm sorry, what was it you wanted?"

One corner of his mouth lifted, hinting at amusement. He clasped his hands before him. "Your company, for the night."

"My company?" She blinked. That couldn't be what it sounded like. "For what, exactly?"

"Sex." His slightly amused expression didn't change.

"Sex." Her heart slammed in her chest. *Danger, danger, danger . . .* She swallowed. "I see." Good God in Heaven, this guy wanted sex? With *her*? Was he out of his mind? She wasn't un-attractive; she'd never had a problem getting dates. Her gener-ous bustline, more than generous butt, and small waist drew the guys out of the woodwork, but this guy was just too pretty to even consider someone who didn't come straight from Holly-wood.

"I'm flattered, really, but . . ." She pushed up from the bench and her coiled hair teetered precariously on top of her head. She made a quick grab for the chopsticks jammed in the twisted knot of her long dark-blond mane. Several of her charcoals rolled from her sketchbook to land on the floor with the tiniest sound of breaking glass.

"Oh, damn . . ." She abandoned her hair and leaned over the side of the banquette sofa, reaching for the fallen charcoals. Her bare foot struck the wall under the night-black window, and three of the vampire paperbacks by her knee were knocked to the floor.

She groaned in annoyance. *It figures. . . . A cute guy, and I am an instant klutz.* Lifting her feet carefully over the backpack that hogged the far end of the sofa, she turned on her belly to get her feet on the floor. Not the sexiest move in the world. *Just call me "Grace".* She hunched down to gather the fallen books and broken charcoals.

The man crouched at her side and collected one of her fallen vampire books. He scanned the back cover, and a black brow rose. "What interesting reading material."

Elaine stood and her cheeks warmed. "Yes, I read trashy romances." She leaned over the sofa to stuff her charcoals and her other two books into her backpack. "It's a girl thing."

"This is a romance?"

"A *trashy* romance—it has sex in it." Elaine glanced over her shoulder and froze.

He was still crouched, but the book was forgotten in his hand. He was focused entirely on the curve of her jean-clad butt less than a foot from his nose. His midnight stare lifted from her butt to capture her gaze. "Then you like sex?"

Elaine swallowed the lump in her throat. *Oh boy, I really stepped in that one.* She stood upright slowly, struggling to gather what dignity she could, then turned around to face him. "Yes, I like sex." It was too late to deny it now. She tugged the hem of her thick white cable-knit sweater down over her hips and butt. She held out her hand. "My book, please?"

He rose to his feet in one smooth effortless motion and held the book slightly out of reach. He was a full head taller, and the bulk of his leather coat crowded the small compartment with his presence. "May I have you for the night?"

Elaine was forced to look up to see his face. The back of her knees were against the seat, and her nose was less than six inches from his broad chest. She took a deep breath. The warm masculine scent of leather caught her attention. He smelled good. He smelled . . . sexy. Her libido awoke with a lazy curl of warm interest.

She turned her head slightly away and shivered. *Down, girl.* "Look, I don't have sex with people I don't know." *No matter how devastatingly cute they are.* She set her hands on her hips. "You haven't even told me your name."

His black brows lifted along with the corner of his mouth. "Pardon me." He stepped back and held out his empty hand, palm up. "I am Aramis."

Elaine wiped her damp palms down her hips and frowned a little. Where had she heard that name before? *Oh yes . . .* A small smile inched its way across her lips. "Aramis, as in *The Three Musketeers?*"

He lowered his hand and his gaze, then let out a soft sigh. "Surrounded by books, I should have guessed you would know."

"Well, Aramis, any friend of Alexandre Dumas is a friend of mine." She grinned and held out her hand. "I'm Elaine."

His head lifted and a smile flashed briefly across his lips. His slightly cool fingers and smooth palm closed around her smaller hand. "Elaine." He turned her hand palm down and gracefully bowed over her knuckles. "I am charmed." He remained bowed but lifted his gaze. A breathtaking smile bloomed across his full mouth, and his eyes narrowed slightly with sudden intent. "Such eyes—the color of new leaves. Do you have any idea how lovely you are?"

Yikes! Elaine sucked in a sharp breath. *They should bottle that smile and label it "raw sex." They'd make a mint.* "Thank you." She swallowed. "You're very handsome yourself."

Aramis straightened, but held on to her hand. "Now that we

have been introduced . . ." He tossed the paperback onto the sofa behind her and reached out to collect her other hand. He focused his gaze on hers, and his smile disappeared. "I should very much like to have your company for the night."

Elaine rolled her eyes. He was certainly persistent.

Aramis lifted her hands and pulled slightly, forcing her to take a step closer. "Am I not agreeable to you?"

She lowered her gaze and twisted her hands slightly. He couldn't be serious?

His fingers tightened. "Elaine?"

She looked up at him.

His dark eyes were dilated wide and his mouth tight. "Please." His voice was barely a whisper. "Let me have you for this night?"

Elaine felt her heart slam in her chest. He was serious—really, really serious. A bead of sweat trickled down her back. *Is it getting warm in here, or is it just me?* She licked her dry lips. "Aramis, I don't just sleep with anybody who wants me."

"That is . . . reassuring." A smile flashed across his lips. "However, I should like it if you made an exception."

"This is all very sudden. . . ." Elaine felt a tiny shiver of nervous amusement. *Hello? Can you say, "heroine in a Gothic romance"?* "May I think about it for a little bit?" *Can I have a little breathing space while we're at it?*

"Of course." Aramis lowered his gaze, released her hands, and stepped back with a sigh. "May I stay while you . . . think about it?"

Elaine smiled. "I wasn't going to throw you out, I just wanted to get . . . used to the idea."

"I see." His head lifted and he smiled, just a little. "May I remove my coat?"

Elaine shook her head. *Aramis and his politeness . . .* "Sure." She turned to collect the paperback lying on the seat and stuffed it in her backpack. "Remove whatever you like." She set her backpack on the floor and picked up her abandoned sketchbook.

A warm chuckle came from behind her. "With pleasure."

Elaine flinched. *Maybe that wasn't such a good thing to say?* She turned back, with the sketchbook clutched before her.

With his back to her, Aramis let the heavy black leather slide from his broad shoulders. He wore a creamy white sweater similar to hers, only his was obviously real cable-knit Irish wool. The long tail of his night-dark hair fell straight and sleek toward a waist that was obscenely narrow. He took two steps toward the door and set his coat on the hook. The slight motion showed quite plainly that his pants were tailored closely, and that he had an ass to die for.

Elaine's nipples tightened in blatant interest; moisture dampened her panties. She had to sit down before she fell down. *God in Heaven, he's freaking beautiful.* And he wanted to sleep with *her*? On second thought, she realized a lot of guys wanted to sleep with her—they just didn't want to be seen in public with someone built like they belonged in the Victorian era.

In two long, unnervingly sensual strides, Aramis stood before her.

Elaine had to remember to breathe. He didn't just look like sex, he moved like sex. The rich scent of leather and maleness drifted over her. She shivered slightly. *God, he smells like sex.*

"May I see?"

"Huh?" Elaine forcibly dragged her mind out from under her libido. "I'm sorry, see what?"

Aramis tapped a finger against her tightly clutched sketchbook. "Your drawings."

She lifted her shoulder just a little. "If you like, but . . ."

"I'd like." Aramis smiled and plucked the book from her fingers. "But?" He turned and sat down on the sofa next to her.

Elaine winced. "But I'm not very good."

"Is that so?" He opened the large book, spreading it across his lap and over onto her knee.

The book had been new when she brought it overseas with her to Rome. Her sketches began with page after page of museum and gallery statuary renderings, then fountains and monuments. A few grave statues were tossed in, here and there, with the occasional portrait. The two-inch-thick book was three-quarter full, and she was already on her third box of fine charcoals.

He leaned close to her, their shoulders and knees in warm contact, while he flipped the pages.

Embarrassed warmth filled Elaine's cheeks. Having Aramis looking at her sketches was more intimate than if he had been looking at her naked body. Displayed across his lap lay her very soul. . . . She rolled her eyes. *Okay, let's not get overly melodramatic here. They are just still life and statuary sketches, not nudes.* She bit back a smile. *Those* were in her other sketchbook.

Aramis stopped and ran his finger down a ragged paper edge, close to the spine. "There is a page missing."

"Anthony, one of the art students I met in Rome, took it from my book when I wasn't looking. It was his portrait, so I understand why he took it."

"He stole it?"

"No big deal." Elaine shrugged. "Anthony got what he deserved later, when he tried to pass it off as his work."

Aramis frowned. "He told someone that your drawing was his work?"

"Yep." Elaine grinned. "Too bad he couldn't actually draw

portraits that well. From what I understand, it got him into a lot of trouble when the drawing master interviewed him for an apprenticeship."

"I would assume so." Aramis raised a brow; his mouth curled into a cynical smile. "A good drawing master always asks for a demonstration."

Elaine chuckled. "Anthony is actually a good artist, just not for portraits."

"He should not have tried to claim another's skill." Aramis turned the page and stopped at one of her better portraits. The young man had been watching something just past her shoulder, and a slight breeze had tousled his hair while she sketched. She had tossed in a slight rendering of the Renaissance fountain behind him, just to give the portrait theme.

Aramis frowned slightly. "I'm afraid I do not understand."

Elaine looked down at the portrait. "Do not understand what?"

Aramis glanced at her with a quick smile. "I do not understand how you could possibly think that you are not good."

She felt heat creeping into her cheeks. "Okay, even *I* know that picture is good. But for every good one, there's about a dozen that are dismal failures."

He raised a black brow. "Indeed? Show me what you consider a failure."

She looked up at him and bit down on a nervous smile. "Do I have to?"

Aramis pushed the book onto her lap. "I insist on proof."

She groaned just a little and flipped to her last sketch, the portrait he had interrupted. The face just wasn't coming out right.

"Ah . . ." He frowned at the page, then turned to face her, his lips barely a kiss away. "This young man does not look drawn from life, imaginary perhaps?"

"Fictional." Elaine reached out to smudge a line with her finger. Nope, the picture was hopeless. "I was trying to draw a character from a book."

"But"—he frowned at the sketch—"the proportions are off on some of the features in this one. The ears, the eyes . . . this does not even look human."

"That's because he's not." Elaine hunched her shoulders. "He's supposed to be a vampire."

Aramis stilled. "Indeed?" His voice was barely a breath.

2

Elaine could feel the tension in his thigh and shoulder where they had touched. Her heart began to hammer.

Aramis's gaze focused tightly on hers. "You have a fascination for vampires?" The word "vampire" was curiously exotic in his lilting Eastern European accent. He turned to gaze at her with intense yet hooded eyes. "The soulless damned?"

" 'The soulless damned'?" Elaine felt a nervous chuckle forcing its way up. "Well, that all depends on whose story you're reading."

His brows rose. "You do not think they are the soulless damned?"

Elaine coughed to keep from laughing out loud. "I really wouldn't know. I've never met one."

"So you would reserve judgment on a creature of the dead?" Aramis lowered his chin and tilted his head toward her drawing. "Is that not a trifle . . . naive?"

"You're sure vampires are creatures of the dead, huh?" Elaine crossed her arms under her breasts and lifted her chin. "Have you met one?"

His black eyes held her gaze. "Perhaps I am one."

Her heart stopped for a single beat; then her pulse leaped in her throat. Suspicion ignited a spark of temper. *If he thinks pretending to be a vampire will get him into my pants, he better think again!* A smile as cold as ice curled her lip as she narrowed her eyes. "You breathe, and you're warm, so you're not dead. Does this make you merely the soulless damned?"

Aramis closed her sketchbook carefully, lifted it from their laps, and turned away to set her book against the wall behind him. "There are those who believe that drinking blood is enough to damn one."

"Oh please . . . ." Elaine rolled her eyes and grinned. "They obviously haven't been around the fetish crowd. Lots of people do bloodletting, and they aren't damned or even vampires. They just think it's . . . stimulating."

"Do you?" Aramis turned to her. His eyes were pits of darkness so large that the whites were nearly gone.

Elaine's breath stopped in her throat. No human being had eyes like that. She'd seen too many Goth kids in spooky contacts to know that she was looking at the real thing. *Good God in Heaven, what if he is telling the truth? What if he really is . . . a vampire?*

Aramis turned his whole body to face her, his bent knee brushing hers. "Do *you* think bloodletting is . . . stimulating?" The gleam of long upper incisors and smaller lower canines showed while he spoke.

Fangs? Elaine bit down on her bottom lip. Those were not dental caps. She had a set of porcelain vampire fangs made by a dental assistant. His were definitely real.

So how the hell did one answer that kind of question to someone who might actually be a vampire? She licked her lips. *Oh, what the hell. . . .* She took a deep breath. "Yeah, as long as I'm not scarred, maimed, or killed in the process."

Aramis raised a brow over an inhumanly dark eye. "It does not frighten you, to have someone shed your blood?"

Elaine gave him a slight shrug. "It's the fear that makes it exciting." She narrowed her eyes at him. "But blood-play is not something you do with someone you don't trust."

Aramis chuckled. "I should say not."

Elaine's heart slowed to a more sedate panic. Weird eyes and long teeth aside, the laugh made him seem less alarming, less . . . alien. "Out of curiosity, I thought vampires only had upper teeth?"

"All predators have both." Aramis looked down, hiding his eyes. "Do I frighten you?"

Do you? Elaine glanced at the back of the couch. "I think 'intimidated' would be a better word."

Aramis lifted his gaze to hers and his brows dipped. "How so?"

Elaine lifted her brow and gave him a crooked smile. "Well, you did come on a little strong with the sex."

His brows rose and his eyes widened; then he scowled. "I am a vampire. I drink blood. This does not frighten you?"

Elaine stared him straight in the eye. "Are you going to kill me?"

He jerked away and sat with his arms folded across his chest. "I do not kill."

Elaine shrugged. "I didn't think so."

He turned sharply to look at her with wide eyes. "What did you say?"

Elaine had to bite her lip to keep from laughing. "Oh, come on! You're way too polite to do something as vulgar as murder."

Aramis glanced to the side and frowned. "So I am too polite to frighten you." He gave her a tight smile. "Should I be offended, or not?"

"Relax." Elaine patted his knee. "You're still sexy."

Aramis raised his brow and gave her a thoroughly cynical smile. "You think so?"

Elaine winced. *Me and my big mouth.* She sighed. "Yes, Aramis, you are incredibly sexy. I don't think I've ever met a sexier man than you." She smiled. "Feel better now?"

His smile faded. "Would you kiss me?"

"Uh . . ." Elaine focused on his lush mouth. Everything in her body leaped to aggravated erotic attention. He might be a vampire, or he might be something even scarier, but he still had the most kissable mouth she'd ever seen in her life. She licked her lips. "Sure."

His eyes widened just a hair; then his brows dipped. "You would?" He lowered his arms and turned to face her. "As I am now?"

She smiled. "I like vampires, remember?"

Aramis turned to sit facing her with one knee up on the sofa. "Elaine, I should very much like . . ." His gaze focused on her mouth and he licked his lips. "Will you kiss me?"

Kiss him? Oh, hell yeah! Elaine brought both knees up onto the sofa to kneel in front of him.

He watched her, his eyes wide, his mouth slightly open. Clearly unsure of what she intended.

Elaine smiled. "It would be my pleasure." She leaned forward, setting one hand on the back of the sofa for balance. Her lips brushed his. *Warmth, breath, velvety softness . . .* Her eyes drifted closed and her tongue swept the fullness of his bottom lip. She felt the edge of one long tooth. It wasn't sharp, exactly, but it was pointed.

His mouth opened against hers. He released a sigh.

She dipped her tongue into his mouth and brushed against his tongue fleetingly, then again to explore. He tasted vaguely

14

of expensive coffee and, oddly, of vanilla. He smelled of rich leather, a little of warm wool, but also of aroused male. Her nipples tightened. She pressed deeper to taste more of him.

He shifted on the sofa while his tongue parried hers, teasing her with light strokes. He released a soft yearning moan and leaned back.

She released the sofa and reached for his shoulders to get closer. One knee jammed against the back of the sofa, the other precariously perched on the edge, framing his knees. His sweater was warm under her palms, and the muscle hard under the thick wool. She pressed her mouth to his, seeking a deeper kiss.

His hands cupped her hips and slowly drew her toward him, his tongue sliding in a wet, sensual flirting dance against hers. He nipped gently at her bottom lip with his long teeth.

God in Heaven, the boy knows how to kiss! Her hands slid around his neck, her fingers tangling in the silk of his black mane. Her knees spread wide to straddle his thighs, and her breasts pressed against the broad wall of his chest.

His fingers slid up and around her waist, his hands pressing at the small of her back. He angled his mouth, pressing firmly, his tongue stroking boldly, tasting her, encouraging her to kiss him the same way.

She stroked his tongue while he stroked hers. *Heat, hunger, urgency...* A small moan escaped her throat. Her thighs tightened around his.

His arms closed around her waist, pulling her tight against his body.

She could feel the hard length of his erection pressing against the seam of her jeans. Her nipples peaked to hard, hot points against the tender irritation of her lace bra. Moisture dampened her panties. She groaned and pressed into him, nipping at his lips and tongue.

Aramis fell backward with a small gasp, his body unfolding to lay full-length on the sofa.

Elaine sprawled on top of him, straddling his hips. The chopsticks fell from her hair, and her dark honey mane uncoiled to tumble down around her hips. She pushed up, her hands splayed on his chest. She shoved the hair back from her face and grinned. "Oops."

"Oops, indeed!" Aramis grinned from among the cushions and reached up to coil a lock of her mane around his finger. "You have me in a compromising position." He chuckled. "Do you plan to ravish me?" He lifted his knees, pressing his cock up against her crotch and her clit.

Carnal heat seared her, and her core clenched with demanding appetite. *God, he feels so good.* She rocked her hips, rubbing against him. Tension coiled with delicious ferocity and a small groan escaped. "You know, that doesn't sound like a half-bad idea."

"Excellent!" He folded his arms behind his head and smiled. "I am ready."

She choked on a laugh. "Eager to be ravished, are we?"

Aramis leaned up on his elbows and grinned at her. "It has been a long time since I was ravished and thoroughly debauched." He raised a brow at her. "You have some experience at this, I assume?"

"I've done some ravishing." She bit her lip. "I don't know about debauchery."

"No?" He rolled his eyes and collapsed, lying limp beneath her. "I am deflated." He sighed dramatically.

She blinked at the unusual word. "Do you mean 'defeated'?"

"No, *deflated.*" He glanced from side to side, scowling. "No, you are right. That is not correct. Ah . . ." He looked her straight in the eye and gave her a tight smile. "Disappointed."

" 'Disappointed'?" She sat up with her hands on her hips. "What do you mean *disappointed*?"

He raised his brows and pursed his lips in a small pout. "If I am going to be ravished, I should like to be debauched as well."

She crossed her arms over her breasts and lifted a brow. "I can do kinky, I don't know about debauchery."

"Oh, that is too bad." Abruptly he pushed up, sitting with his knees raised and his hands on the sofa behind him for support. "Perhaps you should let me ravish and debauch you?"

She lowered her chin and raised a brow. "I am sure you have tons of experience ravishing women."

Aramis smiled. "And debauchery."

She rolled her eyes. "Oh, of course."

"In fact"—Aramis pushed forward, forcing her back, until he sat up completely, while she had to fall back onto her hands to stay upright—"I am something of an expert at both."

Elaine swallowed. "You don't say?" Her heart began to pound with increasing speed.

"Now"—his eyes narrowed and he smiled, showing the full length of his feral teeth—"will you let me have you for the night?"

3

Elaine shivered and nibbled on her bottom lip and stared up at the vampire. "I suppose it's a little late to say no?" According to the howling uproar in her body, it was way beyond too late. Her panties were soaked through to her jeans from excitement.

Aramis pressed forward onto his knees, driving her back. "Much too late." He licked his lips, and flames flickered deep in the heart of his eyes. "I confess that I am quite desperate to have you."

Pressed back, she fell beneath him onto the sofa cushions, with her knees splayed open, framing his hips. Fear mixed with excitement in a boiling morass of unbearable erotic tension. She swallowed. "Um, just how desperate are we talking here?"

"I have a terrible hunger for you, Elaine." Aramis arched over her with his palms to either side of her head. "I would have all of you." His knees spread, urging hers to open, and lowered his hips. "All that can be taken." He came down on his elbows, his chest brushing her breasts. "All that can be possessed." His trapped cock pressed against her crotch in blatant demand. His smile tightened. "But I would have your willing consent before I partake."

Elaine could barely breathe past the pounding of her heart and the hot, wet throbbing in her core. "You're going to drink my blood?"

"Yes." Aramis lowered his mouth. "Only a little, and not all at once," he whispered against her lips. "I need your pleasure as much as, if not more than"—he turned his head and his lips brushed her cheek—"your blood." His lips caressed her ear. "Will you let me have you for the night, Elaine?" His hips ground hard against hers and he groaned.

Heat, fire, hunger . . . She writhed under him. Reckless passion stole her breath. "Yes," she whispered. "Yes, Aramis!"

His breath was hot against her ear. "All of you?" His hands slid under her sweater to brush her waist, his cool fingers drawing shivers from her fevered skin. "Every part that I desire?" His hands slid upward, shoving her sweater before him to expose her lace-covered breasts. "In every way that I desire?" His mouth descended, his tongue sweeping across her swollen nipples, wetting the lace; then he sucked and nipped on the aching flesh beneath it.

She wrapped her arms around his waist and arched, pressing up against his mouth while digging her heels into the cushions to grind up against him. "Oh God, yes!"

His head lifted. His eyes were narrowed to slits and his smile held pure masculine triumph. "Done."

Elaine blinked up at him through her sensual fog. His feral smile was unnerving. *Uh-oh . . .*

Aramis took her mouth in a ferociously possessive kiss.

Elaine moaned and writhed while her tongue parried his, her concerns washed away under a ruthless flood of carnal heat.

Aramis released her mouth with a smile. "At last." He sat upright, bringing her with him. "We shall share such pleasures, you and I." He turned to sit with his feet on the floor, Elaine astride his lap. "Disrobe. I would see you. All of you."

Elaine slid from his knees to stand on her bare feet. Her core throbbed with hunger, and her nipples ached. "Aramis . . ."

Aramis reached down to remove his shoes. "It is too late for regrets, Elaine." He lifted his chin and his smile tightened. "You already agreed—every part that I desire in any way I desire."

Elaine swallowed. She *had* agreed; she just hoped she hadn't done something supremely stupid. She caught the hem of her sweater and lifted it over her head; then she tossed it to the floor. What was a little blood, anyway? She'd done scarier things before. She reached behind and unfastened her black lace bra, releasing the round fullness of her breasts.

Aramis tossed his shoes toward the window and stared fixedly at her breasts. He licked his lips. "Very, very nice." He stood and jerked his sweater up and over his head, revealing a deep exquisitely defined chest, with dark erect nipples. His arms and belly were corded with muscle.

Elaine froze with her hands on the button of her jeans. *Whoa . . .* Those muscles did not look like they had been built in a gym, but rather through use. He looked like a professional fighter. The hair rose on the back of her neck. He could have raped her the moment he walked through her compartment door, and she would not have been able to stop him.

But he hadn't. He had taken the time to talk her into willing sex. Well, okay, he'd done a bit more than talk. That didn't change the fact that he had gone out of his way to get her hotter than she'd ever been. *Seduction . . .* She blinked. That's exactly what he had done; he'd seduced her. A small smile lifted her lips. Well, damn, here she was, back at being a heroine in a romance novel.

Aramis set his hands on his hips. "I am waiting."

Elaine looked away and opened her jeans. He was freaking gorgeous, and he obviously knew what he was doing. It had been forever since she'd been properly laid. What the hell, why *not* go for it? She pushed her jeans and panties down past her rounded hips and full bottom, then bent over to peel them from her legs. She tossed her jeans over to where her sweater lay, then faced him with her shoulders squared, and her chin lifted. "Okay, handsome, I'm naked. Your turn."

Aramis barked out a short laugh. "Now, who is eager?" His gaze drifted across her breasts, then down her belly to her neatly trimmed mound. "You are quite lovely." He opened the button of his trousers and the fly. "I shall very much enjoy having you." His pants dropped to the floor. From a nest of dark curls, his cock rose in a smooth arch to his navel. The broad head peeking from its sheath was flushed with excitement. His ball sack hung plump and ripe between muscular thighs. He stepped free and tossed his trousers to the side. He grasped his shaft and stroked it with slow deliberation. "Come here and kneel."

He wants a blow job. Why am I not surprised? Elaine released a breath and dropped to her knees at his feet. He might have the seduction thing down, but she had read a lot of erotica over the past few years. She had practiced a few of the more interesting things. *Let's see if I can surprise him.*

He pushed his shaft down toward her lips. "Your mouth." His voice was husky.

Elaine stared at the cock pointed at her and worked her mouth to generate saliva. He was big, thick and long. She was not going to be able to deep-throat that monster. That meant keeping her hands on him to make damn sure he didn't shove that thing deeper than she could handle. She licked both palms and reached out to smooth both wet palms along the warm length of his shaft from head to root. She pushed the sheath back to fully expose the blushing purple head.

He groaned and his mouth opened just a little.

Elaine's smile broadened. *Oh, he liked that, did he?* She leaned forward with her very wet tongue extended and twirled it around the top of his cock head. He tasted clean. She could smell the soap he'd used under the rich musk of male arousal. She widened the circling of her tongue until she stroked the flared edges, then took him deeper, and deeper, to the back of her throat. Her hands grasped the rest of his length extending the reach of her mouth. She pulled back slowly while sucking strongly. He slid from her mouth with the sound of wet suction.

Aramis rocked on his heels and gasped. "I have a strong suspicion that you are talented."

Elaine leaned back. "I read a lot." She opened her mouth and took him swiftly to the back of her throat. *Looks like he hasn't had a decent blow job in a while. Good.* Sucking strongly, she pulled back until he slid past her lips with another wet smack.

He choked. "You learned this from books?"

"Some of my books are really detailed." Elaine grinned. "Practice makes better." She took him back into her mouth, lashed her tongue under the shaft, and swallowed him deeper.

Aramis threw his head back and groaned. "Mother Night, ah!" His hips bucked reflexively, fucking her mouth in short jabs. "You are going to make me cum very swiftly."

Elaine smiled around the cock pumping in and out of her mouth. *That's what you think.* She closed one hand around the base of his shaft, pressing a thumb against the thick vein on the underside, right up against the start of his ball sack. At the same time, she used her other damp palm to stroke what she couldn't get into her mouth.

Aramis's mouth opened on a choking gasp, his hips thrusting. He leaned over her to grasp her shoulders and came up on his toes, pushing into her mouth at a frenzied pace. He moaned through clenched teeth.

Elaine felt a pulse against her thumb warning that he was about to come in her mouth. The little shit hadn't bothered to warn her. She applied just a tad more pressure and stopped the flow. *Nice try, buddy.*

Aramis dropped onto his heels, gasping and groaning. His whole body trembled with denied release.

Well aware that he was a lot more sensitive after his misfire, Elaine lashed the head of his cock unmercifully with her tongue.

Aramis gave a frustrated gasp and jerked back, pulling completely from her mouth.

Elaine widened her eyes and looked up at him with her best innocent expression. "What?"

His eyes were narrowed to slits, his cheeks flushed, and he panted for breath, but he smiled. "You are perhaps a bit too talented."

Elaine tilted her head, keeping her eyes wide, but her mouth tipped into a small smile. "Goodness, whatever do you mean by that?"

Aramis pointed a finger at her. "Do not move." He stepped past her to go to his coat, which hung by the door. He pulled the tie belt from the belt loops.

Elaine bit her bottom lip. *Uh-oh . . .*

He stepped behind her. "Give me your hands."

Elaine tucked her hands under her arms and hunched. "I don't want you to come in my mouth, Aramis."

"That is too bad, because I very much wish to. Give me your hands."

Elaine shivered. "Aramis—"

24

"Give me your hands, or I will take them. I will not be denied again."

Elaine lunged from the floor.

Aramis caught her around the waist, lifted her, and shoved her facedown on the sofa in half a breath.

Elaine yelped in surprise and twisted under him. "Hey! Cut that out!"

He chuckled and dodged her kicking feet, wresting her hands to the small of her back. "Oh no, since your hands are too talented to trust, you shall not have them." In two breaths, he had her wrists looped and bound behind her with the broad supple belt to his coat.

Elaine writhed in his hold and twisted her wrists. The knot was just out of finger reach. She was not going to be able to get it off. "Aramis, this isn't fair!"

"It is perfectly fair. You agreed to give yourself to me for the night. It is you who is not fair." Aramis levered her back onto her feet and turned her to face him, pulling her tight against his body. "Make no mistake, I will have you, in every way I desire." He caught her hair at the back of her head and took her mouth in a ruthless kiss.

Elaine fought the kiss, writhing against the sweat-slick muscles of his body, but her own excitement worked against her. She wanted him too badly. A small whimper escaped and she began to return his kiss.

Aramis pulled her head back and smiled. "Much better. Now, on your knees." He shoved.

Elaine dropped. She looked up at him, panting with need and a touch of fear. "I don't mind sucking your dick, but I don't want your cum in my mouth."

Aramis gripped his shaft and stroked the rigid length. "That is too bad, as I need you to drink it that I may feed properly on your blood." He caught the hair at the back of her head and pushed his cock toward her lips. "Open your mouth."

Elaine tried to turn her head.

"Elaine, please." His voice was patient, but his entire body was rigid and trembling.

Elaine focused on the cock, which was less than a breath from her lips. Damn it, it was only cum; it wasn't poisonous. But she was not going to swallow it if she could avoid it. She opened her mouth and took his hot shaft in. A bead of slightly salty moisture spread across her tongue. A tingle of warmth shivered through her, like the tingling buzz from fine whisky but without the numbness. It didn't taste bad; in fact, it tasted rather . . . interesting. She stroked her tongue across his cock head to taste more.

Aramis sighed. "Oh yes, blessed Night. . . ." His hands clenched in her hair and he thrust a little ways into her mouth. "Suck me, take me deep."

Elaine drew as much of him into her mouth as she could, but without her hands to stop him, he went deeper than she intended. Her throat closed slightly. She swallowed to clear it. She took him again, but again he slid just a bit too deep.

"Ah, yes . . ." Aramis groaned and began to pump his hips, fucking her mouth with increasing speed.

Elaine simply held the suction steady and used her tongue while he took her mouth. With his hands guiding her head, and her hands tied, she couldn't control his speed or his depth. His cock struck the back of her throat. She was forced to swallow between snatches of breath to keep from gagging.

His hands tightened in her hair and he rose up on his toes.

Elaine shivered. He was about to come. She spread her knees and tensed to turn away. She was not going to swallow if she could avoid it.

Aramis set a hand on her shoulder and shoved her down

lower, jerking her head back by the hair. He arched over her and shoved his cock straight down her throat. "I come," he choked out.

Her nose pressed into his belly, Elaine couldn't take a breath past the cock deep in her throat. Her throat closed tightly and a whimper escaped her.

Aramis choked and shuddered. "Drink, Elaine. Drink me."

Hot liquid gushed deep in her throat. She moaned and shuddered in panic, unable to breathe and unable to stop him from pouring straight into her stomach.

"Yes . . . ah!" Aramis pulled from her throat.

Elaine fell back onto the floor and sucked in a deep breath. She choked in reflex and had to swallow twice to clear her throat. The thick liquid burned in her stomach. She groaned and rolled onto her side as her vision blurred. *I'm getting drunk?* It didn't have the numbing quality of alcohol; it was hotter, more urgent, and more carnal. "What is happening to me?"

Aramis dropped to his knees and wrapped his arm around her, encouraging her to sit up. "Forgive me, but it was necessary."

Elaine fell back against his arm and shivered, her body coiling and tightening under a hot wave of rampant lust. A needy whimper fell from her lips. "What have you done to me?"

Aramis pressed her head against his heart. "Be at ease, the dizziness will soon pass." He brushed the hair from her face and pressed his lips to her brow. "And then there only will be pleasure."

A solid wall of red lust washed over her and swept her away.

4

Somebody was moaning like a cat in heat.

Then the rest of the moan escaped her throat. Elaine sucked in a startled breath and opened her eyes. She was facedown on the sofa, with Aramis's big, warm body pressed against her back, and his leg thrown over both of hers. "Please tell me I wasn't making all that noise."

Aramis pressed his lips to her temple and tugged at the belt still tied around her wrists. "Oh, but you were."

Elaine turned her head to look past her shoulder at him and stuck out her bottom lip. "You could have lied," she said in a small voice.

Aramis pulled the belt free of her wrists, caught her by the shoulder, and turned her onto her back. "I find the truth far more entertaining."

Elaine rolled her eyes and scowled. "You would." She lifted up on her elbows and moved to get out from under him.

Aramis shifted to stay on top of her and chuckled. "I see that you are feeling more yourself."

"First the bondage, and now you're holding me down?"

Elaine wiggled her trapped fingers. "Has anyone ever told you that you have control issues?"

Aramis rolled his eyes and pursed his lips. "Perhaps once or twice."

"Speaking of issues . . ." Her eyes narrowed. "What the hell is it with drinking your cum? And what the hell did it do to me?"

Aramis lowered his gaze and sighed. "It was necessary, to heat the blood."

"Heat the blood . . . ? You mean it makes my blood pressure rise?"

He smiled. "That, and makes the needs of the body run hot." He leaned down and laved his tongue across a peaked nipple.

Erotic fire blazed from her nipple to her core. "Oh shit!" Elaine gasped and arched under him. He wasn't kidding about the hotness. "Is that all it does?"

Aramis turned his head away, refusing to look at her. "It enthralls."

Elaine's eyes opened wide. "Are you saying that your cum is addictive?"

"You will not crave it, no." He lifted one shoulder in a half shrug. "It makes the will more compliant."

"More compliant. I see." Elaine felt her temper rise hot and fast. "How compliant, exactly?"

Aramis sighed. "It makes denial difficult."

Elaine ground her teeth. "Your cum is a date rape drug?"

He flinched. "I prefer not to describe it as such."

Elaine scowled. "But that's essentially what it's *for;* to make me *obedient* to your sexual demands."

Aramis lifted his head, his eyes narrowing. He spoke through clenched teeth. "It is *for* your survival. It contains a property that allows you to recover from blood loss quickly, so I may drink without endangering your life. It increases your lust so that you will find pleasure in the taking." His lip curled in an angry snarl. "And yes, it makes you inclined toward obedience, to make it easier to take you without force or harm."

"Making me the perfect meal—willing, able, and submissive." She rolled her eyes. "Great."

"Yes." His brows lowered and he locked his gaze on hers. "However, I would not use the term 'submissive' to describe you."

A small smile curled Elaine's lip. "Good."

His brows shot up; then a tight smile appeared. "However, it will be quite difficult for your body to resist the call of mine."

Elaine scowled. "Never mind the fact that I was having trouble resisting you before. . . ."

"Elaine." Aramis's smile disappeared. "What I have given you—"

Elaine set her jaw. "Your cum."

He curled his lip, baring a long tooth. "Yes, my cum will cause you to have great difficulty resisting the demands of *any* vampire that finds you."

An icy chill raced up Elaine's spine. "There are other vampires?"

"Of course, though not many." His hands tightened on her. "I suggest that you stay indoors after sunset for the next three nights."

"Three nights?" *Well, there goes any chance of dancing at any nightclubs in Prague.* Elaine's brows shot up. "Wait a minute. Then vampires do have a problem with daylight?"

Aramis gave her a small smile. "No, we may walk day or night, but night is when our appetites awaken and our senses are at their sharpest. At night is when we hunt, and feed. Night is when you are more likely to be discovered."

"Discovered?" Elaine shivered, just a little. "How?"

Aramis sighed. "A vampire will know by your scent that you have been enthralled, and primed for feeding." He looked away. "They will know that you are . . . easy prey."

Elaine smiled grimly. "I've never been easy prey."

Aramis's brows shot up and he smiled. "Somehow I can believe that."

Elaine smiled, then rolled her eyes. "So how long do I have to worry about other vampires?"

Aramis sighed. "After three days, the scent of your enthrallment no longer rides on your skin, but a kiss will still betray you to one of us. After nine days, you will no longer be enthralled, but you should still exercise caution, day or night."

"Nine days total?" Elaine groaned and closed her eyes. "Great, and I have no clue how to tell one of you from anyone else."

"For all nine days, you will know. For some, it is longer. In fact, you will know one of us before we will know you."

Elaine opened her eyes. "How?"

"A vampire will know you by scent or taste." Aramis's gaze was steady. "But your blood will know us. Your lust will warn you that one of us is near."

Elaine tilted her head to the side and lifted her brow. "So, during the next nine days, if I suddenly find myself wildly aroused by somebody, there's a good chance that he's a vampire?"

"Yes." His eyes narrowed. "You must avoid us at all costs. There are those that will not hesitate to take you and perhaps keep you as part of their . . . harem."

Elaine's brows shot up. "Vampires have *harems*?"

Aramis nodded. "It causes less harm to sip from many than to feed from only one."

Elaine raised a brow at the vampire above her. "But not you?"

"No." Aramis looked down, hiding his eyes. "I do not . . . keep thralls."

Elaine felt a small stab of disappointment. She squashed it immediately. "Are there vampires in Prague?"

"There is only one vampire in Prague. If you sense him, you must flee immediately. He will drain you of your artistic talent if he catches you."

Elaine frowned. "What has my drawing ability got to do with anything?"

"The vampire feeds on the creative spark, the source of your talents. Blood is how we access that essence." Aramis focused on her. "Elaine, this evening I was drawn from across the dining car by the fire that shines from your soul. Others will be drawn to you, primed or not, for exactly the same reason. Make no mistake, it is not your blood we hunger for, but to feed on your artist's soul."

My art . . . ? Elaine stared up at the vampire above her. Drawing and painting, her creativity was all she had. After her parents' nasty divorce, and the hopping from one relative to the next, her ability to put her feelings on paper was the one thing that no one had been able to take away from her. And yet, that's exactly what he said he . . . consumed. Fear seared through her. "No"—she jerked and shoved to get away from him—"not my art!"

"Elaine!" Aramis grabbed her wrists and pinned her under his body. "Elaine, I mean you no harm." His dark gaze caught and trapped hers. "Be calm. I swear that I would never destroy such a talent as yours. Be calm, relax. Trust me."

A wave of warmth and stillness washed through Elaine. She fought to keep struggling, but the languorous heat flooding her body defeated her, until she lay quietly under him. "I want to believe you. I *want* to trust you. . . ." She did—she really, really did, but . . .

"Believe me." Aramis smiled. "Do you not remember? I am too polite to do something vulgar, yes?" He released her wrists and brushed the hair from her brow.

She swallowed. He was pretty damned polite. In fact, he had gone out of his way to get her permission for just a kiss, and then again for sex, when he was fully capable of just raping her. Those weren't the actions of someone who would destroy her talent. And . . . and she wanted to believe him . . . very, very badly.

Was that why she had just stopped fighting? Or was it . . . ? Suspicion burned in her. "I guess you weren't exaggerating about the compliant part?"

"No, I was not." Aramis brushed his thumb across her bottom lip. "Elaine, I have no desire to harm you."

"Okay . . ." Distracted, Elaine's worries seemed to melt away as though unimportant. More important was the gentle pressure of his thumb against her bottom lip. She opened her mouth without thinking about it, touching his thumb with the point of her tongue.

"More," Aramis whispered, and pressed his thumb against her tongue. "Taste me."

Elaine sucked his thumb into her mouth. She could actually taste the salty musk of his arousal on his skin. Moist warmth flooded her core and slicked her thighs. A groan came from deep in her throat.

Aramis smiled. "Ah, I think you are ready."

"Hmm?" She released his thumb.

Aramis rose above her and smiled while licking the thumb that had just been in her mouth. "Mmm . . . yes, I see that you are."

Elaine licked her lips. "Ready for what?"

"For your ravishment, of course." He crawled backward

and then knelt between her knees. "Open and spread for me. I would taste you."

Elaine blinked. He was going to eat her pussy? *Hot damn!* She brought her knees up and spread.

Aramis dropped down to his belly, kicking his feet up and perching on his elbows. His hands swept across her closely trimmed mound. His palms spread her open to expose the pink folds. "Ah, a succulent feast." His mouth descended. His moist warm breath brushed her intimate flesh.

Every muscle in her body clenched in voracious eagerness. Elaine bit back a yearning moan.

His black eyes watching her, he opened his mouth on her flesh and the wet heat of his tongue brushed lightly yet seared across the tender oversensitive folds.

She choked and arched up from the sofa, her body shuddering with violent hunger. "Oh, my fucking God!"

"You are very, very ripe, my sweet." Aramis chuckled and wrapped his arms around her thighs to hold her still. "And this is barely the beginning." His head dropped and his tongue delved among her moist folds, then burrowed into her center, seeking her cream.

It was too much. Elaine bit back a scream and struggled to get away from the searing intensity, but his arms held her still for his lashing tongue. Helpless under the onslaught of torturous pleasure, she cried out and writhed, her hips rising in time to his working tongue.

He smiled and sucked, groaning his delight. His tongue swirled lightly against her clit.

Climax rose with brutal intensity. She threw back her head and cried out, her hips bucking—and went nowhere. She wailed in frustration and writhed against his mouth. "Please?" The word simply slipped out.

Aramis's black eyes creased with amusement. "Please what?" He lowered his mouth and sucked noisily.

Elaine's need coiled tighter, but no closer to the edge. She shuddered and trembled, whimpers becoming cries that escaped her lips, but climax would not come. Something was holding her back, something was missing. *"Please!"* It exploded from her mouth.

Aramis lifted his head, not even bothering to hide his broad grin. "Please what?" He pushed a finger deep into her core and flicked it within her.

Elaine howled and bucked in time to his finger's possession. "Please, Aramis, let me come!"

"I will have to bite you."

"Then bite me, damn it!"

"As you wish." He pulled fingers from her core and lifted his arm to press her thigh against the back of the sofa. He opened his hand on her outer thigh and held it down against the cushions, spreading her wide and holding her perfectly still.

Elaine panted while orgasm retreated and sanity returned. *Oh God, I just told a vampire to bite me. . . .*

His mouth and tongue descended to her tortured flesh. His long finger slid back into her slick core. He pressed rhythmically within, while his tongue slowly circled her swollen clit.

Searing heat, voracious hunger, hammering need . . . Elaine arched and twisted. Gasping cries burst from her lips.

He trapped her leg flat and firmly on the cushions. His mouth moved from her aching flesh to the crease dividing her mound and the softness of her inner thigh. His tongue darted out, wetting a spot close to her thigh's juncture, and his thumb slowly circled her swollen clit.

Elaine's body stilled. The hair rose on the back of her neck. She panted in dread and anticipation. She felt the press of pointed teeth against the softest flesh of her inner thigh. Tension coiled, clenched, knotted.

A small but sharp burn scored her inner thigh. A soft whimper escaped. Wet warmth . . . Her body released in a brutal explosion of icy-hot fire that blazed up her spine to scour the back of her skull. A waterfall of pleasure crashed down on her.

His mouth closed on the burn, and his tongue lapped while his finger plunged and his thumb flicked across her aggravated clit.

She drowned under wave after wave of glorious abandon. Her delighted cries filled the small compartment in time to his sucking mouth.

ך

Aramis raised his head from her thigh and licked the crimson smears from his smiling lips. "More?"

Elaine gasped for breath and trembled with aftershocks, gazing at the vampire's brutally handsome face and night-black eyes. "God, yes! I don't think I've ever come that hard in my life."

He rose from her spread thighs and crawled over her to stare down into her eyes from barely a breath away. "I am glad to have pleased you." His mouth descended to hers.

She opened for his kiss. His teeth gently scored her lips and sweet copper flavored his tongue. It was the taste of blood— her blood. A tiny and illicit thrill raced up her spine.

While straddling her thigh with his knees down on the cushions, Aramis caught her knee, which was pressed back against the sofa, and lifted her leg up onto his shoulder, spreading her wide. Then he turned her hips to the side.

She arched her back and threw out her arms for balance. "What are you doing?"

Aramis sat upright, spreading his knees wide. His cock—a

thick, long, and very rigid curve—pressed against the entrance of her body. "Fucking you."

Elaine swallowed. He looked freaking huge. "Take it easy. I'm not very big in there."

Aramis smiled, and it was pure male. "I will fit." He thrust. Slick from her climax, he slid in deep, taking her, filling her, possessing her to the balls, in one lunge.

They both gasped.

Elaine sucked back a groan, feeling her body stretch to accommodate him. She had no idea how the hell she was able to hold all of him in her, but she had.

Aramis pulled back with a groan, withdrawing partway from her snug body. "You are tight."

"You're not exactly small yourself." Elaine twisted her hips and groaned. "And I haven't had sex in a while." *A long while.*

"Nor have I had sex." Aramis released a breathy chuckle. "I intend to make up for the lack." He thrust, grunting with the impact. "Tonight."

"Great . . ." Elaine grabbed the cushions, biting back a soft whimper. *Oh God, he's big.*

Aramis withdrew in a long, slow slide. He groaned and thrust, and thrust. . . . His hips struck her ass with damp smacks.

Elaine arched under him as pleasure built with a simmering heat that rose and held to just this side of boiling. Each of his strong thrusts struck against something that made her jolt and clench with each entry. It felt incredibly good, but he was going way too slow. She tried to shift under him. "Faster!"

Aramis panted and smiled. "No."

"No?" Elaine clenched her teeth and tried to lift in counter-thrust, but she couldn't move. He had both her legs trapped. "Aramis, fuck me, damn it!"

Aramis licked his lips, his body straining as he took her with strong, hard plunges and slow, lascivious retreats. "I am fucking you, Elaine."

Elaine dug her fingers into the cushions. "No, you're not! You're teasing the shit out of me! Fuck me!"

Aramis released a breathless chuckle. "I fear to come too quickly." He slid deep into her, then groaned and stopped. "So you must suffer."

Elaine lifted her head. "Damn it, don't stop!"

Aramis choked out a small laugh. "I am not, but the urge to come is"—he groaned—"difficult to resist." He withdrew with aching slowness, and drove back in, hard. Then again, and again, taking her with powerful thrusts, yet maddeningly slow retreats, over and over, and over. . . .

Elaine's nipples tightened, engorging from the rocking of her breasts, driven by the force of his hips. She groaned. The burning ache in her nipples transferred straight to her clit and aggravated the clenching need building in her core. "Damn it, Aramis, this slow shit is driving me insane!"

"Good." Aramis flashed a long-toothed grin and fell over her, bracing himself on his hands. Her leg on his shoulder was forced higher, spreading her very wide. "I want you insane." He cupped her breast in one palm. "I want you insane . . . for me." His head lowered to take her taut nipple into his mouth. He squeezed her breast and suckled fiercely while pounding into her with slow, ruthless skill.

Elaine writhed, but it accomplished nothing. "Aramis, please?"

His black eyes narrowed. "Are you begging?"

Elaine licked her lips. "Would begging make you go faster?"

"It might." He stroked her nipple, with a long, wet tongue.

"Then, yes! Aramis, please, I'm begging you with sugar on top. Please fuck me faster?"

"I will consider it." He smiled, and continued with his relentlessly slow thrusts.

Elaine hit the cushions with her fist. "Oh, you bastard!"

His brows shot up. "From begging to insults so quickly?"

Elaine glared at him. "It's going to be threats, if you don't hurry your ass up!"

"Threats?" Aramis stopped and smiled. "In case you have not noticed, you are on the bottom."

"Oh, I noticed." Elaine smiled and slid her left arm under his and up onto his shoulder by her ankle. Being folded nearly in half was not the easiest position to be in. Thank God, she'd kept limber since high school. She licked her lips. "But I think you missed something vitally important, vampire." She grabbed his right wrist, locking her other arm under and around his shoulder.

He smiled from just a kiss away. "Oh?"

Elaine gripped him tight and whispered in his ear, "The person on the bottom has all the leverage." She twisted with every ounce of strength she had, shoving his head and shoulder with her upraised leg and her arm, while yanking his opposite wrist toward her.

Aramis fell sideways and his eyes went wide. He scrambled to stop the fall, disengaging his cock from her body, but she had a firm hold of his supporting wrist.

Elaine released his shoulder to snap her arm out and pushed hard against the back of the sofa while unfolding her leg from his shoulder, wrapping both legs around his hips.

Aramis bared his teeth in a snarl and fought her, but she had the advantage of surprise, momentum, and practiced skill, but especially leverage. He was top-heavy and she was bottom-heavy. It was child's play to tip him over.

The hard part would be keeping him down.

Elaine levered herself on top of him, tucking her heels under his ass, then grabbed both his wrists and pulled them up over his head, using all her body weight to pin him. She grinned and wiggled. "Much better."

Aramis's snarl froze under her lascivious movements against his hard cock. His mouth closed, his jaw tightened, and his eyes narrowed. "And what has *this* accomplished?"

"Oh, come on, don't be so disappointed." Elaine leaned down to lick his pouting bottom lip. "I was a judo champion in high school—four state trophies by my senior year." She smiled. "You never stood a chance." With some judicious wiggling, she found his hard cock and centered the broad head on the mouth of her body.

"What are you doing?"

"Taking the driver's seat." She dropped, sheathing herself over him and taking him deep. "Oh God, yeah!"

He choked. "Elaine?"

Elaine writhed, feeling his deliciously hard length moving within her, while tilting her hips forward to rub her excited clit against his pubic bone. Delight sparked hot and fast. "God, you feel good." She leaned forward, putting her weight on his trapped wrists. His cock slid partway out. She fell back down on him, taking him brutally hard. His cock slid into her slick sheath and hit just the right spot within her. She gasped in raw pleasure.

Aramis bucked under her, meeting her with a thrust. "Fuck, woman!"

"That's the idea!" She groaned and rose again. "Oh yeah, much better." She rose and fell, faster and harder, riding him with ruthless abandon.

Aramis groaned and bucked under her. "Elaine, I will come very fast this way!"

Elaine closed her eyes and twisted above him. "Mmm . . . that's the plan." She ground down on him and proceeded to fuck the living hell out of him.

Aramis panted and bucked under her, but he didn't try to change their positions. His heels dug into the cushions as he thrust upward, meeting her stroke for stroke, until the sweat gleamed and ran on both of them. Their panting breaths were punctuated by the rapid slaps of wet flesh against wet flesh.

The rich scent of sex perfumed the small compartment.

Elaine literally felt him becoming harder and more rigid within her as she took him hard and fast. Soon, very soon, he would snap. . . .

"Elaine!"

"Mmm?" She opened her eyes and gazed down at the vampire straining beneath her.

His eyes were wide, his cheeks were flushed, and his mouth gaped open, showing all four of his long teeth. "Release me. Now."

Elaine's hands flinched back from his wrists. She barely had time to brace her hands on the cushions to keep from falling over. *What the hell?*

Aramis reached up and caught her around the neck, pulling her breast down to his open mouth. His other hand cupped her ass, his fingers digging into the soft plump flesh. His mouth made enthusiastic wet sounds as he suckled hard on her breast and pounded up into her with hard, swift thrusts.

"Oh God, yes!" Elaine forgot all about the way her hands had done their own thinking as she gasped and mewled with delight, her body straining to match his pounding rhythm. "Yes, yes . . . fuck me!" Climax coiled and tightened into a white-hot molten mass. Shivers danced up her spine. This one was going to be strong. She was close, very close. . . .

Aramis growled, a low and liquid feline rumbling deep in his chest. His arm was locked around her neck as he pulled her breast tight against his wide open mouth. His teeth pressed into the soft flesh around the pale rose areola of her nipple. He thrust up into her with frantic speed.

Elaine sucked in a startled breath. He was *not* going to bite her there . . . ? Fear spiked through her, and her climax rose to a vicious crescendo—and held, right on the edge. She writhed and twisted, but she couldn't make herself go past it. She couldn't make her body come. "Damn it!" Her voice was hoarse with raw need.

His gaze pinned hers as his tongue swirled across the taut flesh pressed against his long teeth surrounding her nipple. His arm tightened, and his fingers knotted in her hair, holding her breast locked to his mouth.

Elaine's hair rose on her neck, and her body froze with fearful expectancy. *Oh shit!*

His teeth sank into her breast. Two thin lines of scarlet slid from the corners of his mouth.

Icy shock washed over her, and then sharp pain. Erotic fire flavored by the adrenaline jolt of fear lanced straight down to her core. Climax exploded in a violent skull-burning rush of black rapture, ripping screams of terror and joy from her throat. She howled and bucked in his arms, driven to the edge of sanity by the horrific power of her dark and brutal climax.

She barely heard his groan as his release took him.

Overwhelmed by the sheer power of her climax, she collapsed in his arms, limp, barely conscious, and straining for breath.

The vampire eased her over onto her side, pressing her against the back of the sofa, his legs wrapping around hers as his arms held her securely. He suckled gently, almost purring against her breast as he fed, while grinding his pulsing cock into her, pumping stream after stream of cum into her trembling body.

Elaine's senses returned as Aramis turned her onto her back. She opened her eyes to see him licking, with his long tongue, the four small wounds on her breast. The two on top were actual slice cuts, the two on the bottom were punctures. Still, the marks were a lot smaller than she had expected, and they had stopped bleeding. She drew in a shuddering breath. "I don't believe you bit my *tit*."

Aramis lifted his head, his eyes hot and hard. "I do not take well to aggression."

Elaine snorted. "You just hate to lose—"

Aramis's brows lowered and his mouth tightened. "Elaine, I very nearly took your throat."

She frowned. He seemed angry, really angry. "Biting the neck is bad?"

"A bite on the throat can be fatal."

Ice raced through her blood. "Fatal?"

"I am a predator. My teeth are overlong and curved. A deep-enough bite would tear right through the arteries. Your heart would empty your body of blood within minutes."

Elaine's throat tightened as her breath caught. "That's freaking scary."

"Do not attempt to fight me again." Aramis stared hard into her eyes. "I will not allow you to endanger yourself by defying me."

Elaine tore her gaze away. He wasn't angry—he was furious. "What? Am I supposed to play passive while you have all the fun?"

Aramis gave her a smile, but anger still shimmered in his

eyes. "I do not think you could be passive if you tried. But I will have your submission."

Elaine curled her lip sourly. "If you wanted submissive, you should have picked a better victim."

Aramis raised a dark brow. "I will have you know, I am perfectly content with the victim I have, thank you."

Elaine smiled in spite of herself. "Good."

Aramis sighed and the anger bled from his gaze. He brushed her lips in a light kiss. "You are incorrigible."

Elaine wrapped her arms around him, glad that his anger had passed. "Only with you." She pressed a kiss up to his lips. "I've read an awful lot, but I am very picky with my lovers."

His brows rose, but his smile broadened. "Is that so?"

Elaine gave him a cheeky grin. "I'm not as practiced as I seem."

"Oh?" Aramis pressed his lips to her brow. "Then I suspect that I will need plenty of lubrication when I take you again."

"Lubrication?" Elaine frowned in suspicion. This had better not be what it sounded like. . . .

"Of course." Aramis smiled as his hand snaked between her thighs. His fingers slid down and under to investigate the tight rose of her anus. "I am assuming that you will be quite tight when I take you here."

"No freaking way!" Elaine jerked away from his inquisitive fingers. "You barely fit in my pussy! You are *not* going to fuck me up the ass!" There was no way in hell his big dick was going to *fit* in her ass.

"Oh, but I am." His grin was slow in coming, and malicious when it got there. "Your body is mine tonight, Elaine, and I would have it all."

Elaine twisted under him. "I have a perfectly good pussy . . . !"

Aramis chuckled. "Which I have indeed enjoyed." His arms

closed tight around her, holding her firmly under him. "But I would have all of you."

Elaine stared up at him in panic. "You don't need my ass!"

"Have you never taken a man there?"

Elaine cringed. "No."

"No?"

Elaine shook her head, her body shivering under him. "I tried it, but it hurt too much."

"Ah, then I will be the first." His smile was feral. "You have no idea how much this pleases me."

Elaine twisted hard. "No, absolutely not!"

Aramis trapped her chin and caught her gaze. "Elaine, be still."

Elaine's entire body went limp. Cold sweat broke out on her skin and she shivered. "Aramis?"

"No more defiance." Aramis sat back on his heels, his eyes black and hot on her body. "Turn over and raise your ass. Now."

6

Elaine rolled over onto her belly. Her throat closed with fear. She could not make herself stop from rising up on her knees and balancing on elbows. She couldn't make herself move from the position, either. "Aramis, please, not my ass." She sucked in a frightened breath. "You're too big."

He knelt between her thighs. "I will fit, you will stretch." He stroked a hand down her damp spine and slid a finger into the crease of her ass.

"Aramis, please, I'm begging you, not my ass!"

"You may beg." He chuckled, the sound dark and sinister. His hands cupped the globes of her ass and parted the cheeks. "But since no one has taken this part of you, I am quite determined to claim it for myself."

Elaine ground her teeth. "Oh, you bastard!"

Aramis sighed thoughtfully. "Perhaps you should have a spanking first?"

Elaine's mouth fell open. "What?"

"Perhaps discipline will remind you that your body is mine?"

He rubbed the cheeks of her butt and kissed the base of her spine. "To take however I please."

" 'Discipline . . . '?" Elaine turned to glare over her shoulder at him, her hands fisted with hot anger. "You are not spanking my ass!"

"It seems that I must." Aramis raised his hand.

Elaine blinked, shocked. "Aramis?"

"Oh no, now I am your master." He smiled.

"What?" Elaine heard the sharp slap a full breath before her right butt cheek erupted with hot fire. She hissed and writhed under the burn. "Son of a bitch!"

"I am Master." Aramis's voice was calm, with just a touch of humor. His hand came down hard on her other cheek. "And your body is mine, Thrall." He smacked the first cheek again.

Elaine set her jaw to keep back the whimpers trying to pass through her lips. Damn it, her ass hurt! She just knew she was going to have bruises tomorrow.

Aramis was back on his heels between her thighs. "Now, then, how do you address me?"

Elaine turned and glared at him. *Fuck you.* "I am not going to call you Master!"

"Oh, but you will." Aramis's hand flashed across her butt faster than her eyes could follow.

Smack! Smack! Smack!

Elaine's butt cheeks erupted with fire. She jumped and writhed under the strikes, trying to hold still, but her ass had a mind of its own. The worst part was, each burning smack sent an illicit thrill straight to her clit. She was getting seriously excited, really fast.

Aramis opened his hands on her hot cheeks and rubbed. "You realize that spanking your delicious ass is making me very hard." His fingers dug in. "If this keeps up too much longer, I will not be inclined toward mercy when I take you."

Elaine gasped for breath, but she couldn't stop from writhing under his palms. *Bastard* . . .

"You are very wet." His voice held entirely too much satisfaction. He plunged two fingers into her wet opening.

Elaine was able to hold back her moan, but her body tightened around his fingers with appetite.

"Ah . . . you seem to be enjoying this as much as I." He pressed and rubbed deep within. "I think you desire my cock up your ass."

Elaine ducked her head and bit back a hungry moan. Damn it, he was right, she was hotter than hell. "Fine, your spanking got me hot, but that doesn't mean I want to be ass-fucked!"

Aramis dragged his fingers out. "Are you quite sure?" He plunged them back in.

Elaine moaned, and her hips rocked with uncontrollable eagerness. She couldn't take much more of this.

Aramis scissored his fingers as he dragged them back out. "Elaine, my sweet thrall . . ." He thrust them back in and swept his thumb across her clit. "How do you address me?"

Elaine gasped as her clit throbbed with a raw and carnal pleasure. She released a soft, needy sound.

"The faster you comply, the faster I will let you come."

Elaine groaned. "Fine, okay, whatever . . . Master."

"Very good." Aramis pressed a slick finger to the puckered rose of her anus.

Elaine stilled. He was not . . .

He came up and leaned over her back, whispering in her ear, "Push out against me."

Elaine helplessly obeyed, and his finger slid right in. It felt achingly huge. She shut her eyes and moaned in abject mortification. It felt achingly *naughty*. She felt another trickle of moisture slide from her traitorous body.

"You are very, very tight." Aramis chuckled. "Are you

ready to have your master stretch your ass with his cock, Thrall?"

"I'm ready to die from embarrassment, does that count?"

Aramis snorted. "Your shame will make my possession all the more enticing."

"You're a sadistic bastard . . . Master," she ground out between clenched teeth.

"And your suffering as you come with my cock up your ass will be beautiful to behold, Thrall."

Elaine shivered. "I'm *not* going to come with your cock splitting my ass!"

Aramis pulled his fingers from her ass. "You will come." He rose from the sofa and walked over to his coat. "In fact, you will likely scream." He dug into one of the pockets.

Elaine glared in his direction. "Oh, I'll probably scream, but it won't be because I'm coming."

Aramis turned to glance at her while removing the top of a white squeeze tube. "So little confidence in me?" He squeezed clear gel into his palm, then rubbed his dick, coating the long, threatening length liberally.

With grave misgivings, Elaine eyed the gleaming length of his huge cock. "How about, so little confidence in your big dick fitting in my ass?"

Aramis squeezed more gel into his palm. His smile was broad, but his black eyes were narrowed to slits. "I will fit, and you will come."

"Your finger barely fits!"

Aramis smiled. "So speaks the fear of the virgin."

"Virgin, my ass!" Elaine immediately wanted to bite her tongue.

"I believe that was my point." Aramis walked back over to the sofa and knelt on it. "I promise, you will accommodate me." He reached out to probe her butt with a gel-coated finger. "Relax and open for me."

Elaine took a breath and pushed.

Aramis's finger slid past her tight ring and shoved deep. "Very good." He probed and swirled his finger around, coating her interior with gel. "As with the loss of any virginity, there will be pain, but you will find pleasure in the act, I assure you." His voice was gentle, soothing.

Elaine nearly groaned out loud. The sensation of his finger moving within her was dark, forbidden, and almost pleasant.

"Breathe, and accept," he whispered. He slid a second slick finger into her snug butt, then pressed his thumb into her hungry opening.

Elaine gasped and groaned, shuddering with the darkly erotic feeling of his thumb possessing her pussy while his fingers conquered her ass. Her body clenched with excitement. Erotic heat mixed with the aching tightness. Good God, what if he was right?

"Feel me within you." His hand stroked down her thigh as his fingers moved in her uncomfortably tight ass, curling to rub against his thumb, only a thin wall away. "Welcome the pleasure, accept the pain, and move beyond."

Elaine took a deep breath as pleasure-pain confusion ran rampant through her. She shivered, wanting to hold still to ease the pain in her butt, while desperately wanting to move against his thumb. The hunger in her core won and she moved, rocking back on his hand.

"Yes, that's it." He began to pump his fingers in, then out of, her ass and pussy in a rich and decadent rhythm.

Elaine felt a moan rise as the ache in her butt sharpened the pleasure growing in her belly.

"Very good." Aramis withdrew his hand and shifted behind her. "You are ready."

Elaine swallowed. *Oh God, here it comes....* Panic dampened her back with chilly sweat.

"Push and breathe out slowly." His hands closed on her hips and he leaned into her.

A hard, hot, and slick bluntness pressed against her anus. The small bud burned as it slowly opened under the pressure. Elaine's breath escaped in a hiss. She writhed, but there was no escaping the cock ruthlessly pressing into her ass. "Damn you, it hurts!"

"Of course there is pain!" Aramis groaned, and his fingers tightened on her hips. "Push out!"

Elaine released a small whimper and pushed out with all her strength. The cock's broad head slipped past the snug ring of her anus.

Aramis groaned. "Yes!" He grabbed both her shoulders. "Sit up slowly, sit up and take me."

Elaine slowly came up on her knees and he pressed deeper into her. "Oh God..." He was so fucking big! She could feel him stretching her backside impossibly wide as he progressed. "I can't take it. You're too big!"

"You can. You are." Aramis pulled her back and down onto his brutally rigid length. "Breathe, and push...." His fever-hot length forged slowly but steadily deeper into her tight passage.

Elaine groaned with the vicious fullness of his cock stretching her intimate flesh with his brutal width. Her butt cheeks contacted with his thighs, and she straddled his lap, fully impaled.

"It is done." His hands slid from her shoulder to cup and squeeze her breasts. "Blood and Night, you are a tight fist around me!"

Elaine didn't bother to hold back her moan. "Try having a big fat pole up your ass—then tell me about *tight*!"

Aramis chuckled, the sensation vibrating darkly through her

passage. "You will grow accustomed." His fingers closed on her nipples and pinched, hard. "And you will come."

Vicious delight burned in her nipples and resonated to pulse in her clit. She gasped as a wet, hungry clench echoed in her core, and she arched back against his broad chest. She twisted her hips to relieve the pulsing throb in her clit and the aching fullness in her butt. The huge, hard length in her ass shifted. She released a startled breath. The pain was lessening, or changing into something else under the seditious pulsing in her nipples and the hungry echo in her clit.

Aramis hissed, "Oh yes, my sweet thrall, move and feel me within you." He rolled his hips in complementary rhythm. "Feel my cock spreading you." He kneaded her breasts with his strong pale fingers and rolled her taut nipples. "Feel my possession."

Responding to the inciting fire in her nipples, the image scorching her mind of his cock spreading her impossibly wide, and the rapacious appetite boiling in her core, Elaine rocked in his lap, rolling back and forth. The fiendishly cruel pleasure increased.

"Yes . . ." His lips traced the length of her throat. "And now, your surrender." He reached down between her spread thighs to stroke his fingers over her fevered and swollen clit, while he tugged insistently on her trapped nipple.

Elaine released a soft cry and bucked, jolting the cock in her ass. It didn't hurt any less, but the decadent fire resonating from her clit and nipple was definitely swamping the pain and changing it into a darkly wicked sensation that was far closer to pleasure.

His fingers massaged and swirled around her clit. His hand closed on her breast.

A tight coiling throb hammered through her, and a fresh spat of cream slicked her thighs. She groaned and whimpered, getting hotter by the second, stunned by her body's fierce and greedy response. Her ass still ached around the hard length lodged in it, but the pain seemed to be sharpening the darkly erotic pleasure. There was a real possibility that she *would* come with his dick up her ass.

Aramis chuckled softly. "Ah, the sweet sounds of reluctant pleasure." Aramis pressed her forward up on her knees and began to withdraw.

Elaine gasped with the riveting sensation created by his retreat. It wasn't painful; in fact, it was quite pleasurable, but the pleasure was alien—different and wicked.

Aramis stopped with his cock still halfway in. "Prepare yourself." He looped one arm around her hips and cupped her ass in his other palm, his fingers digging into the soft cheek. He pulled her back onto his lap, his cock surging hot and brutally hard into her body.

It hurt. A lot.

Elaine tossed her head up and shouted, "Bastard!"

Aramis groaned. "You say that now. Later you will scream for my cock in your ass." He began pushing her back up, withdrawing much slower than he had gone in.

That hot, dark pleasure was back, and then some. "Oh, my God . . ." Elaine's toes curled with the exquisite shivering torment of his hardness moving in her backside. She writhed and moaned.

He groaned and his hands trembled as they gripped her. "Ah, you feel delicious." He thrust swiftly again, then pulled back with slow decadence.

Elaine whimpered briefly in distress, then moaned in abject hunger, overwhelmed by the arresting and profane delight. Her core pulsed in ravenous need; moisture slithered down her thighs.

"You are ready." Aramis pressed her forward, onto her hands, leaning over her back.

Elaine turned her head to look over her shoulder at him. "Ready for what?"

Aramis smiled, showing the length of his fangs. "You have been possessed. Now you will be taken." He pressed against her sweating back and wrapped an arm around her waist. "I will accept nothing less than your complete surrender."

Elaine shivered. "I don't think I can surrender."

"You can. You will." He kissed her shoulder briefly. "To me." His hand curled under her to brush against her swollen and frantic clit; then he thrust. Hard.

Elaine bucked under him, her senses confused by the sudden throbbing fullness of his brutal thrust and the ferocious liquid delight of his fingers on her clit. He pulled back, and the dark voluptuous retreat of his cock was compounded by the inciting burn of his fingers dancing on her clit. The pleasure scorched a trail of fire up the back of her skull.

He thrust again, then pulled back. . . .

Shivers skittered up her spine as the delight blazing in her clit, and the aching fullness in her ass, mixed to become a raging blend of avaricious lust. She cried out and shoved back against him in abject need for more of that sinful ecstasy. He retreated, and she thrust back for more.

Aramis groaned, thrusting in earnest to meet her demand, his fingers rubbing with insistence on her clit. "Blood and Night, yes! Fuck me!"

Her gasping cries echoed with the sound of flesh striking flesh as he took her ass with increasing speed. Erotic tension coiled deep and low in her belly. Her body twisted and her thighs spread wider, toes curling tightly with the violent pleasure of being fucked, of being possessed, of being taken. Climax built with savage strength with every stroke of his cock in her backside.

Aramis wrapped his other arm around her shoulders and panted against her throat, his thrusts pounding into her with frenzied speed. "Your surrender is upon you."

Elaine was beyond thinking past the lust boiling and clawing within her. "Fuck me!"

His thrusts hammered into her as his teeth scored her shoulder. "Mine!" The vampire's voice was a soft whisper. He bit down.

Fire exploded in the back of her skull. She shrieked as it swept her under a wave of darkening glory that shredded her sanity.

Somewhere far away, she felt his arms close breathlessly tight around her, taking her, writhing and gasping, down to the cushions. He wrapped himself securely around her as he buried himself in her body one final time and pulsed within, filling her ass with his cum as he swallowed her blood.

7

Elaine awoke, lying on her back on the sofa, with Aramis sitting at her side, pressing a hot cloth on her sore privates. Embarrassing though it was, she groaned under the delicious strokes. "God, that feels good. . . . Oh, my ass!"

Aramis smiled as he cleaned her with gentle attention. "By tomorrow's sunset, the aches will have faded."

"Sure about that?" Elaine raised her brow and tried to look stern. "Benefits of all the cum you pumped into me, I suppose?"

Aramis grinned broadly. "Of course."

She watched his beautiful hands and thought of sketching them. Then another thought crossed her mind. "I don't feel like I lost any of my creativity."

"I barely skimmed the surface of your talent. I teach art, I do not take it from others."

Elaine looked up at him. A vampire who taught art? Okay, that was strange. . . . "What do you teach?"

Aramis smiled and strode back to the tiny turn-of-the-century sink in the corner to run hot water over the cloth.

"Drawing and oil painting, so believe me when I say you are very good, indeed."

Elaine rose up on one elbow. "Wow . . . I hope the instructor interviewing me in Prague agrees with you."

"What?" Aramis stilled. He came back to her in one long stride and gripped her shoulder. "What instructor? A drawing master?"

Elaine frowned. What was with him? "Yes, Dimitri Ivanova."

Aramis's eyes went wide, black, and inhuman. "You must not go to him!"

"What? But I have to—"

"No, I forbid it!"

"You forbid it?" Elaine's mouth fell open. "Aramis!"

"No." Red flared deep in the heart of Aramis's black eyes. "He is the vampire in Prague I spoke of. He will destroy you."

Elaine shivered. The weird glow in his eyes was seriously scary. "Aramis, he already found me. He paid my way from Rome. I have to go. I can't afford to pay him back."

His fingers dug painfully into her shoulder. "How did he find you?"

"You know that picture missing from my book?"

"Yes."

"I got a letter at my hotel with a Xerox copy of the picture asking if the portrait was my work. I think he was the instructor Anthony tried to pass my work off to. The next letter had the train ticket on the *Orient Express* from Rome to Prague."

Aramis turned away and scowled at the wall. He shook his head. "Elaine, you must not meet with him. Dimitri's victims do not recover from his appetites."

Elaine swallowed. Oh God, what if he was right? "Aramis, he paid for everything—food, hotels . . . everything. Are you sure . . . ?"

"Very sure. This is not the first time he has done this. The travel expenses are payment for the talent he will scour from your soul."

Oh shit . . . "Fine, I'll just tell him 'no thank you' and leave."

Aramis turned to her, his fangs bared. "No! If he sees you, he will take you. You are not to meet with him!"

Elaine rolled her eyes. "Oh, come on! I'm not totally helpless. Judo champ, remember?" *How bad could it be, really?*

"Elaine, at this moment, you *are* helpless. Your body is enthralled. You have no resistance to any vampire's will—he will rape your soul dry!"

Okay, that's bad. Elaine swallowed. "I can't avoid him. He's meeting me at the station in Prague."

Aramis turned away. His hands clenched into fists. "Then you will not meet him alone."

"What? Are you out of your mind?" Elaine set her jaw. "Aramis, this is not your problem."

The vampire shook his head. "I enthralled you. You are my responsibility."

I'm a responsibility, terrific. . . . Elaine sighed.

Aramis shook his head and raised his hand. "I will deal with Dimitri."

Elaine frowned in suspicion. "How well do you know him?"

"More so than I would like." Aramis went back to the basin and ran the cloth under hot water, then draped it over the spigot. "I was once an art student myself, a very long time ago."

"What?" Elaine's mouth fell open. "Then the vampire-longevity thing is true?"

"Yes."

"How old are you?"

"Older than I care to mention." Aramis stepped into the small chamber beyond the partition and pulled the blankets off

61

the fold-down bed. He strode back into the main compartment. "It is time for you to sleep."

"But, Aramis—"

"Enough." The vampire shook his head and unfolded the blankets. "I will deal with this when we get to Prague." He climbed onto the sofa with her and spread out the blankets.

Elaine moved back to make room for him. "Are you sure?"

"Sleep, Elaine." He kissed her brow and drew the blankets over them. "I will take care of this."

She snuggled against his heart, her legs entwining with his. "But . . ." A yawn escaped.

"Sleep." He wrapped his arms around her and tucked her head under his chin. "I will take care of you."

Somewhere in the tangled realm of waking dreams, she felt his warm body wrap tight against her back. The hot brand of his cock slid between her thighs. She didn't think she merely arched back and opened to him.

He groaned and slid within, in one swift thrust. His body rocked against and within hers in a slow and comforting rhythm, his hands possessively cupping her breasts and tugging her nipples, his breath hot against her throat.

Passion smoldered, flared, and she writhed within his grasp. His teeth grazed her throat. Lines of fire scored her tender skin. She moaned as her climax flashed in a fierce wave.

He groaned and pulled her tight against him, rocking within her and lapping at the warm wetness running down her neck. His whispering voice was barely audible as it rasped hoarsely against her ear: "Mine, mine, mine . . ."

It was early afternoon by the time Elaine stirred from sleep with the vampire still wrapped around her body and hot against her spine. She ached everywhere. She turned to see him open his eyes. His eyes were sleepy and human brown. He looked perfectly normal, if a little tousled and a touch pale. He looked beautiful.

Aramis gave her a tired smile. "Elaine," he whispered. He kissed her brow and rose. "Gather your things, but do not leave this car until I come for you."

Elaine grabbed the blankets and sat up. "What about breakfast . . . ?"

"Call your steward, and eat here." Aramis caught her chin and stared into her eyes. "You are not to go anywhere without me."

Elaine raised a brow at his command. "Aren't you being a little paranoid?"

"No." He tugged on his clothes with swift efficiency.

"I can't leave? Not even to take a shower?"

"Use the sink in here."

"Aramis, I need a shower! I stink of sex!"

"No shower." He caught her face and kissed her. His smile was swift. "You stink of me." He left her in a swirl of dark leather.

From the window in her cabin, the woods and fields showed that a light snow had fallen in the night. The sky was still gray with the threat of more snow to come.

After as thorough a wash as she was able, with only a cloth, Elaine dug out her warmest socks and pulled on her last clean pair of black jeans. To her dismay, the bite on her breast was too sensitive for her to wear a bra comfortably. She pulled on her softest T-shirt and yanked her heavy white sweater on over it, hoping that no one would notice her unrestrained breasts.

She was tugging her hair into a tight braid, while finishing the last of her tea and toast, when Aramis returned for her.

He immediately dug his fingers into her mane and tugged out the braid. "Leave your hair unbound."

"Aramis!"

"Please." He turned her face and touched his lips to hers. "For me."

Elaine sighed. "Fine, whatever." She brushed out her hair.

With a shuddering rattle and a squeal of train whistles, the *Orient Express* sailed past medieval castles, modern skyscrapers, and Gothic churches of Prague and into the soaring Victorian station in the heart of the snow-dusted city. The broad face of the station's antique clock tower showed their arrival exactly at two.

"It is time." Aramis set sunglasses over his eyes, his mouth set in a determined line. He lifted her backpack over his shoulder and looped her arm through his. "Do not leave my side."

Elaine took one last look at the art deco sleeper car. She was putting all her trust in the word of a total stranger, someone she had met only last night, and yet . . . Aramis had been honest with her. Honest about what he wanted from her, honest about what he was, honest about the power he held over her . . . honest about everything. The real question was, how honest was this man awaiting her in Prague? What did he want from her? A student or a meal?

There was only one way to find out.

Her heart slamming in her chest, Elaine tightened her fingers on the vampire's arm as he led her from her car toward the exits.

Under the soaring steel-and-glass–arched cover of the Victorian station, amongst the sea of shouting porters and disembarking passengers, Elaine held tight to Aramis's arm, while battling her long dark-blond hair and the wind. The sky was gray, the air bitterly cold, and the wind smelled strongly of snow.

With swift efficiency, Aramis organized the collection of

their luggage, a porter, and a rolling cart. He patted her cold fingers on his arm. "I have a car waiting. I will take you someplace safe—"

"Elaine!" The voice was youthful and eerily familiar.

Elaine turned to look behind her.

A tall, slender, and dark-haired young man wove through the crowd toward her. His hair was matted and his face looked sunken. There were dark circles under his blue eyes. His short brown leather coat flapped open over a thin T-shirt. His jeans didn't look particularly clean.

And yet, she knew him.

"Tony?" She frowned. When she had seen him in Rome, he had been ablaze with character, arrogance, and good humor. The girls had swarmed over him. Now he looked nothing like himself. He looked drained, worn-out. *What the hell has happened to him?*

Aramis turned, took one look at Anthony, and growled.

Anthony jerked to a startled halt, less than two yards away. He stared wide-eyed at Aramis, then darted a look at her. "Elaine?"

"Do not speak to her, Thrall." Aramis pulled Elaine behind him. "Where is your master?"

Elaine nearly choked. *Thrall?* Tony belonged to a vampire?

Anthony flinched. "He's . . . he's . . ." He shuddered. "Oh God, he's going to kill me. . . ."

Aramis sneered. "You are already dead."

"Boy, is there a problem?" The voice was cultured and grotesquely erotic.

Elaine felt heat flash through her heart, and yet her stomach churned as though she'd somehow come face-to-face with an open sewer. "Oh, my God . . ." Aramis had *not* been kidding when he'd said she'd know another vampire, but this . . . *this* was disgusting!

Aramis glanced down at her, his expression obscured by his dark sunglasses. "Avoid looking directly at him, and do not answer him."

"No problem," she whispered. "I think I'm going to be sick."

Aramis flashed a smile. "Good instincts."

The crowd parted around a tall, slender man impeccably dressed in a long pale-gray coat and charcoal slacks. His hair was neatly trimmed and silvery. His eyes were hidden behind dark glasses, but his face seemed carved from white marble. He stopped by Anthony and his expression turned frigid as he gazed at Aramis. "You . . ."

Aramis's fingers tightened over Elaine's hand. "Dimitri."

The pedestrians parted and flowed around the two vampires rather than between, as though sensing the two predators in their midst.

Dimitri nodded. "Is that my student?"

"No." Aramis smiled.

Dimitri glanced at Anthony.

Anthony flinched and nodded. He tucked his hands under his arms and refused to look at Elaine.

Dimitri raised his chin. "Elaine . . ."

Aramis smiled, but his voice came out in a growl. "I will thank you not to address my thrall."

"You've taken her?" Dimitri's jaw visibly tightened.

Aramis's smile turned frigidly cold. "In every way possible."

Elaine could not hold back the heat that flooded her cheeks. She looked away.

"Does she know?"

"Yes." Aramis's smile bled away. "She knows why you want her."

Dimitri folded his arms across his chest. "I am an instructor, as are you."

"Oh yes, we can both see quite clearly how you instruct your students." Aramis nodded at Anthony. "Can he still draw?"

Dimitri's lip curled. "He didn't have much to begin with. It's not as if he is a true loss."

Tony stared hard at the ground, his face white and his shoulders hunched.

Elaine stared at Tony's sunken gray face and felt her heart break. Tony was an artist, just not a portrait artist. Or rather, he had been. Even from this far away, she could tell something vital was missing from him.

Aramis released a soft breath. "If you will excuse us, we are leaving." He turned away.

Dimitri took a step toward them. "Aramis, I want her."

Aramis's head came up and he glared at Dimitri. "To destroy her talent as well?"

Dimitri scowled. "Do not pretend that you do not feed on her talent, Aramis. You are no better than I."

Aramis's arm trembled under Elaine's hand. "I do not consume."

Dimitri smiled. "Nor do you keep."

Aramis stiffened and his hand became a fist.

Dimitri tilted his head thoughtfully. "Tell me, have you ever made a fledgling?"

Aramis's fingers tightened on Elaine's arm. "I can—"

"Oh, I know you can, but have you?" Dimitri's smile broadened. "There is only one way to keep her out of my eventual grasp. The same way you escaped mine."

"This conversation is over." Aramis turned Elaine away.

Dimitri's voice snarled out behind them. "If you take her, you know what happens to the boy."

Aramis stopped, but he did not look back. "He is your thrall."

Elaine looked up sharply at Aramis, then back at Anthony. "Aramis, what's going on?"

Aramis looked down at the walk. "He is implying that he will bleed the boy's soul dry, tonight."

Elaine choked. "Drain his soul? And then what? Will he let him go?"

"He will let him go, but"—Aramis sighed—"the body cannot live without a soul. He will die within a day."

"Die?" Elaine looked back at Anthony. "We can't let that happen. . . ."

Aramis turned to look at her. "The boy is already dying."

Elaine gasped as her heart tried to stop in her chest. "What?"

Aramis covered her cold fingers with his warm palm. "Too much of his soul has already been consumed. Even if we took him with us right now, he would be dead in less than a month."

Elaine blinked back sudden tears. Vibrant and alive Tony was dying? "There is no way to save him?"

Dimitri laughed. "Oh, come now, Aramis, you could save the boy."

Elaine looked back at Anthony. "Aramis?"

Aramis refused to look back at Dimitri.

Dimitri pulled off his sunglasses and wiped them with a handkerchief. His eyes were a hard stone-gray. "If you leave the girl, I will let you take him. Make him your fledgling, and he lives."

Elaine frowned. "Is he saying that you should make Tony into a vampire?"

Aramis stared at the ground. "Yes."

"Save the boy. Give me the girl." Dimitri's voice was as soft as a whisper, yet crystal clear.

Aramis's jaw clenched. "Mine." His voice was so soft, Elaine barely heard him. Aramis turned to face the other vampire. "Since you want the boy saved, Dimitri, Rafael still owes me a favor."

Dimitri froze. "You would not . . ."

"Consider it done." Aramis smiled coldly. "I will tell him to expect your car, an hour after sunset."

Dimitri threw his hand out. "This does not concern Rafael!"

Aramis stared steadily at the other vampire. "For me, he would make it a concern, and we both know how he feels about your destructive appetites."

Dimitri's hands balled into fists. "You will pay for this!" He stabbed a finger toward Elaine. "She will pay!"

Aramis's entire body tensed. His lips curled back in a snarl. "You would dare?"

Dimitri snarled right back. "Sooner or later, you will release her, and I will be there to collect!" He turned on his heel and stalked away. "Anthony, come!" The sea of people closed around him.

Anthony stared openmouthed at Aramis; then he turned and darted into the crowd after Dimitri.

Elaine curled her lip in disgust. "Well, that was nasty."

"Aptly put." Aramis lifted his hand and gestured to the porter still sitting by their cart. "It is a long drive to Rafael's . . . house. It is best that we begin immediately." He led her briskly across the busy drive toward the tree-lined car park on the opposite side.

Elaine looked up at the pale vampire walking at her side. "You are taking me to see Rafael?"

"Rafael is having a house party, and I am an invited guest." Aramis nodded to the porter and gestured toward a sleek black car with shiny new tire chains. He tossed him a set of car keys.

The porter caught the keys, opened the car's trunk, lifted the cases, and began stowing the luggage in the trunk.

Elaine stared at the car. It was a freaking Jaguar.

"I intended to invite you to come with me." Aramis looked down at the cobblestoned drive. "I was not willing to relinquish your . . . company."

He was not willing to relinquish my *company.* Elaine's heart gave a silly little leap. It almost sounded . . . romantic. She tried to squash the warmth flooding her heart, but she simply couldn't.

"Once I knew that Dimitri was involved, it was my intent to have you remain under Rafael's protection while I made arrangements to send you home."

Home? Elaine tripped on the pavement. She had to go home sometime. And then it would be over. Europe, the vampire— everything. Over. She looked up at Aramis. "And now?"

The porter tossed the keys back to Aramis.

Aramis caught the keys in a smooth gesture and leaned down to unlock the passenger door. "And now, as before, we must still deal with Dimitri."

⊠
_____

Elaine buckled her seat belt. "Aramis, you own a Jaguar?"

Aramis smiled as he fastened his seat belt, too. "I do, but this one belongs to Rafael." He turned the key and the sleek black vehicle purred to life. "He left this one for my convenience." He turned in his seat and backed the car from its parking space. Aramis turned the car into traffic and glanced at Elaine. "Hold on, traffic in Prague can be . . . adventurous."

Elaine grabbed the door handle. "Adventurous . . . ?"

Tire chains jingling, the sleek Jaguar raced through the narrow, winding, and ill-paved streets. It dodged other vehicles at breathtaking speed. There wasn't a streetlight or street sign that wasn't ignored by every vehicle on the road. In a matter of minutes, the black car blazed out of the aged city and onto a narrow, high-banked, snow-dusted farmland road.

The winter countryside was picturesque. And after about twenty minutes of fallow fields, leafless woods, and steel gray skies, Elaine found it incredibly dull. A yawn came out of nowhere.

Aramis chuckled. "Lie down and sleep. You will likely have a long night ahead of you."

Elaine grinned at Aramis. "Another long night, like last night?" *Full of screaming orgasms?*

"Of course." Aramis smiled broadly. "I intend to avail myself of your company." His smile thinned and his voice lowered. "For as long as you remain in my company."

Elaine set the Jaguar's soft leather seat back, her smile fading. Sooner or later, this Gothic romance adventure was going to end. She curled her hands into her chest and stared at the vampire's spectacular profile. Once he sent her back to the States, it was highly doubtful that she would ever see him again. She took a deep breath, smelling the leather of the seat under her, plus the warmth that was Aramis. A sharp stab of pain arrowed through her heart.

Aramis lifted his hand from the steering wheel and his fingers drifted lightly through her hair.

Elaine pressed a kiss to his fingertips and closed her eyes. The adventure wasn't over yet. She would worry about it when the time came. Meanwhile, she would enjoy what time she had.

"Elaine."

Elaine came out of a deep and dreamless sleep with a moaning and bone-popping stretch across the leather seat. Soft classical music played on the Jaguar's stereo. She smiled at the vampire. "Are we there yet?"

Aramis rolled his eyes and grinned. "Nearly. And you have my permission to do that again."

"Do what?" She grabbed the lever on the side of the seat to set her chair back upright.

Aramis shook his head and changed gears. "Never mind."

The open countryside had turned to a pale and glowing late

afternoon. Snow fell in thick fluffy clumps. Elaine jerked fully upright. "Oh . . . it's snowing!"

"You like snow?"

"I love snow!" Elaine curled her knee under her to get a better look out the passenger window. Everything was coated with a softly glowing blanket of pristine white. "It doesn't snow near enough in the Carolinas." Her breath fogged the glass. She smeared the fog away and spotted a building as they came up a rise. A big building . . . no, a huge building. Tall gray stone walls rose and rose for several stories, stretching across the road. A crenellated stone bridge appeared at the bottom of the hill. It spanned a deep, dry moat and led into a monstrous gateway. Huge floodlights spilled up and across the gateway and the guards.

Elaine faced the windshield and inhaled. "Aramis, are we going to that castle?"

"Yes. Rafael's *palazzo* is within the walls."

" '*Palazzo* . . . '?" She looked over at the vampire. "Rafael has a *palace*?"

Aramis gave her a small shrug. "This one is more of a Roman villa."

Elaine sat back in her seat. "A Roman villa inside a castle?"

Aramis smiled. "Rafael says it reminds him of home."

The sleek Jaguar stopped at the end of the bridge between a pair of well-lit gatehouses posted on either side of the castle's yawning gateway.

Aramis buzzed down both the driver's-side and the passenger-side windows. He turned to Elaine. "Give the guard your hand." He stuck his hand out the window.

A dark-uniformed guard, wearing thick winter gear and carrying a semiautomatic rifle, waited outside Elaine's window. His eyes were black and overlarge. *A vampire . . .*

Elaine stuck out her hand. Snow struck her palm and melted.

The guard bowed over her wrist, sniffed, and nodded at Elaine. He lifted his head and barked out something to the other guard.

Aramis changed gears and the car began to move forward.

Okay, that was weird. Elaine jerked her arm in and rubbed her chilled fingers against her thigh. It was freaking cold out there. "He didn't want my ID?"

The windows buzzed upward and closed.

Aramis smiled tightly. "Your blood is your identification."

"My blood?"

Aramis nodded. "Your identity as my thrall is written in your scent."

Elaine winced. *His thrall—his food.* Her following thoughts were lost while they drove through the ancient stone passage-way that tunneled through the castle wall. It was freaking huge. It was wide enough and appeared tall enough to let a semi pass. There was a soft S-curve in the middle of it.

She blinked. *Whoa, those are some thick walls.*

The tunnel opened up to a snow-shrouded formal garden, with huge bare-limbed trees completely enclosed by the monstrous castle walls. Moments later, the Jaguar rolled onto the broad gravel drive of an honest-to-God four-story Roman *palazzo* built entirely of sculpted white marble. Two curved and floodlit wings arced outward, framing the broad steps of the Corinthian-colonnaded front entrance.

Elaine looked at Aramis. "It's Roman all right, but this is no little villa."

Aramis stopped the car and gave her a wry grin. "Nor is it his palace."

Elaine's breath stopped. *This guy has a real palace?* She

looked over at Aramis, but he was already out of the car. Her door was tugged open by a uniformed guard.

Elaine stared at the open door. *I guess I should get out.* She climbed out and the door was closed for her. She turned and watched as two men in formal black-tuxedo livery pulled their suitcases from the Jaguar's trunk.

Aramis came around the Jaguar's nose to take her right arm. "Stay on my left." Together they climbed steps that were swept clean of snow and onto the gray carpet before the glass double doors.

More liveried men pushed both doors open.

Elaine felt heat wash over her face from the open doors. She followed Aramis into the *palazzo*'s main entry. Just within, two massive wooden doors stood open. Sculptures stood in wall niches under spills of golden light. Black lacquer art deco chairs sat by gilded art deco tables. A crystal chandelier chimed on the distant and sculpted ceiling. Tall flower arrangements were scattered everywhere. Directly ahead of her, a large broad staircase rose upward and curved to the left.

Elaine nibbled on her bottom lip. *This is a private residence? Somebody actually lives here?* It looked more like a really, really expensive museum than a home.

A man in gloves and a tux bowed and gestured for their coats.

Aramis let his long coat slide from his shoulders, showing his charcoal gray wool sweater and black angora trousers.

Elaine felt distinctly shabby in her less-than-authentic cream sweater and her black jeans. Bereft of her coat, fingers of warmth climbed up her legs from the floor. She looked down at the snowy marble. *He must be heating the building the old Roman way, with a furnace pushing heated air through hollow stones in the floor.*

A statuesque woman, dressed in an expensively tailored white suit, with an amazingly short skirt, stepped from the galleried archway on the right. Her sleek black hair was upswept in a smooth French twist and pinned with glittering diamond stars. A matching diamond choker blazed around her throat. Oceanlike blue eyes focused briefly on Elaine; then she bowed gracefully to Aramis. "Welcome, Aramis." She turned and nodded to Elaine. "Welcome, guest of Aramis, to the palazzo of Rafael. I am Countess Sephonie." And she was a vampire.

Elaine bit back a nervous smile. She could feel the pressure of the woman's nature against her heart. *Okay, formal-manners time.* She inclined her head. "I thank you for your gracious welcome, Countess Sephonie, I am Elaine."

Sephonie smiled brilliantly. "My pleasure, Elaine." She raised a slender brow at Aramis. "Oh, I like this one."

Aramis grinned and shook his head. "Be cautious in your appraisal. Elaine has been known to surprise."

Elaine frowned up at Aramis. "What is that supposed to mean?"

Sephonie laughed. "I see what you mean." She turned toward the archway she had just come from. "Rafael is waiting for you in the small salon." She raised her hand. "This way, please."

Elaine marched at Aramis's left elbow as they followed Sephonie into the white marble hall. Striding carelessly on brilliant carpets, they passed incredible art objects and ornate flower arrangements displayed on intimately lit tables within tiny alcoves set into the walls. Broad doorways on the left and the right revealed the occasional person, clad in formal livery, arranging exotic flowers or moving exquisite furniture.

Elaine's heart began to pound for no reason that she could think of. The farther she walked down the hall, the more she felt like she was seriously out of her depth. By the time they stopped at a pair of floor-to-ceiling doors of gleaming bronze, her heart was beating in her mouth, and sweat was trickling down her spine.

Aramis looked down at her. "Is something wrong?"

Elaine licked her dry lips. "I'm fine." She took a deep breath and tried to calm her hammering heart. Unfortunately, her heart was not in the mood to listen.

"I'll have your suite readied." Sephonie pushed the bronze doors open and stepped back.

The room appeared to be at least two stories high and immense. The entire far wall was nothing but floor-to-ceiling windows, framed in dark golden silk, showing the falling snow. A humongous and ornately carved fireplace of white marble took up the left wall. All other available wall space consisted of massive bookshelves crammed with books, papers, scrolls, and odd statuary. The center of the marble floor held a circular carpet in scarlet and gold. A low table of thick glass, which was balanced on the outstretched wings of two angels, was framed by four wing-back chairs of red velvet. A silver coffee service was parked carelessly on the glass table alongside three plain white mugs. One mug sat haphazardly near the table's edge on a small paper napkin.

Elaine stared into the room. She didn't want to go in there. There was absolutely nothing alarming about the room; in fact, it was rather warm and friendly, in a big expensive kind of way. However, something about the room was making her heart pound in her ears, her body sweat cold, and her stomach distinctly unhappy, as though something truly dangerous was in there. Suddenly she wished to God that she had asked to stay behind.

Behind her, the closing doors gave a hollow *boom.*

She nearly jumped out of her skin.

Aramis frowned down at Elaine and caught her clammy

hand, drawing her into the room. "Elaine, you're safe. No one will harm you here."

Elaine nodded, too breathless to speak.

"Is something wrong?" A slender young man stepped from the far corner of the room. He wore an Irish cable-knit cream sweater and fawn slacks. He crossed the room toward them with utterly silent steps.

Aramis lifted his head and smiled. "Rafael."

"Aramis!" His stride lengthened and he smiled with exquisite sweetness. "Pleased I am that you are here." Red highlights gleamed in his dark curls, which were worn loose and tumbling at his brow and across his shoulders. His rounded cheekbones and pointed chin perfectly set off the full Cupid's bow of his mouth, defining the delicately youthful face of an Italian Renaissance angel.

Aramis, smiling broadly, released Elaine's hand to take Rafael's hand. "It is very good to be here."

Rafael looked down at Elaine. Eyes as blue as a summer sky, framed by sooty lashes, peered at her from under the fine arch of black brows. "And you have brought a guest!" His smile turned sly and he glanced at Aramis. "How novel."

Elaine's breath caught. Her eyes told her quite firmly that Rafael was perfectly human and young, barely twenty, but her body knew a predator when it felt one. He was the reason her heart was thundering in her chest. There was absolutely no doubt in her mind that this small and beautiful boyish figure could eat her in one gulp.

Aramis set his hand on Elaine's shoulder, and his smile softened. "This is Elaine."

Elaine couldn't make a sound come out of her mouth, so she smiled and nodded, desperately wishing that Rafael would look elsewhere.

Rafael's head tilted as he watched Elaine. "Very new, I gather?"

Aramis looked down at the floor and then up from under his brows. "Last night."

"Last night?" Rafael raised his brow at Aramis, then focused on Elaine. "And yet, so stout of heart."

Elaine continued to hold her smile and firmly clasped her hands to hide their shaking. *Could you please stop looking at me?*

Aramis peered at Elaine, his gaze flicking from her eyes to her white-knuckled hands. He sighed. "Ah . . ."

"You had not noticed?" Rafael shook his head. "For shame, Aramis, your first visit was not all that long ago."

Aramis smiled. "I have since had time to get accustomed to your . . . presence." He squeezed Elaine's shoulder. "Be at ease, you are safe here," he said softly.

Elaine simply could not make herself believe him, but she kept smiling.

Rafael lifted his chin and smiled at Aramis. "Coffee?" He turned to Elaine. "Colombian, fresh brewed, less than five minutes old?"

Elaine stared longingly at the silver coffeepot. She would dearly love a cup of coffee. She glanced up at Rafael—and still couldn't get a word out of her mouth, so she nodded.

With a smile, Rafael led them over to the glass table and patted one of the chairs absently. "Aramis, perhaps you should pour, and let your guest be seated?"

Aramis nodded at the chair Rafael had indicated and bent to pick up the silver pot.

Elaine perched on the edge of the chair, too nervous to sit back.

Rafael collected the mug at the end of the table, chose a chair on the opposite side, and flopped into it, tossing one leg over the arm. He smiled briefly at Elaine, then focused on Aramis. "Your call said it was somewhat urgent."

"Yes." Aramis handed Elaine a white mug of coffee, which was loaded with cream and sugar.

Elaine took it with both hands. Her hands were shaking so badly, she was terrified that she would drop it.

Aramis poured coffee into the last mug and sat in the chair between Elaine and Rafael. "It is Dimitri."

Elaine felt oddly comforted to have Aramis sitting between her and Rafael. She was able to sit back and actually sip her coffee. It had more cream and sugar than she would have used, but at that moment, she really didn't care. It was *coffee*, her favorite addiction.

"Dimitri?" Rafael rolled his eyes and curled his lip. "What does he want now?"

Aramis closed both hands on his mug and looked over at Rafael. "He wants Elaine."

Rafael's gaze sharpened and his smile tightened. "Explain."

Aramis proceeded to outline the situation with Dimitri, Anthony, and Elaine. He spoke completely without embellishment, as though detailing a military report.

Rafael listened and sipped his coffee. His gaze drifted to Elaine. "How talented is she?"

Elaine froze in the middle of her sip. She simply could not swallow until his gaze moved away.

Aramis set his cup on the glass table, then sat back in the chair. "Better than I."

Embarrassed warmth filled Elaine's cheeks.

Rafael's brows lifted and his lips parted just a tiny bit. "I see. . . ." He leaned forward to set his cup on the table. "I will make arrangements for the boy's care." He sat back and folded one knee over the other, focusing fully on Aramis. "However, this will not resolve the situation."

Aramis looked over at Rafael. "I was hoping to leave Elaine under your protection while I made arrangements to send her back."

Send me back. Elaine jolted, just a hair. She took a firm breath. She had to go back. It wasn't so much that she was needed at home, it was more that she obviously did not belong here. Her gaze flicked to Rafael. He was watching her again. She lowered her gaze. *Nope, I definitely don't belong here.*

Rafael's smile completely disappeared. "That will not stop Dimitri's pursuit. This is the second, and if you count the boy, the third time you have taken what he feels is his. He will not rest until he has what revenge he can collect. You know this."

Aramis shook his head. "I cannot allow—"

Rafael leaned forward. "I know this, and I agree, but there are only two ways to prevent his eventual success. You must remove temptation, or even the battlefield. If she is as talented as you say, only one choice is completely beyond Dimitri's reach. He has time on his side."

Aramis stared at his hands. "I am not ready."

"No one is ever ready." Rafael smiled. "But this decision comes to us all. I've had to make these choices myself, if you remember." He shrugged and pursed his lips. "I do have a few regrets, but these are things we must all face in time."

Elaine was well aware that they were discussing her, but she wasn't quite sure what they were discussing. At the same time, she was desperately glad that she was not included in the conversation. Her pounding heart simply couldn't handle the attention.

Aramis scowled at his clenched hands. "I do not have your sound judgment."

Rafael glanced at Elaine. "I think you underestimate yourself." He tilted his head. "Have you asked?"

Aramis sighed. "No."

"Ask." Rafael leaned back in his chair. "Whatever choice is made, my suggestion is not to delay. Dimitri knows that either possibility exists. With his long military history, he is more likely to act very swiftly rather than wait. Tonight would be best for all."

Aramis's head came up. "Tonight?"

Rafael smiled at Elaine. "Tonight you will have resources that you may not have at another time."

Aramis smiled tightly. "Are you perhaps volunteering?"

"Absolutely!" Rafael smiled. "The will is there, I assume?"

"Very much so." Aramis chuckled. "I barely have a grasp on it."

"Excellent!" Rafael grinned. "Can you imagine such a pairing of talent and power with such a will?"

"No one of the court would stand a chance." Aramis sighed and sat back. "The education will be challenging, to say the least."

Rafael's brow shot up. "I have not enjoyed the challenge of strong potential in quite a while." He smiled warmly. "Not since your youth."

Aramis released a long breath. "You would truly be willing to do this with me?"

Rafael snorted. "I would be grievously insulted to be left out!"

Aramis nodded. "I will ask."

Rafael arose from his chair. "Do not delay, Aramis. It is possible Dimitri will act on arrival."

"I will ask as soon as I have a private moment." Aramis stood and held his hand out to Elaine.

Elaine set her empty mug on the glass tabletop and stood. A

sound like falling leaves hissed in her ears, nearly overwhelming the *thump* of her hammering heart.

"Then by all means let us gain you that privacy immediately." Rafael strode to the wall and tugged on a long, dangling ribbon. He turned back and frowned. "Have you eaten?"

Aramis shook his head. "There wasn't time."

Elaine snorted. *Well, there goes that vampire myth.* Apparently, vampires ate normal food. Aramis had to be seriously hungry. She doubted he'd stopped to eat even a Continental breakfast of coffee and toast. She felt her stomach roil. She was hungry, but she wasn't sure she could eat a bite. Heat flushed through her entire body. She had to open her mouth to breathe past it. The rushing sound in her ears escalated to a windstorm.

Rafael nodded. "I will notify the kitchen."

Aramis rolled his eyes. "I can order dinner—"

Rafael's gaze flicked to Elaine. "You have more important tasks to attend to, such as acquiring privacy." He grinned. "I will notify the dressers that you have a guest in need of a costume for this evening's masquerade."

"Your masquerade!" Aramis groaned. "It slipped my mind entirely."

A liveried young man pushed the bronze doors open.

As Elaine listened, their voices began to fade under the loud windstorm in her head; then as she watched, Aramis's face seemed to be going away, as though down a long tunnel. She didn't quite notice when her knees buckled. One minute she was swaying on her feet; the next minute, the nice warm carpet was under her back, and she was staring at a blue sky and clouds painted on a ceiling very far away.

9

Someone was speaking to her. She could barely hear them through the loud rushing wind in her ears. "What?" Elaine opened her eyes. She didn't remember closing them. The room passed by her eyes in a blur. She was being carried in someone's arms. It smelled like Aramis. Her cheek was against his gray sweater. *God, he smells good. . . .* Someone's fingers pressed in the hollow under her jaw. She was pretty sure it was Aramis.

"Her pulse is strong." It sounded like Aramis.

"Too strong." That sounded like Rafael somewhere past Aramis's shoulder. "I can hear her heart beating."

Her heart gave a hard lurch.

Rafael's voice softened. "It's getting stronger."

"She's reacting to your presence."

"She's reacting to both of us. You forget your own strength. She needs to be bled."

"It's too soon. . . ."

"Rather than too late. Bleed her, you don't have much time."

Cool shadows fell around them.

"I will leave you in here. Ask her now."

Aramis's arms tightened around her. "Now?"

"Now. I expect an answer when I return with the Aquinas."

Elaine felt the world shift, then become still. She opened her eyes again, and again she didn't remember closing them. She looked up at Aramis. She was sprawled across his lap in a small room that was dark and, thankfully, cool. Her long hair spilled over his supporting arm, nearly to the floor. She was pretty sure they were on some kind of sofa, but she was having problems focusing on details. The one thing she was perfectly aware of was that Rafael was not in there with them. The pressure in her chest loosened.

Aramis stared down at her, his eyes black and inhuman, his brows drawn together. "Elaine, can you hear me?"

"Aramis?" Her tongue was as thick and dry as leather in her mouth. Her whole body was hot as a furnace. "Thirsty."

He smiled briefly. "You'll have plenty to drink in a moment." He levered her up against his shoulder. "Elaine, I need to ask you a question."

She smiled tiredly. "Sure."

Aramis tilted her chin to peer into her eyes. "Elaine, would you like to be a vampire?"

Elaine frowned. She could not have heard that right. "What?"

Aramis's mouth tightened. "I need to bleed you, to ease your heart." He pressed his palm over her pounding heart. "If I drink deeply enough to ease you while you remain my thrall, it will take time for the soul to heal, and your creativity to return."

A fist squeezed tight around her already slamming heart. Without her art, she was nothing . . . nothing. "No . . ." She struggled, pushing at him tiredly. "*Not* my art."

Aramis held her easily. "Elaine, be calm. I will not take more than you can recover from, but if you are a vampire, you won't

86

lose it at all. It will not be quite the same, but you will not lose what you have."

"I won't?" Elaine stilled. "Wait, what do you mean, *not* 'quite the same'?"

Aramis sighed. "To make you a vampire, I take part of your soul and you take part of mine. This . . . changes things, within."

Elaine latched onto the one important aspect of what he said. "I won't lose my art?"

"No, your gift will be safe." Aramis smiled briefly. "In fact, you will have a part of my art, as I will have a part of yours."

"And Dimitri can't feed on me if I'm a vampire?"

"Yes, he or any other vampire can." Aramis's gaze turned to ice. "Your art will be safe, but your blood will carry other properties that will be just as alluring. You will be far more difficult to hunt, but you will also be the least among us."

"Oh . . ." Elaine let that tumble around in her head. "Then . . ." She licked her lips. "Either way, I'm still at the bottom of the food chain?"

"I am afraid so." Aramis smiled briefly. "It is different . . . taking from a vampire. The soul of a vampire is not the same. It does not give, or enthrall, so easily. Taking from a vampire does not destroy them, as it does an artist."

Elaine frowned. "If I am a vampire, will I *have* to drink blood?"

Aramis held her gaze. "You must drink the souls of others to remain alive."

"Oh"—she shook her head—"but I don't want to take anybody else's soul."

"Nor do I." Aramis rolled his eyes and his smile soured. "A sip or two from a talented artist will maintain us for quite a while. The greater the artist, the less we need to take, and the less harm we cause to them. As a very young vampire, weeks may pass before you need to take more than a single sip. However, as you gain in age, the need becomes greater." He brushed his hand across her hot brow. "Rafael is very old and does not feed on humans at all. He cannot, without consuming them completely."

"He doesn't feed on humans?"

"No. Rafael is a maestro of the violin. He would starve before destroying another artist." He shook his head. "I've seen him do so."

Then who . . . ? Elaine looked up at Aramis's beautiful profile. If Rafael didn't drink from humans, there was only one option left. "The party . . . Rafael needs to feed."

"Yes." Aramis smiled tightly. "This is why Dimitri did not wish to come. If he appears at the door, he is offering his blood to Rafael."

Dimitri definitely hadn't wanted to come. "But if he doesn't come . . ." Elaine's breath caught. "What about Tony?"

"Oh, Dimitri will come, and he will bring the boy. His pride will compel him." Aramis smiled coldly. "And Rafael will claim his due, you may be sure."

"And that's it? Rafael has a taste from everybody, and then everybody goes home?"

Aramis sighed. "Yes and no. From among his guests, Rafael chooses a vampire to become his lover. During that time, they enjoy unlimited wealth and an enormous amount of influence, but they are completely subject to his will. They are his thrall, as you are mine. When he is ready to release them, he throws another party to choose another."

Elaine bit her lip. "Aren't you worried he'll pick you?"

"Elaine." Aramis caught her chin and focused fully on her. "Pay attention to what is important! Dimitri will be very, very angry when he arrives. You will be in great danger. You will need protection, even after he leaves. As my thrall, I can keep you safe for only as long as you remain my thrall. . . ."

Elaine shivered. "And also feeding on my art."

"Yes, but if you are a vampire, your art remains yours, and you will be under Rafael's protection, as well as mine."

"Rafael's too?"

"Rafael is willing to partner me in making you a vampire."

"I'm going to have two . . . ?" What was that term she'd read in her books? *Oh yeah* . . . "Two . . . sires?"

Aramis smiled wryly. "What child does not benefit from two parents?"

Elaine snorted. "Very funny." *Very scary, actually.* For all Rafael's sweet looks, he frightened the living hell out of her. Her heart was still pounding in her chest.

"Having two sires is best." Aramis sighed. "New fledglings cannot be parted from their sires, as the sires carry the fledglings' souls. To be physically separated too young is to kill them. By having two sires, you will always have one available when the other must be elsewhere."

"Oh . . ." Elaine shifted restlessly. "Do I have to be a thrall . . . ?" *A sex slave.* "Or a vampire? I can't just be myself?"

Aramis gave her a small, sad smile. "Dimitri would see you drained of your talents, and possibly your life, before the year ended."

"But I don't live in Europe. . . ."

Aramis shook his head. "It does not matter where you live. Dimitri has the resources to follow you wherever you go." He gazed at her with wide, dark, hypnotic eyes. "And he has all the time—that you do not—to wait."

Elaine folded her hands under her arms. "I don't have much of a choice, do I?"

"Nor do I, Elaine." Aramis stroked her brow. "This is as

difficult for me as it is for you. You will mean a great deal of responsibility."

"Oh, come on!" Elaine scowled. "I'm not a child."

"But you will be." Aramis smiled tiredly. "A new vampire is very childlike in a lot of ways. They require just as much guidance and protection as any mortal child."

"Are vampires immortal?"

"No, we can be killed, like anyone else, though it is far more difficult to do so."

"You just stay young forever?"

"We stay young, as long as we feed well."

"Oh . . ." Elaine stared into the shadows. It was a lot to think about.

"Elaine." Aramis tilted her chin to focus his gaze on hers. "Would you like to be a vampire?"

"You mean I have to decide right now?"

The door behind the sofa opened. Elaine's breath caught, and her pulse pounded in her ears. Rafael was in the room.

"Now would be an excellent time to decide." Rafael moved around them and set a tray with a large metal pitcher and a plain tumbler on a small table at the far end of the sofa. He turned and locked gazes with Elaine. "Dimitri is on his way, and my contacts say the boy with him does not look at all good."

10

Aramis lifted his head. "If we do this now, we will miss your masquerade."

Rafael smiled. "Merely the beginning."

Elaine jerked upright. She simply could not sit still, and prone, with Rafael so close. Her head ached and her heart slammed painfully in her chest with the movement.

Rafael dropped to one knee at the side of the sofa. "Aramis, a decision?"

He was too close. He was too big against her heart, too loud in her head, too scary altogether. . . . Elaine tried to scramble away.

Aramis trapped her in his lap. "Elaine."

"Let go!" Elaine's fist cocked back for a vicious punch. She focused on her target, Aramis's throat.

"Stop!" Aramis's voice cracked like thunder.

Elaine froze.

Aramis's lip curled, baring long teeth that had appeared out of nowhere. "Put it down."

Elaine vibrated with a terror that was almost closer to fury, but she set her fist down in her lap.

Rafael snorted, and a smile tilted his perfect mouth. "Are you *sure* you took her?"

"Four times." A rolling liquid growl rumbled from Aramis's chest. "The Aquinas."

Rafael stepped back and poured what looked like ordinary water from the pitcher into the glass. "Full glass?"

"Yes." Aramis's inhumanly black and furious eyes locked firmly on hers. "Vampire or not? Choose, Elaine."

Elaine's mind went completely blank. She couldn't think past the blood pounding in her veins.

Rafael held the glass out to Aramis. "She may be too frightened to think straight." Amusement colored his entire expression.

Aramis's eyes narrowed at Elaine. He bared the full length of his teeth at her, and shouted, "Predator or prey! *Choose!*"

He shouted *at me?* White-hot fury seared the back of her skull. She shouted right back: "Predator, you bastard!" Her fist shot out, straight for his mouth.

Aramis caught her fist in his hand and grinned. "Good."

Elaine froze, startled. *Oh God, what did I just do?*

Rafael chuckled. "This one is going to be quite entertaining to educate."

Aramis pushed her hand down into her lap and reached back to take the glass from Rafael. "I am thrilled that you think so." He smiled sourly and lifted the glass to her mouth. "Drink."

Elaine licked her lips and reached for the glass. She was dying of thirst.

Aramis pulled it away. "No." He set the glass to her lips. "Drink."

Elaine let him tip the glass and drank. It didn't quite taste like water, too pure, too sweet. Also, the more she drank, the more she wanted. She finished the glass far more quickly than she thought she would.

Aramis handed the empty glass back to Rafael.

Elaine's head began to swim, and her panic slid back under a thick wave of exhilaration, quickly followed by a wave of relaxation. She suddenly felt really, really good. Almost happy. "Whoa . . . what was that?"

Rafael rose to his feet. "We will need to hurry." He moved around the sofa and pushed the door open.

Aramis scooped her up into his arms and rose to his feet. "Aquinas relaxes the will."

Elaine flopped back, completely relaxed in his arms, and groaned. "More compliance stuff?"

Aramis winced. "Yes." He followed at Rafael's heels, striding across the huge room with Elaine nestled in his arms.

Rafael glanced back as they passed the open bronze doors. "Aquinas tempers the fear. If we try to take you without it, your instinctive fear will not let you feel anything beyond pain."

Oh, that's right. They're making me into a vampire. She knew damned well she should be alarmed, but for some reason, she couldn't quite summon the energy to do more than wonder. Elaine watched the hallway pass in a blur of white walls and smears of color. Doors slammed opened and then closed. People scurried around them. A long, winding staircase . . .

Elaine's shoes were tugged from her feet, and she started awake. "Huh?" She was lying on an enormous bed, in a black-as-night room, with walls and columns of black-and-silver marble. She was looking up at a huge black dome painted with clouds and studded with glittering crystal stars. In the center of the dome, a round chandelier blazed with rainbow-tinted crystals, like a moon. She moved her arm, and something crinkled under her. *Plastic?* A glance showed that a clear plastic sheet had been spread over the bed's scarlet silk duvet.

Aramis leaned over her to tug at her belt, then opened the button on her pants. His sweater was missing. His bare chest shifted in an amazing display of muscle. Rafael was off to one side of the bed, hastily tugging his cream sweater off and revealing a body built like a Greek statue.

Her pants slid from her thighs and Elaine's attention returned to Aramis. "Hey, um . . . am I about to have sex with both of you?"

Aramis's smile was tight as he tossed her jeans away. "Something like that."

Elaine released her breath. "Oh." She frowned. Her thoughts were muddy and hard to collect. "What's with the plastic sheet?"

"It is to save the silk." Rafael crawled across the bed toward them. "From bloodstains."

Elaine stared. Rafael was freaking gorgeous in motion, and totally naked. He seemed to glow against the room's darkness. Her eyes were drawn from his predatory smile, all the way down his sculpted body, to his jutting cock. He was clearly happy to be there.

Before she had more than a moment to wonder, strong hands pulled her upright, then drew her sweater up her body and off her arms. She vaguely watched it fly across the room.

Rafael crawled behind her. His arm closed around her waist, supporting her back against his smooth, cool body. His lips brushed her shoulder. "She smells incredible."

Aramis licked his lips. "She tastes better." He opened his trousers and dropped them. His cock was thick, heavy, and rigidly erect.

Fingers pressed against the side of her throat. Rafael's voice was soft. "Her blood pressure is very high. Between the two of us, this will be very swift."

The bed dipped as Aramis knelt on the mattress. "I have not done this before."

"Of this, I am well aware." Rafael chuckled softly and drew Elaine backward toward the center of the bed. "It is quite simple—you bleed, you fuck, you drink, and you bleed."

Aramis shook his head as he crawled, following them to the center of the bed. "I do not know how to hold a soul."

Rafael let Elaine fall back onto the bed, her honey mane spilling everywhere. "Your heart will know." His eyes had changed to narrow rings that were a vivid sky blue, around pits of infinite shadow. "For the heart is where the soul of another is kept." He smiled, showing fangs that would have done a lion proud.

Elaine shivered, but panic seemed to be a small flutter, very far away.

Rafael's eyes narrowed at Aramis. "You will need to drink first, and very deeply, to catch her. She will need your scent to ease her as I take the rest."

"Agreed." Aramis stretched out beside Elaine. He cupped her hip and pulled, tilting her onto her side, facing him. "But she has only been debauched once."

"Oh?" Rafael stretched out along her back. "You, I assume?"

Aramis smiled. "You assume correctly." He leaned close to brush a kiss across her mouth.

Elaine closed her eyes and opened for his kiss. Her tongue brushed by his long teeth, then stroked against his tongue. Heat speared straight to her core and tightened everything. She caught the perfume of expensive oil.

Rafael groaned. "I am oiled, I am ready."

Aramis brushed loose hair from Elaine's shoulder. "Forgive us, but we must be swift."

Rafael leaned up and pressed his lips to Elaine's ear. His black curls swept across her bare shoulder. "There will be time, and then some, for more thorough exploration later. This, I promise." He lifted his head. "Aramis, you know what must come first?"

Aramis's gaze slid to Rafael. "I know." He rolled Elaine on top of him and lifted his knees, forcing her body to spread wide while pressing the heated length up against her intimate and rapidly creaming flesh.

Elaine felt the hard heat of him seek, find, center, and thrust, sliding deep into her. She gasped, her legs tightened, and she rocked, to feel him move within her. She moaned. God, he felt good.

Aramis groaned and his hand pressed against her butt to still her. "Save your eagerness." He smiled.

Rafael slid in close, along her right side, one leg covering theirs with the hot length of his cock pressing against the side of her thigh. He set his arm across Elaine's back, holding them both in his embrace.

Aramis took her mouth in a voracious kiss and turned his head away from Rafael, easing Elaine slightly to one side. He closed his eyes and explored her mouth.

Elaine groaned under the skillful caress of Aramis's tongue against hers, but she couldn't close her eyes.

From less than a kiss away, Rafael knotted his hand in Aramis's long hair, then brushed his lips against the throbbing hollow on Aramis's neck above his collarbone. His lips came back, showing the points of his teeth pressing into the skin of Aramis's throat. His gaze focused on Elaine, and his arm tightened around them both.

Elaine's breath stilled, and the hair rose on the back of her neck.

Aramis's arms closed hard around her, his tongue working deep and slow in her mouth as his heart hammered against hers.

Rafael bit down very carefully, but deeply, stabbing the full length of his fangs into Aramis's throat.

Elaine felt shock—and a flare of erotic heat.

Aramis tensed and moaned into her mouth, his eyes closed tight. He surged hard into her body and held perfectly still, deep within her, his entire body taut and trembling under hers.

Rafael's eyes closed, and a feline purr rumbled as he swallowed. He pulled his lips away and used his tongue to stroke the four wounds on Aramis's throat, leaving not a trace of blood. There was a terrifying sweetness and a haunting beauty in the act. He opened his eyes and licked smears of scarlet from his lips.

Her turn was coming. Those long lion's fangs would be in her throat, very soon.

Aramis pulled his mouth from hers and licked his lips. He centered her on his belly and pulled her head down to his neck. His wounds were at her lips. His tongue stroked her throat, along her jaw. Throat bites could be fatal, he had said.

Elaine shivered hard.

Behind them, Rafael settled between their entwined legs. He rose on his knees and then arched over them, supporting himself on his palms.

Aramis lifted his knees, making room for Rafael, and slid more deeply into Elaine.

Elaine groaned. Rafael's chest was cool against her back, as cool as Aramis's chest against her breasts, but Rafael's cock felt burning hot against the seam of her butt. Her heart ached as it pounded, but, oddly, the fear she knew she should be feeling was kept at a distance.

Rafael's breath rasped against her right ear. His fingers and then his slick cock centered on the tight rose of her anus. "Push out, my sweet. Push out and let me in." He pressed for entry.

Elaine pushed and groaned as Rafael's broad cock head began to spread her anus. The pulling ache was intense. She was already stretched full with Aramis's cock within her. She gasped for breath.

Rafael groaned as he forged inward, a white-hot brand sliding against the hard length already lodged within her. "Mother Night, she is tight!"

Aramis groaned under her. "Of course, and you are not a small man!"

"Neither one of you is small!" Elaine whimpered between them. "You're going to split me in half!"

Rafael chuckled, vibrating the invading pole stretching her backside. "Oh yes, we will indeed split you in half, but not with our cocks."

Elaine groaned and shifted in an attempt to ease the fullness. "Was that supposed to make me feel better?"

"Not quite." Rafael's hips pressed against her ass. "Ah, I am in."

"Good." Aramis grunted and moved in a long, voluptuous withdrawal.

Elaine moaned. He felt so good. . . . Erotic heat flared.

Aramis groaned and surged back in as Rafael moaned and began to withdraw.

There was pain, but it was blunted under a swell of horrifically decadent pleasure.

Rafael surged in and Aramis began to withdraw. Slowly, relentlessly, they thrust against each other in counterrhythm, fucking her.

Elaine writhed between them, but their hands held her still.

She was in a marble palace being fucked and reamed by a pair of beautiful men—who were going to drink her blood.

Cruel lust welled with a ruthless haste, which made her gasp. A climax viciously tightened in her belly, her muscles locked and trembled.

"She rises," Rafael whispered. "Be ready."

Elaine felt her hair grasped and wound tightly against the base of her neck. Aramis's lips and tongue whispered against the pulse in her throat. The points of his teeth pressed against her tender skin. *Brutal pleasure, rapacious hunger, liquid heat . . .*

Their bodies tensed around and within hers. Anticipation perfumed the air with the salty aroma of lust and the sweet sweat of her fear. Tension coiled to unbearable tightness, thick and heavy with danger.

White heat flared at the base of her skull, climax boiled in her core—and held, burning and roiling, holding her back from the edge. A soft whimper escaped.

Teeth sank into her throat. The pain was sharp and swift.

Release exploded and crashed through her, but she didn't have enough breath to scream.

II

She was falling with the rushing sound of a thousand wings. She could almost see the black feathers beating around her. *Am I dreaming?* She could still hear her heart matching the pounding rhythm of theirs—or were their hearts matching hers?

It was getting colder.

There was a pull in a direction she couldn't name. She was going somewhere. . . .

She opened her eyes and saw . . . her face, eyes dilated wide to blackness. The four cuts in her throat were frighteningly large and very deep. Thick scarlet threads ran down her shoulder, and over the curve of her breast.

Rafael hung over her shoulder, still thrusting up into her body. His teeth were bared; he had a look of joy and hunger.

Her lips moved. "I have her." It wasn't her voice; it was Aramis's.

She felt the shift of muscles, and an overwhelming lust was centered low on an unfamiliar muscle wedged in a deep, hot, wet, delicious place. A moan escaped her, but it didn't come from her body.

Something cool, and dangerous, yet oddly comforting, pressed against her thoughts. *Hello, love . . .*

She stiffened, surprised. She wasn't in her body—she was in Aramis's. It was so strange. She could feel his urgency and her own body, soft and pliant, in his arms. At the same time, she could feel his presence wrapped around her mind, waiting for something vitally important.

Rafael lifted her body upright against him. He tilted her head to the side, baring the bite mark on her throat. Her skin was so white. His mouth closed on her throat. Her body shuddered in his arms as his tongue stroked the wounds on her throat. "She tastes like fire." He smiled and licked his lips.

Elaine released a soft cry. She was back in her own body, and she was about to come again. Rafael's arms held her upright, both cocks still thrusting into her, her body rocking with the strength of their thrusts. She could see the blood running down her breast.

Aramis rose, sitting up. He cupped her breasts in his hands and lapped at the rivulets of blood running down from her wounded and aching throat. His lips closed on her nipple and suckled with ruthless ferocity. His teeth scored her skin.

She whimpered. This climax was a snarling and angry beast. It clawed her vitals, fighting its way toward release.

Rafael's teeth sank into her throat.

Heat, fire, the scorching erotic ferocity of the teeth in her throat . . . she screamed this time.

Rafael moaned, and swallowed.

She could feel a tear in her heart; then something vital was pulled apart, torn asunder, and ripped away. The sound of wings drowned her screams.

A flash of light and she saw . . . the back of her head, and Aramis's face. His mouth was stained with scarlet, and he looked frightened.

"I have her," she whispered with Rafael's voice.

She was in Rafael. Oceans of lifetimes lived in there. Thousands of faces, places, sights . . . burning cities, books.

"Ah, she is inquisitive, this is good." Rafael's voice had come again.

Waves of feeling washed against her in a powerful tide—humor, hope, joy, love—for Aramis, and for herself.

"And you must go now. . . ."

The darkness of black feathers smothered her sight. She was falling among the deafening sound of feathers. They brushed against her skin, chilling and razor sharp. They pressed against her, and closed around her, encasing her in ice.

Liquid fire burned down her throat.

She swallowed. Heat and warmth burned in her belly and spread. Hunger bloomed for more warmth to battle the spreading, sharp-edged cold. She drank it down, and sought more.

Burning water ran down her skin.

Elaine gasped and shuddered. "Too hot!" She struggled against the hot arms that held her. "No, too hot!"

"Be at ease, Elaine, you need the heat."

She knew that voice. "Aramis?" Elaine lifted her head and struggled to stand. She was in a white-tiled, glass-walled shower suspended between Aramis and Rafael. Both of them held soapy cloths, and suds rolled down her body. "What's going on?"

"I should think it would be obvious." Rafael smiled.

Aramis rolled his eyes. "We're bathing you."

She stared at Aramis—and *knew* him. Knew his rage for the pain Dimitri had caused, knew his desperate love for Rafael, and knew his aching guilt for making her a vampire. She twisted free of them until she could wrap both her arms around his warm body. She pressed her cheek to his heart. She took a deep breath, laden with the aroma of his body. "I can't go back, can I?"

Aramis closed his arms tight around her and pressed his cheek to the top of her head. "I hope you can forgive me."

Elaine dug her fingers into his back. "You did it to save my life."

"So quickly I am forgotten." Rafael sighed at her back. "Should I be jealous?"

Elaine turned and blinked through the water up at Rafael, and knew him. Knew his ancient pain, knew his grief for friends long lost, knew his protective love for Aramis, and knew intimately the aching loneliness caused by the sheer power of his incredible age. She snaked an arm around him and pressed her face against his heart. The tears exploded from nowhere, along with the gasping sobs.

Rafael gently embraced her. "Perhaps she saw a little too deeply."

"I did the same, if you remember." Aramis's voice was quiet.

Rafael swept a hand down her wet hair. "Why, so you did."

Elaine grabbed for Aramis to hold them both. He came into her arms and they leaned together in silence under the running water.

Eventually the washing continued and then the water stopped. Towels were scrubbed down her body and through her hair; then they led her from the white marble bathroom.

Guided between them, Elaine felt dazed and wrung out. She flinched back from the light in the black-and-scarlet master bedroom, her eyes aching.

Rafael chuckled. "Her change is going to be swift, it seems."

"Is this safe?" Aramis caught Elaine around the shoulders and knelt to peer into her face.

Rafael snorted, striding naked and glorious past the bed. "Aramis, if it was not, I would tell you."

Elaine stared at the deep bite on Aramis's throat. She raised her hand to her own aching throat.

Aramis caught her hand. "No, do not touch."

"It is time to attend to our guests." Rafael opened a mirrored door against the far wall and dug among the clothes hanging within. He drew a long length of black silk and another of white from the closet, then a length of deep scarlet velvet. He turned to face them. "Are you ready to be presented, my hearts?"

Elaine frowned. "In bathrobes?"

Rafael smiled. "In dressing gowns. It is traditional."

Elaine walked between Rafael and Aramis with their hands hot on either shoulder. Her long robe of crimson velvet was warm, but her hair, though combed back, was still wet from the shower and soaking the back of the robe. The two bite marks on her neck were still seeping, just a little. She felt empty and raw, as though her skin didn't quite fit properly. She was glad to have their support. She wasn't quite sure where her feet were, and it felt as though she were about to tip over.

Aramis's black mane was also combed back, soaking the thick cream silk of his robe. The marks on his throat were bright red and angry, but not bleeding. His left wrist bore a slender knife cut surrounded by a deep bruise.

Rafael's shower-damp curls dripped just a little on shoulders of the black silk of his robe. There was a raw bite on his throat and a knife cut on his bruised wrist as well. She hadn't seen when those had happened.

Side by side, they walked down a broad gold-and-white marble staircase with a polished oak handrail. The staircase curved until it overlooked what could only be a ballroom.

Mirrors and massive flower arrangements lined the gold-flecked marble walls of the huge circular room filled with people in an incredible collection of glittering costumes. Tuxedo-liveried men and women circulated through the throng as they carried trays holding snacks and champagne-filled flutes. Small tables held seated guests all around the crowded dance floor. In an alcove one level up from the circular and column-lined dance floor, a twenty-piece orchestra played.

Elaine stared in openmouthed astonishment. "Wow, this is some house party."

Aramis grinned. "This is nothing compared to his formal celebrations."

Rafael stopped them at the landing; all three of them robed, barefoot, smelling strongly of soap, and slightly of sex, with just a touch of fresh blood. There was no mistaking where they had been, or what had happened.

A gong rang softly.

The band stopped in midnote. People stopped dancing, voices stilled, and silk rustled. The entire crowd turned to look up toward them. Elaine was startled to recognize more than a few faces from Hollywood among the gathered throng. *I guess it makes sense.* Every vampire there was painfully beautiful.

"My friends," Rafael called out. "May I present, Aramis and Elaine, *ma famille.*"

Polite applause flowed like an ocean.

Ma famille . . . my family? Elaine's breath stopped. She was a vampire.

Tuxedoed staff carried a long Victorian red velvet couch into the ballroom and set it in an alcove a few steps up from the dance floor. The music played, the catering staff circulated, and guests whispered in a hundred different languages.

Elaine sat curled between Aramis and Rafael, her bare feet tucked under her scarlet robe.

A plate of roast beef with potatoes and new asparagus was brought by a staff member and presented to Aramis.

Aramis thanked them politely and unfolded the napkin on his lap.

Elaine stared, rapt at the plate. God, it smelled good.

Aramis shook his head. "No, Elaine, you are not ready for solid food yet."

Elaine jerked back. "What do you mean, 'not ready for *solid* food'?" She hoped to God that didn't mean what it sounded like.

Rafael turned and patted her knee. "You are an *enfant.* Your body is still too new to digest anything but liquids."

Elaine shivered. "You mean, I can't eat anything but . . . blood?"

Aramis wiped his mouth with his napkin, then leaned close to press his lips against her brow. "Correct."

She took a trembling breath. "How long will I be"—she swallowed hard—"on a liquid diet?"

Aramis looked up and shrugged. "A few months. No more."

"Months?" Elaine groaned. That sucked. That really, really sucked. She leaned back against the couch and crossed her arms. "God, I'll never make it without chocolate!"

Rafael smiled. "Relax, you may drink anything that is a liquid, such as coffee or cocoa, but your sustenance will come only from living blood."

Elaine pressed a hand over her heart in relief. "I can still have coffee and cocoa." She gave Rafael a small smile. "Okay, the world isn't ending."

Rafael chuckled and signaled a staff member. "You will adjust. I promise." He spoke softly to the man in the tuxedo, then settled back among the cushions. "Aramis tells me you are an artist?"

Elaine nodded and told him about the museums she had toured while in Rome and Venice.

A staff member entered the alcove with a silver tray and a steaming mug.

Rafael took the mug and a napkin, then passed them to Elaine. "A mocha latte, coffee, cream, and chocolate."

Elaine took the mug with undying gratitude. "You are a god!"

At her back, Aramis choked.

Rafael nodded and smiled. "Of course."

Elaine sipped her heavenly drink, while Aramis finished his plate.

A young man in a tux collected Aramis's empty plate and Elaine's empty mug.

Rafael nodded to the staff member. "You may let them begin."

Guests began to arrive in their alcove. They greeted Rafael, and spoke to him about one thing or another in dozens of different languages. Some smiled and flirted, others knelt immediately and presented a petition, or a grievance, but all were very respectful.

Elaine leaned back in Aramis's warm embrace to watch.

Rafael responded to his guests with gravity or levity, but also with respect to each.

Each visit ended with the guest kneeling and presenting an upturned wrist.

Rafael took each person's wrist gently and bit. Some, he barely pierced the skin with his upper teeth and gently licked. With others, he held their gaze as he bit down hard, piercing their arms with all four teeth and taking strong swallows.

Aramis was a warm, soothing heat against Elaine's back as she watched the proceedings. It was as fascinating as it was frightening. It was obvious that Rafael was not liked by everyone; in fact, he terrified more than a few, but it was clear that he commanded an enormous amount of respect and trust from them.

Elaine found that comforting. She knew, just from the single peek she'd had from within Rafael's heart, that these guests were his personal court and his responsibility. And he took his responsibilities very seriously. He had been trained almost from birth—a very, very long time ago—to be a prince among men.

Elaine was very near to dozing off against Aramis's shoulder when Dimitri walked up the steps to the alcove. He had changed into a tailed tux. He bowed respectfully when he entered.

A dirty trembling shadow knelt, hunched, at the foot of the stairs. He looked up briefly, his face too thin, but still familiar.

Elaine released a soft breath. *Anthony?*

Dimitri's gaze flicked to Aramis, and his eyes widened just a hair; then he gazed down at Elaine. His gaze lowered, noting the marks on her throat. It was obvious that he didn't quite recognize her, and then, abruptly, he did. His nostrils flared and his jaw tightened, as did the rest of his entire body.

Elaine's temper flashed white-hot and then arctic cold. *He's pissed?* Dimitri had kept his word and brought Anthony, but Anthony looked really awful. Her eyes narrowed at Dimitri, and something welled in the base of her throat. She had the most overwhelming urge to—to *bite* him.

Rafael leaned back and patted the seat at his side. "Elaine."

Elaine shifted those few inches to lean up against Rafael.

Rafael dropped his arm around her shoulder and pressed his lips to her temple. "Be calm," he whispered with barely a breath. He turned to Dimitri and smiled. "Dimitri, I hear you have a grievance with my children?"

Dimitri took a deeper breath and frowned, but only slightly. "Then she is yours?"

"Elaine? Oh, she is both of ours." Rafael reached out to catch Aramis's hand. "Aramis allowed me to participate in the making of his first."

Dimitri's eyes narrowed and he vibrated with anger. "Yes, I have a grievance." His voice was tightly controlled, but there was a hint of a snarl at the base of his words. "She was supposed to be mine. She was coming to me when Aramis . . . took her!"

Rafael turned to Aramis. "Aramis, did she carry the mark of Dimitri on her person?"

"Why, no." Aramis managed to look mildly surprised, as though Dimitri's accusation was unexpected. "There was no trace of his scent anywhere on her." He looked over at Dimitri and smiled. "Or in her. She was completely untouched."

Elaine almost smiled. She recognized this game. Rafael was fully aware of exactly what had happened, but they were provoking Dimitri, very slyly. The idea being that the more Dimitri lost his temper, the more innocent Aramis would look to the guests watching with great interest around the bottom of the stairs.

Dimitri scowled and focused on Elaine. "She carried a letter stating that she was traveling under my name."

Rafael turned to Elaine. "Did you carry such a letter?"

Elaine pursed her lips. She wanted to help this little game of "let's piss off Dimitri."

"I had a letter inviting me to an interview, but I didn't think it was something that would matter to Aramis, so I didn't show it to him." She looked over at Dimitri and did her best to look as innocent as possible. "I don't tell everybody my private business."

Dimitri glared at her.

Rafael leaned back to look at Aramis. "When did you discover that Dimitri had any connection to Elaine?"

Aramis tilted his head and attempted to look dismayed. "Shortly after my third taking."

Dimitri's neck flushed red.

Aramis nodded at Elaine. "We were speaking of her drawing ability, when she casually mentioned who she was visiting in Prague." He sighed and rolled his eyes a little dramatically. "But by then, it was far too late." He shook his head sadly. "I'm afraid that Elaine is a very willing lover."

Elaine raised her brow at Aramis and seriously considered mentioning something about persistence, but she held her tongue. The idea was to piss off Dimitri, and to make Aramis look innocent. She was pretty sure Rafael already knew what kind of determined seducer Aramis actually was. Instead, she leaned closer to Rafael. "I'm afraid I read a little too much erotica. It gives me ideas." She couldn't stop the warmth from blooming in her cheeks.

Rafael's brows shot up. "Indeed?" He looked over at Aramis.

"She is very . . . creative." Aramis's smile was more than a touch smug.

Dimitri loosed a low growl. "She was supposed to be *mine*."

Aramis turned to Dimitri, his smile still in place, but his eyes were chips of black ice. "You obviously cannot take proper care of your current thrall. Why should you have another?" He waved a hand toward Anthony, who was huddled at the foot of the stairs.

Anthony had his face buried in his own arms, trying to look as small as possible.

Rafael raised his chin. "Ah, yes. Aramis mentioned that you wanted another to take over the care of the boy." He leaned toward one of the waiting staff, but he did not take his arctic cold gaze off Dimitri. "Would you please ask Countess Sephonie to join me, and have someone bring Aquinas for our young guest?"

Dimitri froze. "You're going to take him?"

Rafael's smile broadened. "Is that not what you wanted?"

Anthony peeked up from his arms. He glanced up at Elaine, then at Rafael.

Dimitri turned to glare at Anthony.

Anthony buried his face back in his arms and tried to huddle smaller.

Sephonie appeared at the bottom of the stairs, as if by magic. She curtsied, gracefully resplendent in a low-cut, full-skirted black velvet gown. Her dark blue-black hair was down about her shoulders, but was still studded with diamond stars. The diamond choker blazed at her throat. She flicked a hard look toward Dimitri, then smiled at Rafael. "I am here, my prince."

Rafael nodded. "Countess, have you met Anthony?" He held out a hand toward the boy at her feet.

Sephonie looked down at the huddled boy. "No, I have not." She knelt, her black skirts billowing around her. She leaned close to the shivering Anthony and whispered.

Anthony looked up from his arms and fell straight into Sephonie's gaze.

She whispered again and held out her hand.

Anthony's mouth dropped open. He nodded and took her hand.

Sephonie smiled deeply into Anthony's eyes. "My prince, I accept."

Rafael sighed very softly. "Thank you, Countess."

A liveried young man knelt at her side and offered the countess a tall, clear tumbler full of what looked like water. She took the glass and held it out to Anthony. "You must be very thirsty."

Anthony gingerly took the glass, then gulped down the drink.

With a soft sigh, Anthony's eyes slid closed and he began to slump.

The countess plucked the glass from his hand.

Anthony fell over, barely conscious.

Sephonie stood, gestured to someone, and stepped back.

A man in a plain black suit knelt to lift Anthony from the floor, then carried him away.

Sephonie turned to Rafael. "All hope is not lost. I may still be able to recover him, with time and proper care." She glanced hard at Dimitri. "But he has been severely damaged."

Rafael nodded. "Thank you, Countess. If there is anything my offices can do to assist, please notify me at once."

"Of course." Sephonie curtsied and left.

Rafael settled back on the couch and sighed. "Now that that small matter is attended to, what ever shall I do with you, Dimitri?"

12

Dimitri glared at Rafael, stiff with obvious outrage. "I have endured one too many insults—from him!" He jabbed a finger toward Aramis. "I demand satisfaction!"

Elaine sat up. Was Dimitri actually asking for an old-fashioned duel?

Rafael grinned. "Dimitri, are you serious? In this day and age?"

Dimitri clenched his hands into fists. "As my right as an elder, I demand blood!"

Rafael leaned back. "Dimitri, if anyone is going to shed blood on my floor, it shall be I."

Dimitri flinched but held his ground. "I demand satisfaction."

Rafael sighed. "You are determined on a duel?"

Dimitri's eyes gleamed. "Nothing less will satisfy me."

Elaine focused on Dimitri's posture and bearing. His stance was arrogant—his movements sharp, precise, and very stiff. *I wonder, how long has it been since he was in an actual fight?* She strongly doubted Dimitri was any good at hand-to-hand. It was possible that he had been at one time, but she seriously doubted he'd bothered to learn anything new, like judo. Elaine sat up and licked her lips. "How about a modern-day fight, bare-handed?"

Rafael frowned at Elaine. "Boxing?"

Elaine narrowed her eyes at Dimitri. "Free-style, boxing, kicking, grappling . . . whatever."

Aramis grabbed her arm. "Elaine . . ."

"Her idea has merit." Rafael nodded to Dimitri. "You may have your duel, but no weapons."

Dimitri focused on Aramis. "I demand blood."

Rafael narrowed his eyes at Dimitri. "The victor shall drink his fill. That shall be your blood."

Dimitri lifted his chin. "Agreed."

Rafael looked over at one of his waiting staff. "Prepare the large salon, thick rugs, no furniture." The man bowed and left. Rafael focused on Dimitri. "You may go."

Dimitri bowed and stepped out of the alcove.

Rafael rose from the couch and rolled his eyes. "It seems we are having a duel."

Elaine stood up and caught Rafael's sleeve. "Let me do it."

Rafael blinked down at her. "You?"

"Sure, it will drive him nuts." Elaine rubbed her jaw. It was seriously starting to ache.

"No!" Aramis came over and grabbed her arm. "You will do no such thing! He is immeasurably older than you."

Elaine rolled her eyes. "He's immeasurably more set in his ways, too. Did you look at him? He's stiff as hell! Look, I took you down, I can take him."

Rafael choked out a laugh. "She took you down?"

Aramis shot Rafael a glare. "She surprised me."

Elaine grinned. "Trust me, I'll surprise him, too."

Aramis caught both her shoulders. "Elaine, he's a vampire."

Elaine shrugged. "So am I."

Rafael cleared his throat. "Do you have any training for this?"

Elaine smiled. "Does twelve years of judo count?"

Aramis frowned. "I thought you said four years?"

Elaine nodded. "I was a champion in high school, but that was only the last four years. I've been in fight training since I was little."

Rafael shook his head. "Dimitri was a soldier and a general long before he began teaching art."

Elaine folded her arms. "I seriously doubt he's practiced in a long time. He's too stiff."

Aramis tightened his hand on her shoulder. "In his day, he was very, very good."

Elaine raised her brow. "Yeah, but how long ago was that? And does he know anything about the Asian arts?" She rubbed her jaw again.

"Elaine." Rafael caught her chin in his palm and tilted her head up. "Open your mouth."

Elaine opened her mouth.

Rafael peered in. "I think perhaps we should let her fight."

Aramis stiffened. "What?"

Rafael straightened. "Her teeth just came in. Her appetite will follow very soon after." He delivered a sly smile. "Can you think of a better target for her first hunt?"

Elaine blinked. *My teeth?* She probed with her tongue and discovered points along the flat line of her teeth. Four points, two on top and two on the bottom. She stabbed her tongue. "Shit . . ." They were sharp.

Aramis caught Rafael's arm. "Rafael, she could be killed."

Rafael shook his head. "Not without a heart stab or removal of her head. She'll recover from anything else."

Elaine swallowed. *Gee, that's nice to know.*

117

Aramis's eyes darkened and his mouth tightened. "He'll rape her."

Rafael's gaze turned to ice. "He will try. He will not succeed."

Elaine looked up at Aramis. "I've handled rapists before." She smiled grimly. *Once you break a bone or two, they stop.*

Aramis's hand visibly tightened. "If he finds a weapon?"

Rafael raised his chin. "If he gains a weapon, then he forfeits the duel, and his blood is ours."

Aramis folded his arms and turned away. "Dimitri challenged me."

Rafael stepped behind Aramis and looped his arms around his shoulders. "He challenged us all." He pulled him back against his chest. "Truthfully, my heart, how much training do you have?"

Aramis sighed and looked up at the ceiling. "What you have given me."

"A handful of years of fencing will not be useful here."

Aramis hunched his shoulders. "I know."

Rafael closed Aramis in a tight hug, then looked down at Elaine. "What do you need to prepare?"

Elaine rubbed her hands together. "My big suitcase and a place to change."

Left alone to change in the midnight-draped master bedroom, Elaine opened her suitcase on Rafael's scarlet bed. *I can do this.* She pulled out her brush and dragged it through her long mane. *This is just like any other competition I've been in.*

Well, except that her opponent was a vampire.

So what? She ruthlessly plaited the whole pile into a long tight French braid. Sure, he had speed and strength on her, but that type always underestimated her. A grim smile lifted her lips. She was looking forward to kicking his arrogant ass.

She let the velvet robe slide from her shoulders and reached into the suitcase to pull out her competition *gi*. With the speed of long practice, she wriggled into her snug sports bra, then pulled on a plain sleeveless black T-shirt. She shook out her hip-length scarlet satin *keiko-gi* top and slid her arms into it. Once she had the side ties fastened, she stepped into her voluminous black satin pleated trousers, and pulled them up over the bottom of her top. After wrapping the long ties around her waist, she knotted them in a perfect overhand square knot.

Last, but not least, she unrolled the long length of thick black silk that stood for her rank. It wasn't a proper judo *obi*, it was more of a sash. She was betting that Dimitri would not realize what her black belt meant. She knotted the silk around her waist with a feeling of ferocious satisfaction.

It was time to kick some ass.

She stepped out of the master bedroom and walked over to Aramis and Rafael, who were speaking by a tall Oriental vase.

Rafael's mouth fell open. He burst out laughing. "Ah! Now you see? It is clearly destiny!"

Elaine stopped. "What?"

Aramis shook his head. "You are wearing the heraldic colors of his house."

Elaine frowned. "Black and red?"

Rafael grinned. "Of course . . . blood and night." He waved a hand toward the hall. "Shall we go, my hearts?"

They walked down a narrow staircase and Aramis groaned. "Dimitri is going to explode."

Elaine raised a brow at him. "I thought that was the point?"

Rafael chuckled. "Very astute."

The large salon was a huge cream-and-gold room, with an entire wall of floor-to-ceiling windows showing black night. There was absolutely no furniture, not even drapes. Brilliantly costumed guests lined the walls, chatting. A number sat on the floor, but most leaned against the walls. Layers of thick Indian carpets were strewn across the center of the black marble floor.

Elaine nodded. *Perfect.*

Dimitri stood facing the windows, barefoot and wearing only his dress slacks. His entire upper body was muscular and gleamed with oil.

Elaine stared at the oil. *Okay, that's gonna make grabbing difficult.* She'd have to make damn sure she had a firm grip before she tried anything. However, if he hit those carpets often enough, the oil would eventually rub off.

Rafael raised his hands and all speech stopped. The liveried staff fled, closing the doors behind them and leaving the room to the vampires.

Dimitri turned around and focused on Aramis. He smiled.

"The rules are simple," Rafael called out. "No weapons, remain on the carpets, and no interference. The first to succeed in pinning and biting wins the right to drink his, or her, fill."

Dimitri walked toward the carpets.

Elaine stepped out to meet him.

Dimitri stopped and flung out his hand. "What is *this*?"

Elaine propped her hands on her hips. "You wanted me, you got me. The question is, can you take me?"

Dimitri scowled. "You stand no chance against me, girl!"

Elaine stepped toward the center of the carpets. "Then what the hell are you bitching about, old man?"

"Stupid child." He bared long teeth and lunged, lightning fast.

Elaine stood her ground. At the last second, she twisted out of his way, slapping the back of his passing shoulder hard.

Dimitri tipped forward and fell in an untidy heap on the carpets.

She blinked. *I didn't think I hit him that hard.*

120

Dimitri rolled gracelessly back onto his feet, cursing in a language she didn't know.

She grinned. "I'm sorry, you were saying something about stupidity?"

The entire collection of guests tittered. A few laughed outright.

He didn't charge again. He stalked her, instead. "I'm going to rip your throat out."

"You have to catch me first." Elaine waited, watching his movements, waiting for him to telegraph what he intended to do.

"I'll catch you." He was in her face in less than a breath.

She barely saw the punch coming, but she *did* see it, and blocked it, snapping out a punch of her own. "Think so?"

He blocked her punch clumsily and lashed a foot out at her. "Bitch!"

She slid behind his kick and lashed out a short side snap, which took out his supporting leg at the knee. "Asshole!"

He dropped, rolled clear, and came back, snarling, punching, and kicking. "I'm going to rip you apart and fuck the remains!"

Wow, nasty temper. Elaine was forced to move out of the way, a lot. His moves were definitely rusty, but it was clear that he had been a vicious fighter at one time. Unfortunately, it was just as obvious that as he warmed up, his body moved cleaner, and faster. She dodged and twisted around him, staying as close as she could to confuse his aim. He had a longer reach on her, and it wouldn't do her any good for him to figure out exactly how far he had to go to hit her.

She slipped into the fighter's serenity of perfect calm and perfect awareness. His threats got nastier, but they rolled past her hearing. They traded blows at increasing speeds. He was remembering his training and getting harder to hit, but, then, so was she.

He grabbed for her sleeves, and the satin slid right out of his hands.

"Missed me." She caught him around the wrist, just long enough to divert his follow-up punch, and grinned. "Got you!" She ducked under him and rolled him right over her back.

He went flying ass over teakettle and slammed flat on his back, his eyes wide in stunned surprise.

Someone doesn't know how to take a fall. Elaine simply could not stop grinning, or rubbing it in. "Oh look, the big bad vampire is getting his ass kicked by a little girl!"

Dimitri regained his feet, snarling with fury. "This game is over!" He lunged and feinted to the side, catching her just wrong by the braid. "Got you!" His punch to her stomach slammed her back onto the carpet, with his weight riding her down. He snapped at her throat with long teeth. "Your blood is mine!"

She caught him just right with her legs and flipped him, riding the roll until she sat on top of him. "Guess again, fang boy!" She was going to win, and soon. She could smell it on his skin. She could smell it *under* his skin. She could hear the slamming drumbeat of a heart and the rushing surge of blood, and knew for a fact that it wasn't her blood she was listening to.

She *wanted* it.

She felt her teeth lengthen in her mouth and focused on the throbbing in the hollow on the side of Dimitri's throat. Moisture dampened her panties.

Dimitri's nostrils flared and his eyes widened. He screamed obscenities and swung upward, with both fists together.

She flipped back and off him before his double-fisted blow could catch her. She rose smoothly onto her feet and closed in on him, blocking his enraged swings.

Dimitri cleared a space for himself and jumped back, all the way to the far side of the carpets.

Confused by the raw sensations running rampant in her body, Elaine paused on the far side of the carpets. The sound of soft moans, whimpers, and softly shredding silk flooded her ears.

All around her, the guests writhed against the walls or on the floor. Ripped and parted clothing gave access to seeking hands. Bared breasts were clutched tight, skirts were lifted, and trousers were opened as guests mounted guests. The scent of sex washed over her in a choking wave—and blood. The vampires were feeding all around her.

Her perfect calm shattered under a lava flow of raw red hunger. Thirst mixed with lust in a boiling combination that choked her and burned a trail up the back of her skull. It ached, in her belly and in her core. She moaned and reached down to clutch her crotch, but that only made the ache worse. She lifted her head and stalked toward Dimitri. He was her prey, and she *needed* him.

On the far side of the carpet, Rafael cleared his throat. "You should have been swifter in your defeat, Dimitri."

Dimitri swung toward Rafael. "What?"

"Elaine has yet to have her first feeding." Rafael smiled sweetly. "And it seems that her hunger has come upon her."

Aramis lifted his chin. "There were the two of us in the making of her. Her hunger is likely very strong." He delivered a nasty smile. "We'll pull her off, once she tastes you."

Dimitri snarled. "Her blood is mine!"

Rafael smiled. "We shall see."

Dimitri turned toward Elaine.

Elaine was nearly upon him. The idiot hadn't been paying attention.

He snarled, and attacked with everything he had.

Elaine shifted around him, feinting, looking for a good opening. She could smell the sharp, sweet stink of his fear, sweat, and anger. She could also smell the musk of his arousal. He was afraid, but he was also hard. *Good.* She needed to get him on the floor and under her.

He got a hand on her long braid again and they tumbled to the floor in a tangle of flailing limbs and snapping teeth. He rolled above her, ripping at the silk of her top, her T-shirt, and tearing it free, baring one breast. "Mine!" He lunged down, lips curled back from savagely long teeth.

She speared her hand up into his bare stomach. Rich, thick, hot wetness spilled down onto her. The smell of raw blood perfumed the room.

He choked and froze, stunned.

She twisted hard and rolled on top. Her mouth latched onto the side of his throat, her teeth stabbing into his flesh. Hot, sweet blood spewed into her mouth, pumped straight from the heart. Her fingers knotted in his hair to hold his head still.

He arched under her and howled. His arms closed around her, holding her against him with punishing strength.

She tightened around him, gulping the hot stream, and writhing against the hardness pressing urgently against her hungry core. Her wet fingers slid on the satin. She couldn't get her pants open to take him into her.

He gasped and bucked frantically under her. The perfume of male cum scented the air.

Lightning burned down her throat and struck her heart. She almost let go. A vibrant warmth spread from her heart. It was the most incredible sensation, like an orgasm.

Hands closed on her arms and on her braid. "Enough, Elaine."

Her head was yanked back, her teeth tearing flesh. She was pulled away and off, screaming and fighting. "No! I'm not done!" She was rolled facedown on the wet carpets. A heavy knee was set in the small of her back, and her hands were ruthlessly pulled behind her.

"You have won. You are finished."

She screamed and kicked out. "No, I'm not!" Something soft was knotted around her wrists. Her kicking feet were caught and tied at the ankles. "I'm not done!" She was rolled onto her back.

Aramis stared down at her with his huge dark eyes and long teeth. "Yes, you are."

Tears filled her eyes. "No, I'm not! Please?" Her voice broke on a sob. "Please . . . more?"

13

Slung over Aramis's shoulder like a sack, Elaine was hauled back upstairs. Her tears had fled and she was pissed as fucking hell. The guests had laughed when they'd carried her out. It was utterly humiliating. "Put me down!"

Rafael ignored her as he walked ahead of them, his black silk robe clutched closed in his hand. Aramis's robe was pinned closed with a diamond star. They had tied her wrists and ankles with the belts from their robes.

"Damn you, I need . . . !" She writhed and twisted. "I want . . . !" But she didn't quite know what her heart was hot and aching for. On top of that, her entire body was screaming for a good hard fuck. "I'm gonna kick both your asses for this!"

"Be still!" Aramis's hand came down hard on her butt.

Elaine jerked. *He hit me?* She opened her mouth and lunged down to bite his back.

Aramis's grip on her braid kept her teeth from his skin, barely. "Stop!"

Elaine trembled with white-hot fury. "I hate you!"

"You do not hate us." Rafael opened the bedroom door. "Straight to the shower. She's dripping on the carpets."

"Yes, I do!" Elaine kicked out. "I hate you both!"

Aramis slipped past Rafael and crossed the midnight bedroom to the white marble bathroom. A growl rolled from his chest. "Stop fighting!"

"No!" Elaine twisted in his grasp. Her body *wanted*... whatever it was, and she needed to go back there to get it.

Rafael opened the glass door to the shower stall and grinned. "We are not dealing well with frustration."

"Fuck you!" Elaine lunged at him, snapping.

"That is enough, Elaine!" Aramis let her drop from his shoulder.

Elaine fell hard on the shower's tiles. It knocked the wind out of her and bruised both elbows. "Ow! Shit!" She twisted on the floor and bared her long teeth at him. "Fuck you, too!"

Aramis glared down at her. "That attitude requires a swift adjustment."

Rafael lounged against the shower door and tsked. "She's a fledgling that just took down a fully mature vampire. Of course she has an attitude."

Aramis glared at Rafael. "At whose design?"

"Mine, of course." Rafael stepped out of the shower stall. "Look at it this way. After this, the others will be less likely to try cornering her, as they did you. Dimitri will certainly not try again."

Aramis left the shower. "But now, she is completely uncontrollable!"

Rafael chuckled softly. "Not completely."

Elaine panted and wriggled, trying for a more comfortable position than lying back on her bound arms. Her heart hungered for something she couldn't name, and her crotch was a wet, throbbing ache. The inciting smell of the blood all over her was making everything worse.

"She hates me." Aramis's voice was barely a whisper.

A stab of guilt struck Elaine's heart. She didn't really hate them, but she was seriously pissed at them. And desperately horny. Her elbows and bare heels rasped on the tiles as she fought the ties on her wrists. God, she was dying for a fuck!

"She does not hate you. She is frustrated. We interrupted her feeding."

Elaine finally succeeded in rolling onto her side and curled up tight. "Frustrated" was too small a word to describe the burning hunger eating her alive. She couldn't even get her fingers on herself to do something about her throbbing clit. A small moan escaped her lips.

Aramis groaned. "She had something, I could smell Dimitri's release."

"But you did not smell hers."

Clothing rustled.

Elaine looked up. According to the shadows on the glass, they were both getting undressed. Were they going to fuck her? God, she hoped so.

"She is going to be very difficult to control."

"If we had let her finish, that would have been so." Rafael chuckled. "As we did not, we will master her very swiftly."

Elaine stiffened. What the hell did that mean?

"Is that why . . . ?"

"That is precisely why."

"Ah." Aramis sighed. "Restraints?"

"No, I do not want to make this easy for her."

Elaine shivered. That definitely did not sound promising. She just hoped it involved fucking. As long as it involved fucking—whatever it was—she was all for it.

129

Rafael appeared at the doorway of the shower. He was naked, and disconcertingly gorgeous. He was also rigidly erect.

Elaine focused on his thick, heavy cock. The blushing purple head was peeking out of its sheath. It looked mouthwateringly delicious. A tiny sound of hunger slipped past her lips.

Rafael leaned against the frame, folded his arms, and smiled. "Elaine, would you like a fuck?"

Elaine opened her mouth—*God, yes!*—and closed it. She was pissed at them. She was also in desperate need of that long, hard cock. A small sound of frustration slipped past her lips. *Fuck it.* "Yes."

Rafael raised his brow and waited.

Elaine winced. "Yes, please."

"Better." Rafael tilted his head. "Are you willing to be obedient to get it?"

Elaine swallowed. That was so obviously a trick question. "How obedient?"

Rafael shrugged and pursed his lips. "Oh, the usual . . . totally, completely, and utterly obedient. If we give you an order, you follow it without question, without argument, and without delay."

Elaine's breath stopped. *Oh . . .* She took a breath and caught the warm perfume of his lust. Her body clenched. She tried very hard not to writhe on the cold tiles. "What if I . . . can't?"

Rafael straightened and shook his head. "I'm afraid that I must have your complete submission. If you cannot give it, then you will remain as you are, bound hand and foot. We will bathe you, then bed you down on the floor. Perhaps tomorrow you will feel different?"

Elaine froze, shocked. They would leave her tied up? On the *floor*? She glared at him. "You can't leave me tied up. That's inhumane!"

Rafael's brows shot up. "But, Elaine, you are not a human. You are a newborn vampire who nearly killed a fully mature vampire. I could never allow such a vampire—a vampire who cannot control her actions—loose among the non-vampiric staff."

Elaine gasped, completely appalled that he would even think that. She rolled onto her back. "I would never hurt one of your staff!"

Rafael shrugged. "If you cannot control your actions enough to be obedient, you are too dangerous to be trusted amongst the staff. Therefore, you give me no other choice but to restrain you."

Elaine jerked at her wrists. "That's totally unfair!"

"Indeed?" Rafael pursed his lips. "How so?"

Elaine's breath stopped in her throat. She didn't have an answer. Her head fell back on the tiles. The more she thought about it, the more what he was saying made perfect sense. Nearly every staff member was human. And she . . . wasn't.

Oh God, he was right. She *was* dangerous. She *could* kill people if she wasn't careful. Her fight with Dimitri proved that. She looked over at Rafael and felt a burning in her eyes. "Just how dangerous am I?"

Rafael's voice softened. "You are a vampire, a predatory creature that preys on the most dangerous animal of all—mankind."

Elaine felt something other than hunger crushing her heart—profound guilt. She had to take a breath to speak past the hard lump in her throat. "I don't want to hurt anybody." Tears began to trickle down her cheeks.

Rafael sighed. "This does not concern *want*. This concerns control. You have to give me your complete obedience to prove that you have enough self-control to be allowed among those weaker than you who live and work here."

Elaine had to close her eyes. It hurt too much. "Am I . . . evil?"

Aramis's voice came from the doorway. "That depends on what stories you read."

Elaine jolted with the memory of saying those very words to him. *Was that only last night?* So much had happened since then. She took a deep breath. "Okay." She took another deep breath. "I'll be obedient."

"Totally, completely, and utterly obedient?" Rafael's voice was firm and uncompromising.

Elaine flinched. When said that way, it sounded awfully permanent, but what choice did she have? "Yes."

"If we give you an order, you will follow it without question, without argument, and without delay?"

Elaine chafed at Rafael's words. She desperately wanted to curl up and die. Unfortunately, death was not coming anytime soon. Not by a long shot. "Yes."

"Good. You may begin by addressing me as 'my prince,' and Aramis as 'my sire.' "

He's not serious? Elaine lifted her head from the floor.

Rafael stood rigidly in the doorway, shoulders back and head up. His icy blue eyes were hard on hers, and his mouth tight.

Elaine swallowed. *He's serious.*

Rafael raised his brow.

Elaine blinked. He was waiting for something. *Oh.* "Yes . . . m-my prince." It stuck in her throat, but she got it out.

Rafael smiled, but his eyes remained hard. "Excellent." He nodded toward Aramis. "Cut her free so she may bathe us."

Elaine blinked. She was going to bathe *them*?

Aramis stepped toward her with his right hand behind him. "Close your eyes."

132

Elaine knew he had a knife behind him and trembled. It wasn't fear, exactly. *Of course he does, stupid. He has to cut the belts off.* She closed her eyes. A hand on her shoulder shoved her over onto her belly. She held as still as possible. She couldn't quite stop the trembling. Her clothes were soaked through and were getting clammy fast.

A swift rip freed her ankles. Another rip freed her wrists. Elaine exhaled and relaxed on the floor. *Thank God!*

Aramis grabbed the back of her robes. "Be still."

Elaine froze. *Huh?*

The knife skimmed down her back. In three breaths, Aramis sliced her silks open from the neck to waist and ripped them apart, baring her skin from shoulders to hips.

Elaine shivered hard. Her competition silks were destroyed beyond repair. She would never wear them again. She closed her eyes to hold back the burning in her throat and tried to breathe past the tightness in her chest. It wasn't as if she could have ever worn them in competition again—she wasn't human anymore. She was too dangerous to compete. She was almost glad that she was already crying.

Aramis stepped back. "Now you may rise."

Elaine decided quite firmly that she should have taken the other option and let them keep her tied up. Bathing both Aramis and Rafael was freaking hard work. They had allowed her to wash the blood from her body, then insisted the water be turned up to scalding.

Cloth and soap in hand, she practically attacked Aramis, scrubbing him from the neck down. The livid bite mark on his throat had completely closed. It was pink and shiny, as though it was days old, rather than hours. The cut on his wrist had faded to a pale line, and the bruise around it was gone entirely.

Rafael, on the other hand, was completely unmarked. Both the bite on his throat and the cut on his wrist had completely vanished.

They wanted every finger cleaned. They wanted every toe cleaned. She nearly lost it when Aramis asked her to clean his hard, hot cock and succulent balls with her bare hands. Down on her knees, the purple head less than a kiss from her lips, she had to swallow back the urge to lick him. A lot.

By the time she started washing Rafael, most of her temper had bled off. Her body was still insane to be fucked, but she could ignore it, as long as she kept moving. Bathing them—rubbing her cloth and palms across their warm hollows, their muscular bulges, and their sleek planes—was painfully absorbing. Their pleased moaning did not help, however.

After a while, all the "yes, my sire" and "no, my prince" responses came easier, too. Most of the time, they were too busy chatting in a language she couldn't recognize to need more than a yes or no answer.

It was degrading. She'd had to get down on her knees a lot. It was also somewhat peaceful. They pretty much let her do her work without interference. Unless you counted all the "clean this" and "clean that" demands.

She utterly refused to look at the pile of ripped bloodstained silk in the corner of the shower.

Elaine had far better control of herself when it came time to cup Rafael's erection in her soapy hands. She finished rinsing Rafael completely clean of soap and stepped back. *Done, thank God.*

Rafael dropped down on one knee, with his back to the shower's hot flow. "Aramis, retrieve the shampoo and conditioner for Elaine." He smiled at Elaine.

Elaine stilled. *Oh shit, I have to wash his hair?*

Aramis wore a sly smile as he handed her the two plastic bottles.

Elaine saw it, but she was more worried about getting soap in Rafael's eyes. She tilted his head back. "Please close your eyes, my prince."

Rafael closed his eyes.

Elaine filled her palm with soap and dug into his curls. Rich lather was just beginning to form when Aramis stood behind her and reached around to cup her breasts.

Elaine froze under a wave of raw lust. Cream slathered her thighs.

"Is something wrong Elaine?" Rafael sounded slightly amused.

"Ara—ahem, my sire has his hands on my . . . breasts"—she almost said "tits"—"my prince."

Rafael gave a slight nod. "You may continue."

Continue? Like this? Elaine took a breath. *Okay.* She bit down on her lip and massaged Rafael's scalp with soap.

Aramis caught the tips of her nipples and tugged, then squeezed, then tugged.

Elaine opened her mouth, panting for air. The fire in her tormented nipples was stabbing straight to her frenzied clit. She desperately wanted to moan. Her belly tightened with violent yearning. If he kept that up, she was going to come just from his hands on her nipples. Somehow she kept massaging the soap into Rafael's silky hair.

Aramis released her.

Elaine nearly gasped, with both relief and disappointment. She tilted Rafael's head back farther to let the shower rinse off the soap. She reached down to collect the conditioner and poured a bit into her palm.

Aramis plucked the bottle from her hands and knelt behind her.

Elaine's hair stood at the back of her neck. Aramis was up to something. She set her hands into Rafael's hair and ran her fingers through his wet curls to condition them.

Aramis slid one hand up between her thighs and cupped her hip with the other. He pushed two fingers into her aching pussy.

Elaine's head came up and she whimpered. Her heels jerked apart, all by themselves, to give him access.

Aramis pressed his slick thumb against her anus and pushed. His thumb slid past the muscular ring and surged deep into her ass, then out, then in . . . finger-fucking her pussy and ass.

Elaine gasped. Rapturous liquid heat blazed in her core. She clutched at Rafael's shoulders to keep from falling over.

"Is something wrong, Elaine?" Rafael sounded very amused.

Elaine could barely think past the exquisite delight stirring up her spine. She had to take a breath before she could answer. "My sire has his fingers in . . ." She stopped to groan and catch another breath. "He has his fingers in my pussy and ass." She whimpered. "My prince."

Rafael made a calm but indecipherable inquiry.

Aramis replied with polite deference.

Rafael rose and stepped into the water to rinse out the conditioner.

Elaine simply stood there and groaned, savoring the delightful torment of Aramis's clever fingers. She was definitely going to come.

Rafael returned to stand before her. "On your knees, Elaine."

Aramis pulled his fingers from her.

Elaine let a small whimper of disappointment escape. She got down on her knees and stared at Rafael's cock, only a breath away from her mouth.

"Take me into your mouth, suck me to climax, and swallow my cum. All of it."

Elaine looked up at Rafael. *Damn it, what is with all this cum drinking?*

Rafael set his hands on his hips and raised a brow, clearly waiting.

Elaine lowered her gaze to his hard cock pointed at her. *Okay, fine, whatever . . . as long as I get fucked after.* She stared at Rafael's cock and worked her mouth to generate saliva. He was not quite as thick as Aramis, but definitely longer. She was absolutely not going to be able to deep-throat him.

She licked both palms and reached out to smooth both wet hands along the warm length of his shaft. Although she wasn't going to stop him from coming, she fully intended to hang on to him. She didn't want a repeat of having a cock jammed all the way down her throat. She stroked his cock from head to root, pushing the sheath back to expose the blushing purple head. She could smell the soap she'd used under the rich musk of his arousal.

Rafael groaned and smiled. "Your tongue, my child. Give me your tongue."

Elaine flashed a sour look up at him. *Don't rush me.* Somehow she kept her words in her mouth. She leaned forward with her very wet tongue extended and swirled it around the top of his cock head. He tasted clean, but he also tasted different from Aramis, more potent. She widened the circling of her tongue until she stroked the flared edges; then she took him deeper, and deeper, to the back of her throat. Her hands grasped and stroked the rest of his length, extending the reach of her mouth. She pulled back slowly, sucking strongly, massaging the rest with her palms.

He slid from her mouth with a wet *pop,* rocked on his heels, and groaned. "Aramis had mentioned your talented mouth."

Elaine allowed herself a small smile. "I try, my prince." She opened her mouth and took him swiftly to the back of her throat. Sucking strongly, she pulled back until he slid past her lips with another wet smack.

He choked. "Delightful. We will have to do this more often."

Elaine winced. *Great, just what I always wanted, to drink cum on a regular basis.* She took him back into her mouth and lashed her tongue under the shaft as she swallowed him deeper.

Rafael threw his head back and shuddered. "Blood and Night, ah!" His hips bucked, fucking her mouth in short jabs. "Very good. I will come very swiftly."

Elaine closed her lips and palms tight around the cock as it pumped in and out of her mouth. *Let's get this over with.*

"A moment, my prince." The amusement was crystal clear in Aramis's voice. "Elaine is more talented than even I suspected." He reached around to catch Elaine's wrists and tugged them behind her.

Elaine jerked back, releasing Rafael's cock from her lips. "Hey!"

Aramis leaned to the side to catch her gaze. "Disobedience?"

Elaine turned her gaze away. "No, my sire." She glanced back at him. "But I wasn't going to do *that.*"

Rafael's brows shot up. "Do what?"

Aramis lifted his head. "Elaine has clever hands. She knows how to still the climax at release."

Rafael blinked, then grinned at Aramis. "Experience has taught you this, I assume?"

Aramis released a breath. "Yes, my prince."

Elaine scowled. "I wasn't going to do that, my prince."

"No matter. I desire a deeper penetration of your throat, so you would eventually have had to remove your hands." Rafael smiled at Aramis. "But, if it pleases you, you may hold her, Aramis."

Aramis brushed his lips against Elaine's ear. "It pleases me, my prince."

Elaine groaned, but she didn't struggle. *Damn it!* She didn't want another cock shoved down her throat, but it looked like it was going to happen, anyway.

Rafael nodded. "Your mouth, Elaine."

She stared at Rafael's cock. Her belly clenched with chafing eagerness. Once she sucked down his cum, they would fuck her. She was sure of it.

She opened her mouth and took in his heated shaft. A bead of slightly salty moisture spread across her tongue. A tingle of warmth washed through her. It was a clear reminder of the blood-thickening drug in his semen. *Shit . . .* As if she wasn't insanely horny enough?

She stroked her tongue across his cock head and tasted more. *Pre-cum . . .* He was seriously ready to spill. Eagerness gripped her vitals and she lashed the underside of his cock with her tongue.

Rafael sighed. "Such a talented tongue." He set one hand on her shoulder and grasped her hair with the other. Holding her still, he thrust into her mouth. "More. Take more of me!"

Elaine drew him in as far as she could.

He surged past the back of her throat.

Her throat closed slightly. *Good God, he is long!* She swallowed to clear it. She took him again, and again he slid too deep. She whimpered.

"Be at ease. I rise quickly." Rafael groaned and pumped his hips, fucking her mouth with increasing speed.

Elaine trembled but held the suction steady and used her

tongue while he took her mouth. His cock slid partway down her throat on every thrust. She was forced to swallow between snatches of breath to keep from gagging.

Rafael's fingers tightened in her hair and he came up on his toes.

Elaine shivered. *Any second now . . .* A small moan escaped.

From behind her, Aramis set a hand on her shoulder and shoved her down lower; then he jerked her head back by the hair, making the path down her throat one long tube.

Rafael arched over her and shoved his cock straight down her throat. "I come," he choked out.

Her nose pressed into his belly, her throat closed tightly. Elaine couldn't take a breath past the cock deep in her throat. Not even a whimper escaped past it.

Rafael thrust and shuddered. "Drink, Elaine. Drink it all."

Hot liquid gushed deep in her throat. She moaned and shuddered, unable to breathe and unable to stop him from pouring straight into her stomach.

"Yes . . . ah!" Rafael groaned and pulled from her throat, trailing cum into her mouth and across her tongue. His cock was a gleaming, wet length, and still erect.

Aramis's hands held her upright on her knees while Elaine gasped for breath and choked. Her eyes watered and she swallowed hard to clear the taste from her mouth. Heat flooded outward from her belly and she began to tremble. "Are you sure that was a good idea, my prince?"

Rafael stepped back and leaned against the tile wall, grinning and panting. "What makes you ask?"

Elaine looked up at Rafael, and her head began to swim. She teetered on her knees. "Because . . ." She had to concentrate past the urgency clawing through her in order to get the words out. "Because I think I am about to"—raging lust forced a gasp from her throat—"to lose control, my prince."

"But of course, Elaine." Rafael chuckled. "That was the point."

That did not make sense, but Elaine was past caring. She leaned back against Aramis, shifting her butt to feel the heat of his cock. Damn it, she needed a fuck!

Behind her, Aramis obligingly rubbed his cock against her butt, and a liquid purr rolled in his throat. The sound was startlingly feline. He released her wrists to cup her breasts and rubbed the aching burning tips of her nipples. "The question is, can you remain obedient in the throes of your lust?" His tongue rasped her throat.

Elaine gasped and arched, baring her throat to his mouth while reaching back to grab his muscular buttocks. She couldn't give a rat's ass about obedience, but she'd do anything to get a cock in her aching pussy. Anything at all to quench the wildfire of lust consuming her. "Please!" She rolled her butt back against his deliciously hot length. "Please, my sire, my prince!" A wail boiled from her throat. "Please fuck me!"

Rafael grinned. "Of course we will fuck you."

Aramis's hands tightened on her breasts while his lips caressed her throat. "You are ours."

Rafael raised a brow. "But first, turn off the water and fetch the towels, Elaine. We need to be dried."

Elaine lunged off the floor.

14

Rafael pulled back the scarlet-colored silk duvet on the monstrous bed, revealing midnight sheets. He turned around and regarded Aramis and Elaine with a small smile. "My two hearts." His eyes became wide pools of shadow ringed by pale blue. Indigo lightning sparked deep within. "Pleased I am, to have you both."

Something powerful and urgent washed against Elaine's skin, bringing the small hairs on her neck and arms to attention. Her heart thumped, and heat flushed from her core outward.

Beside her, Aramis's hands tightened to fists, and his eyes became wide pits of shadow. He took a deep breath and opened his hands.

Rafael focused his vampiric black gaze on Elaine. "To the foot of the bed, and await my call."

Boiling with carnal urgency, yet skittish with the thick palpable tension, Elaine gladly walked away to the foot of the bed.

Rafael turned his gaze to Aramis. "My dark and troubled heart . . ." His voice was only a whisper, but it echoed with age, and power.

Aramis shivered and stalked toward Rafael, his breathing labored and his jaw tight. His expression was shuttered and neutral, but his entire body trembled. Less than a breath away, he gazed into Rafael's eyes. His hands tightened into fists.

"I have missed you," Rafael whispered. "Have you missed me?"

Aramis scowled. "That was a supremely stupid question." He caught Rafael's angelic face and kissed him full on the mouth.

Rafael jerked, as though surprised, but didn't pull away from the kiss.

His eyes closed tight, Aramis's fingers knotted in Rafael's black curls to hold him still. He angled his head, his throat and jaw flexing. It was not a gentle kiss.

A soft moan escaped Rafael while his mouth was thoroughly plundered. His eyes fluttered closed. Rafael's hands slid down to cup Aramis's muscular buttocks, pressing the full length of his body against the taller man. His hips shifted restlessly.

It was the most incredible thing Elaine had ever seen. Two brutally handsome men kissing as though starved. Her nipples tightened to painful points. Erotic pressure slammed and clenched tight in her core. Cream slathered her thighs.

Aramis pulled back, his mouth tight and bitter. "I told you before, I would die for you."

Rafael slid his arms up around Aramis's waist and pressed his cheek against Aramis's. "And I told you, I could not allow that."

Aramis closed his eyes and wrapped his arms around Rafael. Muscle bulged, embracing the smaller man with brutal strength. "You will not send me away again."

"Perhaps it will not be necessary this time." Rafael's whisper was almost too soft to hear.

"Good." Aramis released a rumbling growl. "Because this time I will not leave."

Within her heart, Elaine felt the exquisite torment of black wings. They were in love. She turned away and wiped her scalded wet cheeks with her palms.

Rafael pulled back with a small smile. "Now that you have brought us all to tears . . ." He tilted his head just slightly toward Elaine.

Aramis sighed; then his mouth lifted in a partial smile. "I will endeavor to repair the damage."

Rafael grinned and stepped back. "You may begin by getting into my bed."

Aramis shook his head and climbed onto the bed. "Ever the demanding one."

"*I?*" Rafael followed him across the sheets. "You are the insatiable one!"

Elaine grinned and still wiped at her cheeks. "He has a point. You're pretty insistent."

Aramis shot a glare at Elaine.

Elaine bit her lip to restrain her smile. "Well, it's true, my sire."

Aramis flopped back against the mound of embroidered pillows against the bed's marble headboard. The pile of pillows was large enough that he sat nearly upright. "Now that I have two of you, I'm sure my insatiable needs"—he glanced at Rafael and grinned—"can be met."

Rafael dropped down among the pillows at Aramis's side and rolled his eyes. "We shall certainly try." He turned and focused on Elaine. "Speaking of needs that must be met . . . Elaine, come. On your hands and knees, come and make us want."

"Yes, my prince." *About damned time!* Elaine licked her lips and set her hands on the scarlet silk of the folded duvet. She lifted her knees onto the bed. Her long dark-gold mane draped her back and fell to the sheets in a thick damp cloak. *Ready or not, here I come.* Gripping with her fingers and digging in her toes, she moved from the folded scarlet silk onto the midnight sheets toward them. Cream dripped down her thighs while she crawled in a tiger stalk toward the two handsome men who waited for her.

Aramis smiled and gripped the shaft of his cock. "Ah, truly a lovely sight."

Rafael licked his lips and gripped his cock. "It seems you have found us a huntress." He glanced at Aramis and smiled. "A truly exquisite catch."

Aramis smiled slyly. "Beware, she is ever a surprise."

Elaine's cheeks warmed with the compliments. She stopped at their feet, unsure of what to do next.

"Come." Rafael shifted away from Aramis, making space between them and held out his hand. "And show us your love."

Love? Elaine stared at Rafael, frozen by the black feathered pain that surged in her heart. Oh God, she did love Rafael. *But what about . . . ?* She looked over at Aramis, and the razor-edged pinions sliced her heart in half. She loved him, too. She looked from one to the other, shocked. She loved them both. She had no idea how the hell it had happened. But it was there, burning and bleeding, in the depths of her soul.

Aramis raised a brow at Rafael. "I think you frightened her."

"Ha! Nothing frightens our Elaine!" Rafael patted the bed and smiled. "Come, Elaine, come to us."

Elaine remembered to breathe. She would think about love later, when it didn't hurt so much. Her fingers clutching the sheets, she eased between the two men, slowly stroking their rigidly erect cocks. Their legs were hot against the sides of hers. They both smelled of clean water and soap, a little of blood, but more strongly of aroused maleness. Her nipples throbbed in time with her pulsing crotch. She glanced over at Aramis.

Aramis watched her with wide black eyes, his mouth was tight and his dark nipples were pointed with arousal, but he made no move. He was clearly waiting to see what she would do. He glanced toward Rafael.

She turned and focused on Rafael.

As before, Rafael's eyes were wide with rings of sky blue. Indigo lightning flashed deep within. It was breathtaking. It was also terrifying. There was so much in the depths of his eyes.

To escape his gaze, she pressed a soft kiss on his chest, just a little to one side, over his heart. The muscle moved under her lips. She had startled him. *Good.* Her knotted muscles loosened. *Seduction . . .* It was her turn to seduce. That's what they were waiting for. *I can do that.* She almost smiled.

She lifted her head. "My prince, may I kiss you?"

He blinked. She'd surprised him again. He smiled. "Of course."

She pulled her gaze from his frightening eyes and focused on his lips. She reached over Rafael, spanning his waist with her arms, then leaned forward. Her lips brushed his. *Heat, breath, satiny softness . . .* Her eyes drifted closed and her tongue swept the bow of his full bottom lip. She felt the edge of one long tooth; she shivered.

His mouth opened against hers. He breathed in, and stole her breath.

She set her hand on the pillows by his head to get closer and dipped her tongue into his mouth, brushing against his tongue fleetingly. He tasted of expensive coffee and slightly of chocolate, and familiar. Even though she knew damned well that she'd never kissed Rafael before, she *knew* him. And some part of her . . . missed him. She explored his mouth as though redis-covering something she'd forgotten.

His tongue swept against hers with light, teasing strokes, and he released a softly pleased moan.

She released the pillows and reached for his shoulders. His skin was warm under her palms and the muscle solid. She an-gled her open mouth against his to taste more of him.

A purr rumbled in his throat, vibrating on her tongue. His hands cupped her thighs and he tugged her astride his lap. He nipped gently at her bottom lip with his long teeth; then his tongue swept in a wet, sensual glide against hers.

Her knees spread wide to straddle him. She slid her hands around his neck, her fingers tangling in the damp silk of his black curls. She stroked his tongue, while he stroked hers.

He angled his mouth, pressing firmly; his tongue stroked boldly, tasting her. His fingers slid up and around her waist; then his hands pressed downward at the small of her back, urg-ing her down and tight against his body.

Her bare breasts and hot nipples rubbed against the broad wall of his chest and the small pale nubs of his nipples. His cock was a long, hot ridge against her wet, hungry pussy. *Fire, long-ing, need* . . . She writhed against him and a small moan escaped her throat. Her thighs tightened around his.

Rafael groaned, pressing up against her wet heat, then pulled back from her kiss. He licked his lips and smiled just a little, concealing his teeth. "A huntress, indeed."

Elaine leaned down to kiss him again.

Rafael dodged her mouth with a grin. "Save some kisses for Aramis!"

"But I haven't finished with you yet!" She kissed the side of his neck.

Rafael jumped under her lips, laughed, and pushed her back.

"Ah, but we must not make him jealous." He shoved her over, tumbling her onto her back and between them.

Elaine yelped in surprise.

Aramis grinned and pounced, framing her body with his arms. "Too late, I am already jealous." His mouth fell onto hers.

She arched up to him in delight, nipping at his full lips and chasing his tongue with hers. He tasted of cinnamon and vanilla. His taste was familiar and achingly dear. His long teeth clicked lightly against hers. They stopped and grinned, breathless.

She reached up to kiss him again—this time more softly. Against her tongue, his lips were velvety soft. Their tongues entwined gently, touching, tasting, exploring.

He groaned and rolled fully on top of her, his leg sliding between hers, his cock hot, heavy, and throbbing against her hip. His mouth moved against hers with hunger. His hand closed on her breast and squeezed.

Heat rolled up her body in a stifling wave. She moaned with the carnal need that raged in her hungry core. She wanted that cock inside her. She closed her arms around him and dug her fingers in, rolling her hips up against him to encourage him to take her.

He pulled his head back, his eyes full of shadows and scarlet heat. His heart thundered against hers.

Elaine shifted under him impatiently, but he didn't move. Disappointment crushed her utterly. Tears fell. "Please?"

Aramis smiled and touched her tears with a finger. "Our *enfant* needs to be fed, my prince."

Rafael leaned over her, embracing them both. He brushed a thumb across her damp cheek. "Why, so she does." He looked over at Aramis.

Aramis nodded and rolled back and away.

Elaine cried out with the loss and reached for him.

Rafael caught her hands gently but firmly. "No, I will feed you this first time." He pulled her upright, then smiled at Aramis. "Your sire will feed me." He focused on her. "You will feed your sire."

Elaine panted, trying to think through the fever raging and clawing in her. "I don't know how."

Rafael smiled and swept a hand across her brow. "Your body knows." Rafael pressed a swift kiss to her lips. "Sit up."

She sat up with speed, too frenzied with urgency to think past the fact that fucking was clearly going to happen, and this all-consuming howling need would stop.

"Good." He shifted to sit behind her. "Lean forward on your hands and knees, and spread wide."

Facing the foot of the bed, Elaine dropped forward onto her hands and rose up on her knees.

Aramis moved before her and sat back on his heels.

Rafael eased his legs between hers and sat back against the pillows. "Good." He stroked her back. "Sit back and take me within."

Straddling Rafael's strong legs, Elaine reached between her cream-slicked thighs for the strong column of Rafael's cock. It was hot and very rigid in her fingers. Trembling with eagerness, she pushed farther back, centering the broad head on the hungry and slavering mouth of her pussy. She licked her lips and sat down hard, impaling herself. His rigid shaft struck the limit of her depth, then bumped the nub of her cervix, within. The pain was sharp. She flinched.

Rafael caught her hips. "Easy, my heart. You are snug and I"—he chuckled—"I am long. This way." He guided her hips in a small circle, rubbing within.

Elaine winced and felt him work around her cervix. It actually felt rather . . . stimulating. Something gave, she had no idea what, and suddenly he slid deeper within. "Oh!"

"Yes." He sighed. "Much better. Now sit up."

Elaine pushed upright, off her supporting hand.

Rafael caught her around the waist with one arm. "I have you." He pushed up behind her, guiding her legs farther back alongside his hips, and spread her wide.

Elaine groaned with the feel of her muscles stretching.

"Very good, and relax." Rafael sighed. "Lie back against me."

Elaine leaned back, impaled and spread incredibly wide. *Thank God I'm limber from judo, or this position would be a hell of a lot less comfortable.*

Rafael set his cheek next to hers and took deep breaths, his chest rising and falling against her spine. "Set your hands behind my neck."

Elaine lifted her hands and tangled her fingers in Rafael's black curls.

Rafael lifted his hands to cup her breasts. "Very nice." He squeezed, then tugged on her nipples.

Bolts of fire darted straight to her clit, and Elaine gasped. She pulled with her hands, arching against him.

Rafael sighed. "Oh yes, and now to fuck." He rocked his hips forward, his cock sliding a little out, then lifted his knees, sliding deep within Elaine's pussy. "So good, yes . . ."

Elaine released a soft cry of delight. Filled at last. She shifted restlessly and discovered that she could only move by rocking side to side.

Rafael groaned. "Ah, delicious, do not stop!"

Elaine panted and shifted to the sides.

Slowly Rafael slid outward, and then just as slowly inward, pushing with his heels.

Aramis licked his lips, his gaze focused down where Rafael's cock pumped within the spread folds of her pussy. "I believe that is quite the most enticing view I have ever seen."

"Is that so?" Rafael chuckled, vibrating the cock jammed tight in Elaine's pussy. "Then the next time I take you, we shall do it in front of a mirror so you may see yourself."

Elaine stiffened with the image of Aramis impaled by Rafael, as she was. A spat of cream slathered the cock within her.

Rafael groaned and ground up into her, his hands tightening on her breasts. "Ah, even our *enfant* is inspired."

Aramis's head came up, his mouth tight, but his cock quivered and a drop of moisture appeared at the top.

Rafael sighed and licked his lips. "Aramis, your mouth, on us, please, where we are joined."

Aramis grinned and moved between Rafael's thighs. "With pleasure." He dropped forward onto his elbows, and his loose mane fell in a blue-black cloak across the sheets and Rafael's feet. He extended one arms to cup Elaine's thigh.

Hot breath scalded Elaine's intimate flesh; then a broad wet tongue stroked from the tight rose of her anus up her stretched folds, lingering on the pumping cock, then continued upward to her aching clit, then back down.

Erotic fire scorched her, her core clenching in exquisite torment. She arched, crying out.

Rafael's breath exploded from his chest. "Oh yes!"

Aramis's fingers closed tight on Elaine's thigh. He lapped and sucked with obvious and noisy relish.

Elaine writhed as much as she could, trapped in her position and devastated by the viciously intense pleasure of being licked and fucked at the same time. She whimpered helplessly.

Aramis's hand moved under her butt.

Rafael stiffened. "Aramis, is that your finger within my ass?"

152

Aramis chuckled. "Why, yes, it is, my prince." He continued to lap.

Rafael groaned and pumped harder up into Elaine. "This will end very quickly if you continue rubbing in there."

Aramis peered up from between Rafael's thighs. "That is the idea." He flashed a grin, then lowered his head.

Rafael glared at him. "Impatient!"

Aramis chuckled and continued to lap, slathering Elaine's hot flesh and Rafael's pumping shaft with his saliva.

Elaine's core tightened with ruthless urgency. Her hips bucked in reflex, uncontrollably forced into action by the unbearable tension clenching in her belly. Soft gasps and cries slipped from her lips. She was going to climax really soon. . . .

Aramis's mouth lowered, leaving her tender flesh. The inciting burn eased. But the sound of him lapping continued, with the addition of wet sucking noises. He moaned in delight.

Rafael tossed his head back and gasped. "Oh, foul play! Remove that talented mouth from my balls and put it back on Elaine!"

Elaine groaned. "No, you keep it! It's too intense!"

Rafael snarled. "Aramis!"

Aramis groaned in clear disappointment. His mouth moved back up to Elaine's flesh. At the same time, his hand moved from her thigh and he stretched to reach under the pillows.

Elaine jerked and bucked. Aramis's assaulting tongue was a scalding brand on her far-too-tender flesh. "No! Too much!"

"Yes." Rafael held her firmly, fucking her. "Let go and come so you may feed."

She threw her head back and writhed. It was too much. The tension was too high. She shuddered in resistance. "I can't!"

"You can!" Rafael lifted his hand from her breast and pressed her head back against his shoulder, his cock ferociously driving into her, and into her. . . . "Let go!"

Aramis's hand came out from under the pillow and he came up on his knees. His tongue lapped directly on Elaine's infuriated clit.

Battered by a carnal torment, Elaine bared her teeth and howled voraciously.

"Ah, there!" Rafael surged with determination into her arched body. "At last she rises."

The scent of expensive oil perfumed the room, and Aramis sat up. He leaned forward and caught Rafael around the thighs, lifting them over his folded knees. He smelled of sweat, sweet oil, and violently aroused maleness.

Rafael looked up at the other vampire, panting with his efforts. "Aramis?"

"Rafael." Aramis lifted Rafael's legs higher, tipping Rafael back a little. Aramis pressed in hard and grunted.

Rafael arched back and gasped, shuddering. "Aramis, what are you doing?"

Aramis grinned with long teeth. "I should think"—he pressed in with determination—"it is obvious."

Rafael gasped and writhed under her, his hips lifting hard under hers. "Mother Night!"

Aramis's belly pressed against hers, and he arched over them both, one hand reaching up to clutch the pillows by Rafael's head. Aramis pulled back and thrust; his chest brushing against her breasts and rasping against her swollen nipples. But he wasn't within her.

Rafael gasped and rose hard under her, driven by Aramis's stroke. He bucked again, and again, echoing Aramis's repeated thrusts.

Elaine reeled in shock. Aramis was fucking Rafael. It was unbelievably, sadistically, exciting.

Aramis lowered his hand from the pillows and embraced

154

them both, his thrusts driving hard into Rafael and his belly rubbing against Elaine's clit exactly right.

Elaine's climax swelled and crested with horrific intensity. A scream rose within her.

Aramis groaned. "She is there."

Rafael shuddered. "I too."

"As am I." Aramis groaned and stroked harder. "It has been too long. I have no control."

Rafael shifted Elaine's head to his right shoulder. "Come, feed."

Aramis set his head between them, his breath hot on Elaine's left shoulder.

Rafael lifted his right arm and groaned. "Aramis, the knife!"

Aramis leaned against Rafael's chest. "I have it. Lift your arm."

Rafael's arm lifted out of Elaine's sight just as she felt the tiny tremble that marked her fall into climax. Her orgasm exploded and clawed angrily through her. She screamed, "I need it!"

Rafael's bleeding wrist pressed against her open mouth.

Her teeth sank into the wrist to hold it to her mouth. She sucked and gulped with crazed abandon.

Rafael cried out under her and his cock pulsed in her core.

Lightning burned down her throat and ripped through her heart in a howling climax that seared her entire body.

Teeth stabbed into her shoulder.

A second scarlet-edged climax slammed and scoured through her. She couldn't even scream. The sound of rushing wings filled her ears, and black lightning seared her heart.

All three shuddered and were consumed in a black whirlwind of soul-searing fire.

15

Elaine moaned softly. A hot, wet tongue stroked against the ache on her left shoulder. She winced and shifted on her back among the pillows. A hand gripped her right shoulder to still her. She opened her eyes. Aramis's warm and sweaty body was draped over hers. It was his tongue on her left shoulder. A fresh bite mark was on his right shoulder.

Rafael reclined against her right side, gripping her right shoulder. His wrist was scored by a healing slash, with four jagged holes on either side. A bruise was fading all around it. The scarlet duvet had been drawn up to their waists. The smell of sex and fresh blood was thick in the air.

Rafael smiled. His eyes were a very human sky blue, and the long points of his teeth had retreated to hide among his more human teeth. "How do you feel?"

Elaine blinked. How did she feel? She couldn't seem to grasp hold of anything beyond the fact that the clawing urgency in her was finally gone. "Um, better?"

"Better?" Rafael snorted, but his smile remained. "You're not sure?"

"How about *relaxed*?" Elaine smiled. "Really, really relaxed, my prince."

Rafael chuckled and pressed a kiss to her brow. "That is acceptable."

Aramis lifted his head and smiled. His eyes and teeth had also returned to their more human dimensions. "I feel quite refreshed."

Rafael scowled. "And very pleased with yourself, no?" He swatted Aramis's shoulder. "You, impatient beast!"

Aramis flinched but laughed. "Oh come, Rafael! How could you expect me to miss the taste of my fledgling's first feeding?"

Rafael raised a brow. "Her ass does not have your cum in it."

Aramis grinned. "Imagine that."

Elaine tried to hold back her chuckles.

Rafael turned a stern look her way.

Elaine knew Rafael wasn't angry. She could tell, though she wasn't sure how. She pulled up the duvet over her nose in mock fear, and promptly burst out laughing.

Rafael rolled his eyes and shot a glare at Aramis. "I shall have to think of something truly inventive as punishment for you."

Aramis rested his chin on his hand and smiled. "I shall expect nothing less."

Rafael fell back among the pillows with a groan. "Incorrigible!"

Elaine rolled toward Aramis and looped her arm over him, laughing hysterically against his chest.

Aramis pressed a kiss to her brow.

"You are not setting a good example." Rafael's tone was dry.

Aramis didn't quite laugh. "I?"

The lights began to dim, and Rafael sighed. "Just remember, it is your turn to feed the *enfant*."

Aramis stretched out his arm and pulled Rafael up against Elaine. His leg shifted to cover them both. "When?"

Rafael chuckled in the darkness. "In about four hours."

Aramis sucked in a breath. "Four hours?"

Rafael rolled up against Elaine's spine and spooned against her back, his arm snaking around her waist. "Every four hours for the next few days."

Aramis groaned. "We are both taking responsibility, yes?"

Rafael pressed a kiss to Elaine's brow. "Of course."

Aramis closed his arm tight around them both. "Good."

Elaine snuggled against Aramis's warm breast. "Can we go to sleep now?"

Rafael vibrated with the chuckle he did not release. "Ah, she has your impatience."

Aramis snorted. "And your tendency toward mayhem."

Rafael sighed, and silence fell.

Elaine felt sleep pressing down on her, arriving to the rhythm of Aramis's heart.

"I am pleased to share your child, Aramis." Rafael's voice was very soft.

Aramis took a very deep breath. "I would have one with no other." His voice was barely above a whisper.

Rafael took several small breaths. "My heart."

Aramis leaned over Elaine to reach Rafael. "My life."

Elaine held very still between them, making her breaths shallow. She closed her eyes to hold back the sudden and inexplicable onset of tears.

Rafael sighed. "You have made the *enfant* weep again, Aramis."

"I? It was you this time!"

"I'm sorry," she said in a very small and tight voice.

The two of them shifted around Elaine, locking her tight between them.

"You are sorry?" Rafael tsked. "For what? You have done nothing."

"Elaine." Aramis sighed. "Why are you weeping?"

Elaine had to swallow to speak. "I'm sorry I caused so much trouble. I didn't mean to get between you."

Rafael lifted his head. "Get between us?"

Aramis lifted his head. "Where did you get such a foolish idea?"

Elaine shuddered. "If I hadn't . . . If you didn't make me a vampire . . ."

Aramis growled. "You would have died otherwise."

"I know, but . . . ." She took a deep breath. "Now I'm in the way."

Aramis groaned. "In the way of what?"

Rafael sighed. "I was correct. She saw us too deeply."

"I see." Aramis released a long, slow breath. "Elaine, if we, the both of us, had not wanted you to be with us, we would have found another to make you."

"What?" Elaine blinked. They wanted . . . her?

Aramis groaned. "It would not have been difficult to find a sire."

Rafael's arm tightened around her waist. "With her fire?" He snorted. "There would have been a line of vampires looking to have her for their *enfant*."

"There would have been several duels fought to gain her." Aramis's voice was laced with humor.

"Duels?" Rafael snorted. "I would have had to hold an entire tournament!"

Elaine shifted onto her back. "Then I am not interfering in your lives?"

Aramis choked out a small laugh. "Not in any way."

Rafael brushed her cheek with his fingers. "You have, in fact, brought us together."

Elaine sniffed and wiped her damp cheeks. "But you two are obviously in love. What kept you apart?"

Aramis turned his head away.

She flinched. "If that's too private . . . ?"

Rafael sighed. "No, it is best that you know." He snuggled against her right side. "When Aramis came to me, he was near death from Dimitri's abuse."

Elaine turned to Aramis. "Like Tony?"

Aramis released a breath. "Yes."

"I made Aramis my *enfant* to save him. I loved him from the first moment, and he was a delight to have, but I am very old, older than you can imagine."

Elaine snorted. "I don't know. I can imagine pretty far back."

Aramis pressed against her left side. "The passing of time is different for a vampire. As they gain in age, they gain in power, and that power needs to be fed. Rafael is possessed of a need that a human soul cannot survive." He took a deep breath. "Nor can a fledgling."

"I could not let him stay." Rafael pressed his head against hers. "I needed to feed, and I could not feed on a soul so young, without eventually consuming it, but I had no desire for any other when he was near." He took a shuddering breath. "It was very . . . hard. He was fully half my heart." His arms tightened. "I did not think Aramis would forgive me."

Aramis lifted his head. "Of course I forgave you!" He snorted. "After a while." He released a long breath. "A long while."

Rafael sighed. "You do not know what joy I felt when I saw you again."

Elaine winced. "With me tagging along."

Rafael pressed her shoulder. "When I saw you, I was hoping

Aramis had finally decided to make a child. I knew the moment we met that you were an excellent choice."

Aramis turned to face her in the dark. "I hope you can forgive me for taking you from your life?"

Elaine took a deep breath and released it. "It's okay, I didn't have much of a life." She slid deeper under the covers. "I don't have much of a family. I doubt they'll miss me. I lived for my art, and that's still here." She touched her heart. "I can feel it."

Rafael stirred at her side. "Not much of a family? How could this be?"

Elaine squirmed. "My parents didn't exactly want kids. They stayed together for a little while, and they still provide for me. That's how I got to college, and to Rome, but most of my life has been with one relative or another." She took a deep breath. It hurt, but it was an old hurt. "My art is . . . all I have."

"Ah . . ." Rafael sighed. "That explains what I saw."

Aramis turned toward him. "And I."

Elaine turned from one to the other, but she couldn't make out anything in the darkness. "What?"

Rafael pressed his palm to her heart. "There is a great deal of scarring where the love from your family should be."

Elaine's breath stopped. "You saw that?"

Aramis set his palm over Rafael's hand. "It was difficult to miss."

Rafael lifted his head. "This is how you keep making the *enfant* cry."

Aramis pressed his cheek to Elaine's. "Elaine, your making did not, and cannot, come between us, because you are a part of us. We hold your soul in our bodies, as you hold a part of ours."

"But I was just a total stranger—"

Aramis pressed his fingers to her lips. "With my first glance, I desired you. With our first kiss, you made me smile. With my first taste, you became precious to me. Dimitri only quickened my decision, but eventually I would have made you mine."

Elaine shivered. "That fast?"

Rafael sighed. "Elaine, do you know that every staff member in this house drinks Aquinas with every meal?"

She turned to Rafael. "What?"

"I am very, very old." Rafael drew in a long breath. "Humans cannot live here and work here without it. They cannot abide my presence."

Aramis stroked her arm. "Their hearts would not survive the constant fear."

Rafael sighed. "A human will not walk into a room that I occupy, unless he is drugged, and a thrall is far more sensitive. You should have been as your young friend was."

Aramis snorted. "Cowering on the floor."

"I could not believe you actually sat in my presence, drank coffee, and smiled at me!" Rafael chuckled. "I was absolutely charmed from that moment."

Elaine frowned. "But, Rafael, you aren't bad, just scary. Dimitri turned my stomach—you just made my heart try to pound its way out of my chest."

"Not bad, just scary?" Rafael touched her chin. "Elaine, I am not *scary*. To a human, and more so to a thrall, I am *terrifying*."

Elaine felt the slightest touch of bitter black feathers. *Loneliness . . .*

Rafael released a breath. "I knew the moment you sat down and drank that coffee, that you had will, strength. No . . . how do they say it in America? Ah, *guts*! A vampire must face many things that are terrifying, often within themselves. Your inner strength, your willingness to endure fear, proved to me that you were perfect to be a vampire."

Elaine shifted in the blankets. "Twelve years of judo doesn't hurt, either."

Aramis leaned over her. "Without being a vampire, your judo would not have saved you from Dimitri. Did you not notice that you were far stronger and faster than before?"

Elaine frowned. No, she hadn't. "Oh . . ."

"She is going to be formidable when she matures." Aramis groaned, but Elaine could hear the pleasure in his voice.

Rafael leaned over her. "I tell you now, if Aramis had decided not to make you his child, I would have, with or without your acquiescence."

Aramis turned to Rafael. "You would not . . . !"

Rafael snorted. "I would so."

"It is not within you to do so!"

"It is well within me to save a fire such as this one, just as I saved you."

Aramis growled. "I gave you my consent!"

"Actually, if you will remember, I tricked it out of you." Rafael's voice held traces of amusement.

"Ah!" Aramis rolled onto his back. "So."

Rafael looked down at Elaine. "So you see? You were wanted by both of us. It was inevitable that you would be one of ours. It is better that you belong to both." He looked up. "If not, the other one of us would have been quite upset to be left out."

Aramis snorted. "*There* is a profound understatement."

"Oh." Elaine shifted uncomfortably. It was . . . strange to be wanted. "Okay." Her heart filled with something she couldn't name, and it overflowed.

Aramis rolled up against Elaine's side. "Ha! This time it is you who made the *enfant* cry!"

Elaine choked out a laugh through her tears. "I'm okay, really. I'm just trying to get used to being . . . um." She didn't know how to put her feelings into words. It felt too big, it felt too different.

Rafael brushed his lips against her brow. "The word you are searching for is 'loved.'"

Aramis caught her hand and squeezed it. "Elaine, I thought you knew?"

Rafael sighed. "When you get up in four hours to feed her, she will know."

Elaine groaned. "Oh, come on! It's not like I am a real baby!"

"Oh yes, you are," they both said together. They looked over at each other and laughed.

Elaine squeezed Aramis's hand and searched for Rafael's. "What is that supposed to mean?"

Rafael chuckled. "You will understand when you are older."

Elaine jerked upright. "When I'm *older*?"

Aramis pushed her back down into the pillows. "Go to sleep."

Elaine struggled to sit up. "What do you mean when I'm older?"

Aramis shoved her back down and rolled on top of her. "Sleep now." He turned his head. "She is not going to take well to napping, I can tell."

Rafael laughed outright. "Ah, the pleasures of parenting!"

Elaine gasped. "Oh, come on, guys!"

They both leaned over her. "Sleep!"

Elaine groaned in protest, but the yawn nearly cracked her jaw. "Okay, fine. Whatever." She rolled into Aramis's chest.

"Again she goes to you for comfort. I think I shall be jealous."

Aramis sighed. "You may come to me for comfort, too."

"Oh?" Rafael rolled up tight against Elaine's back. "Good."

Elaine chuckled.

Aramis set his arm over them both and sighed.

The night became still, but for the beating of three hearts filled with the rustling of black-feathered wings.

16

The sun was only moments from setting when Elaine was pulled free of the gigantic bed she shared with Aramis and Rafael, and dragged by them into the shower for a thorough scrubbing.

She groaned under the exquisitely hot water. It felt really good on her sore shoulders, but it wasn't doing a damned thing about the hungry ache in her core. Her body wanted blood, and the sex that went with it. The hunger wasn't too urgent. She could hold it off for a while.

She couldn't wait for her last two weeks of "no solid foods" to be over. It wasn't that she had a problem drinking blood, she didn't. In fact, she'd kind of gotten used to having . . . breakfast in bed. *And lunch in bed, and dinner in bed . . .* But her diet of strictly liquids was *boring*! Her taste buds were screaming for a decent hamburger. *Two all-beef patties cooked medium rare, mayonnaise, Swiss cheese, onions, lettuce, tomatoes . . .*

Rafael abruptly shut off the water. "Towels, Aramis?"

Aramis nodded and gently pushed Elaine out of the shower

stall. She was toweled dry, shoved into a short white terrycloth bathrobe, and towed back into the bedroom proper.

Blinking sleepily, she looked to her right at tall, elegant Aramis in his rich blue velvet dressing gown, and not a stitch else, then to her left at the more delicate yet undeniably powerful Rafael in his black-and-red velvet dressing gown. "Guys, are we in a rush or something?" She lifted a hand to cover her yawn.

Rafael sat her on the end of their huge bed. "We will be leaving in less than an hour by helicopter."

"Leaving?" Elaine snapped completely awake. "By *helicopter*?" She'd never ridden in one of those before. "Where are we going?"

Rafael cupped Elaine's chin to peer intently into her left eye, then her right. "We are going to my more permanent home in the Carpathian Mountains."

Elaine blinked. "Carpathian . . . as in, we're going to Rumania?" *Where Dracula used to live?* She couldn't quite hold back her smile. "Isn't that a bit . . . cliché?"

Rafael lifted his chin and sniffed. "I made my home there long before that paranoid prince decided that impaling people on pikes was good for his country's morale." He lifted his index finger and tapped her lightly on the nose. "And despite what you have heard, he was not a vampire."

Elaine almost snickered. *Hello, ego . . .*

Aramis opened one of the mirrored doors to Rafael's wall of closets and began pulling out clothes. "Elaine, you will need to dress warmly." He handed Rafael a pair of boxers, a black wool sweater, and a pair of leather pants.

Elaine hunched her shoulders. *Oh crap . . .* Over the past two weeks, she'd destroyed nearly every stitch of clothing she had in her suitcase just trying to get in and out of them. "Uh, about that . . ."

Rafael turned to look over at her. "Is there a problem?"

Elaine winced. "I'm kind of . . . running out of clothes." She clenched her hands to keep from tugging on her robe, and tearing it. "I keep . . . ripping them."

Rafael's eyes widened briefly; then he chuckled. "I see."

Elaine lifted her chin. "I'm not used to being this strong!"

Aramis smiled and turned back to the closet. "I'm sure we can find you something to wear."

Elaine plucked at the cable-knit off-white Irish sweater made of lamb's wool. She was wearing it without a bra. That had been one of the first things to quite literally come apart in her hands. One of Rafael's plain white T-shirts was the only thing between all that itchy wool and her skin. As it was, the sweater fell to her knees and practically hid the black fatigues they'd scrounged up for her. She hadn't been able to wear Aramis's jeans, or Rafael's, though their boxers fit just fine. *Go figure.* Elaine rolled her eyes. "Me and my big butt."

Aramis came up behind her and draped his arms around her shoulder. "Your butt is a masterpiece of feminine perfection." He pressed his lips to her brow. "It is time to put on your coat. The helicopter will be arriving momentarily."

"Okay." Elaine picked up her long wool coat from the end of the bed and slid into it carefully, treating it like tissue paper. "I've never ridden in a helicopter."

Aramis slid into his long black leather coat and his lips twisted into a grimace. "They are very . . . loud, and can be . . . erratic."

Erratic? Elaine shook her head. *Was he talking about turbulence?* "Are we flying all the way to the mountains in it?"

Aramis nodded and began applying a hairbrush to his long mane. "An airplane cannot land where we are going." With swift gentle tugs, he braided his hair into a lone long tail.

Elaine grinned. "Why? Is it on the side of a cliff or something?"

Aramis's brows lifted. "How did you know?" He offered her the brush and a small black elastic.

"A cliff . . . ?" Elaine stared, her mouth falling open. "You're serious?" She took his brush and began the task of brushing and braiding her long hair.

"Aramis is quite serious." Rafael stepped into the bedroom. "My home residence is on the side of a cliff."

Elaine handed the brush back to Aramis. "*Long* flight . . . ?" She started on the delicate task of buttoning her coat, without tearing off the buttons. "How long?"

Rafael smiled. "Quite long. We are just outside of Prague. The border of Rumania is eight hundred and ninety kilometers, or five hundred and fifty miles, away."

Over five-hundred miles . . . ? Startled, Elaine felt her fingers tighten, and the button she was trying to fasten popped off in her fingers. She winced and tucked the button in her pocket. "Can a helicopter make it that far?"

"So little faith. . . ." Aramis gently pushed her fingers away from her coat buttons and set to closing her coat. "It is a *large* helicopter."

Rafael stepped over to the closet and withdrew a long leather coat, very much like Aramis's. "There will be stops to refuel along the way."

Elaine shook her head. "Won't that still take a long time?"

Rafael nodded. "Nearly the entire night."

A knock came on the bedroom door.

Rafael went to answer it, then turned to face them. "It is time to go, my hearts. The helicopter awaits us."

Elaine shouldered her battered brown leather backpack, and followed her two men down the broad hallway in the opposite direction from what she'd been used to taking. A simple white door led onto a much smaller corridor, with plain gray carpeting and bare whitewashed walls. The door at the very end led to an unpretentious wooden staircase that led downward. Another door led outside to the broad grassy field behind the monstrous *palazzo*.

Two men in black fatigues, holding what appeared to be semiautomatic rifles, stood at attention on either side of a rollaway staircase, which led to the open hatch of the helicopter.

Elaine eyed the sleek black shark-shaped vehicle with more than a little surprise. It wasn't large—it was enormous. She'd seen tour buses that were smaller, even without the long tail and the propellers. It was also bone-rattling in volume. She'd had no idea helicopters were so loud. She could actually feel the pulsing sound of the engine pressing against her skin.

Her braid firmly in hand against the wind created by the slow-spinning propellers, Elaine followed Aramis up the metal staircase, and into the passenger cabin, looking around in fascination.

It was very posh, with a polished black interior, black leather seating, subtle floor and ceiling lights, which glowed a soft blue, and smoke-tinted side windows. It was also less roomy than some minivans she'd ridden in. The passenger cabin only sat five, with two front-facing tall-backed seats separated by an armrest-table sort of thing, and a back-facing bench, with seating for three.

Aramis urged Elaine to the left, toward the long bench. "You will be more comfortable there." He moved toward the chair seat on the far side, and fastened himself in.

Rafael took the chair seat closest to the door.

Elaine sat down next to the window directly across from Aramis, and set her backpack next to her. Figuring out the heavy rounded seat belt was an interesting adventure, but all that mattered to her was that it didn't fall apart in her hands.

Rafael leaned forward, set his chin on his upraised fist, and smiled. "So what do you think of your first helicopter?"

Elaine grinned. "Loud, very loud."

The hatch door was closed with a loud *thunk*. Abruptly all exterior sound was muffled to the level of a hum.

Elaine blinked. "Whoa . . . I can hear again!"

Rafael chuckled. "From what I understand, this particular interior was designed with our delicate hearing in mind."

The helicopter vibrated, then lurched under them.

Rafael smiled. "And we are away."

Elaine leaned over, practically pressing her nose to the glass. The helicopter tilted to the side and the curved *palazzo* came into view, bathed in floodlights. The helicopter rose higher, and the surrounding floodlit castle walls came into view as well. Everything else was blackness, except for lonely headlights marking distant roadways. Eventually even the roads disappeared, obscured by darkness.

Elaine continued to stare through the glass anyway, wondering what the forests and farmland below would have looked like in daylight. "Rafael, when will I be able to walk around in daylight again?" With their reflections in the window glass, Elaine saw Aramis and Rafael exchange a long glance that spoke volumes.

Rafael looked over at her and smiled a little sadly. "It will be several years before your body will be able to withstand full direct sunlight for any length of time."

Elaine nodded. "Okay." She turned to face him with a determined smile. "How about, how long will it be before I'm *awake* during daylight hours?"

Rafael grinned. "Only two more weeks."

Elaine rolled her eyes. "Oh, thank God! I am so tired of sleeping through everything."

Rafael's smile broadened. "You will also be able to see daylight through specially tinted windows."

Elaine practically bounced in her seat. "Yes!"

Rafael rolled his eyes toward Aramis. "I suddenly have the suspicion that getting our *enfant* to go to sleep will become more difficult."

"That's to be expected." Aramis crossed his arms and raised his brow at Rafael. "She clearly takes after you in that respect."

Rafael lifted his chin and stared down his nose. "And what exactly are you trying to hint at?"

Elaine rolled her eyes. They were at it again.

An electronic crackle sounded. "My lords and lady, we have achieved traveling altitude. You may remove your seat belts until further notice."

Rafael grinned. "Excellent!" He disengaged his seat belt and looked over at Aramis. "Shall we proceed?"

Aramis removed his seat belt and nodded to Rafael.

Elaine poked at the buckle of her seat belt to disengage it, then frowned at Rafael. "Proceed with what?" She shifted in her seat, and a throb stabbed her under both shoulder blades. Elaine winced.

Rafael's brows dipped. "Is something wrong?"

"My back . . ." Elaine shifted her shoulders in an attempt to relieve the ache. "It hurts."

Aramis stepped across to take a seat next to her.

Elaine stiffened. "What . . . ?"

"Relax, Elaine." He pressed a hand against her shoulder to urge her to turn away, then yanked up the back of her sweater. His fingers slid down her spine. "Where does it hurt?"

Rafael's smile vanished. "Check under her shoulder blades."

Elaine stared at him. "How did you know?"

Aramis shook his head slightly. "I do not see any bruises."

His fingers slid lightly over the affected area. "There is some warmth and a slight touch of swelling."

She shivered under Aramis's light, cool touch. "Probably just muscle strain." *From all the sex.*

Rafael's frown held for a heartbeat more, then dissolved into a smile. "I see no need for concern, as long as I receive your most solemn promise that, should there be the slightest increase in pain, you will tell your beloved prince at once?"

Elaine nodded. "I will."

Rafael nodded. "Very well, then, it's time to take off your clothes."

17

Elaine stared at him. "Take off my clothes?"

Aramis leaned against her cheek and spoke softly against her ear. "We did leave without feeding you, yes?"

Elaine turned her head to frown at him. "Yeah, but . . . here? Now? In a helicopter?"

Aramis's black eyes sparked with humor and heat. His hands slid around her to cup the full curves of her breasts. "Did you not promise to follow our orders without question, without argument, and without delay?" He squeezed.

Elaine sucked in a deep breath. *Damn, his hands feel so good.* "Yeah, I did. . . ."

"Then this sweater needs to come off, yes?" His hands slid down to grab the hem of the sweater. He tugged it up.

"Yes, my sire." Elaine raised her arms and let the sweater slide off, taking her T-shirt with it.

Aramis let loose a deep, rumbling laugh and tossed the sweater behind him. "That's my obedient *enfant.*"

Rafael lifted his brow. "No bra?"

Elaine successfully fought the reflexive urge to fold her arms across her breasts, but her cheeks filled with heat. "I, um, ruined them." She'd torn them apart just trying to fasten them around her. *Damned vampire strength!*

Aramis pressed against her back and reached around her to palm her breasts. "All of them?" He slowly squeezed.

Elaine sucked in a breath. His hands were really warm. Her nipples tightened deliciously. "Yeah, all of them." Well, she'd only brought three of them to begin with. She bit her lip to stop a moan.

Aramis's thumbs slid back and forth across her taut nipples and the bumpy ridges that surrounded them.

Tiny bolts of sharp pleasure streaked straight down to her core. Tension coiled tight in her belly, and a wet throb struck her. A soft sound escaped her lips.

He leaned close and his breath brushed against her ear. "Stand up and face me."

Elaine rose to her feet, bracing her feet apart against the helicopter's slight shifts and sways.

Still seated, Aramis looped his arm around her waist, angled her a little to the side, giving her a clear view of Rafael, and pulled her closer. His hand lifted her breast toward his mouth, his breath warm against her flesh. He opened his mouth wide and took her in. He sucked, pulling hard on her nipple.

Hot, wet, and exciting stabs of pleasure burned from her nipple, straight down to throb in her clit. A gasp broke free from her throat, and a fine trembling started in her limbs. Her back arched, pressing her breast tighter to his mouth. She was forced to put her hands on his shoulders or collapse. The wet sounds of his suckling and her own soft moans filled her ears.

Aramis's arm left her waist and tugged at the buttons of the fly on her borrowed black fatigues. The pants came open and he pulled them down to her hips.

Cool air brushed her sensitive flesh. She hissed and shivered.

Aramis tsked. "No panties, either?" He tugged her fatigues all the way down to her ankles, helped her step free of them, then tossed them to the far end of the bench to join her discarded sweater and T-shirt. He captured the other nipple with his lips.

Rolling under a wave of jolting delight, Elaine gasped for breath to speak. "Yeah, I ruined those, too." She dug her fingers into his shoulders. "Harder . . ."

His long teeth pinched her nipple. Clearly, it was a warning not to rush him.

She jolted with the sensual ache and offered a soft whimper of surrender to his will.

Aramis released his pinch on her nipple, then stroked it soothingly with his tongue. His fingers brushed the plump lips that protected the secret folds of her moist flesh.

Delicious shock made her flesh shudder. "Yes!"

He released her breast with a wet smack. His eyes were dilated wide to blackness. He licked his lips. "Impatient?"

Elaine narrowed her eyes and let a low growl into her voice. "Yes."

Rafael chuckled. "Ha! That is from *you*, my heart."

Aramis rolled his eyes. "Oh, what is that saying our *enfant* uses? Ah, yes . . ." He leaned to the side to aim a narrowed gaze at Rafael. "Fine, rub it in."

Elaine couldn't quite suppress her chuckle.

Aramis looked up at her and lifted a brow. "That is not laughter I am hearing from you, correct?" His palm covered her heat, and two fingers slid up into her moist channel. He touched something utterly exciting deep inside, then flicked it.

She rocked forward and moaned. "No, absolutely not!" Her eyes fluttered closed. "I wouldn't dream of it!"

Aramis's fingers thrust within her, making sounds of wet suction. "This lack of . . . undergarments is rather convenient."

Rafael nodded. "There is something to be said for immediate and unobstructed access."

Aramis smiled wickedly at Rafael. "Perhaps we should continue this ... affectation?" His thumb slid across her swollen clit.

Elaine jolted hard, then shamelessly ground down on his hand. She could care less what they were talking about; she was too busy paying attention to Aramis's wicked fingers.

Aramis licked the middle finger of his free hand, then reached around her butt and slid his long finger down the seam of her butt to press against her anus with clear intent. "Open for me."

She sucked in a breath and pushed out. Her body opened under the pressure of his finger and it slid within.

Aramis smiled. "My sweet *enfant...*" His long finger swirled around within her anus, inciting little delicious tingles. "Ah, there is still some in here from before."

"Huh?" Elaine could barely think past the sensations inundating her. "Some what ... ?"

Aramis looked up at her with a hungry gleam in his eye and grinned, showing the points of his fangs. "Cum."

Elaine flinched, but only a little.

Rafael grinned broadly. "And I was very pleased to put my ... love there."

Aramis snorted and wriggled his fingers within her. "I am beginning to suspect that *this* has become your favorite place to put your ... love."

Rafael's eyes narrowed and he grinned, showing all his fangs. "Feeling deprived, my heart?"

Aramis lifted his brow and delivered a wide, fanged grin of his own. "I wouldn't dream of denying you the pleasure of receiving my ... love."

"Is that so?" Rafael set his elbow on the armrest table and rested his chin on his fist. "Speaking of receiving love . . ." He nodded toward Elaine.

Elaine gasped and rocked, grinding down on Aramis's hand. He felt so good. . . . Everything felt so good. Pressure and heat rose in waves. She was going to come. . . .

Aramis pulled his fingers from her flesh.

She dug her nails into his shoulders, whimpering with the loss. "Damn it. . . ."

Aramis rose to his feet, sucking on the fingers that had been in her pussy. He smiled. "I'd say that you found that enjoyable."

Elaine clenched her teeth together and swallowed down the growl that was trying to rise. "Not quite enjoyable enough."

Aramis lifted his brow and crossed his arms. "A display of temper will not give you what you wish for, any sooner."

Elaine stiffened. *Uh-oh* . . . An annoyed Aramis was more than capable of leaving her exactly as she was, naked and twitching on the edge of orgasm, for an hour or more. *Time to do damage control. . . .* She leaned forward and pressed a kiss to Aramis's temple. "Please? Pretty please, can I come?"

Aramis cupped her face in his palms and pressed a soft, sweet kiss to her lips. "Much better." He patted the seat. "Kneel here, and place your hands on the back." He stood and unzipped his fly.

Elaine climbed up to kneel onto the seat, spread her knees, and set her hands on the headrest.

Rafael groaned. "Hard and fast, my hearts. I want to see it hard and fast."

Elaine turned her head to the left to look at Rafael.

He had unzipped his leather pants and was pulling the length of his cock free. He spread his booted feet wide and stroked the pale column of flesh from the base to the deeply blushing crown. His blue gaze narrowed and heated. His fangs visibly extended, showing just how excited he was.

Elaine shivered with raw hunger. Rafael was particularly beautiful when he was aroused. The cool slide of moisture trickled down the inside of her thigh.

Aramis stepped behind Elaine and cupped her hips in his palms. He set one knee up on the seat beside hers. "You're dripping." The heated length of his cock slid down the seam of her ass. "Enjoying the view?"

Elaine nodded, her mouth dry.

"Good." The broad head of his cock pressed between her thighs. He found her wet folds, grabbed her hip, and thrust hard, slamming all the way in.

Elaine rocked under the impact, her hands barely enough to keep her face from hitting the back of the chair, and yelped in surprise.

Aramis leaned over her shoulder. "Elaine?"

"I'm fine, I'm fine." It hadn't hurt, by any means, just startled her. In fact, it felt rather . . . exciting to be taken so swiftly. She rocked her hips from side to side, grinding back on him.

Rafael grinned. "I think our *enfant* likes it . . . rough."

Aramis closed his hand on her shoulder and withdrew slowly, agonizingly slowly. "I think you may be right." He lunged back into her, hard.

Elaine braced her forearms on the chair, then shoved back to meet him. Their bodies made contact with a loud smack. They both groaned.

"Yes . . ." Rafael released a hungry growl. "Just like that, my hearts. Fuck each other just like that."

Aramis replied with a growl of his own and dropped over her back to cup her breasts with brutal strength. Closing her tight in his arms, he thrust up into her wet, and more than willing, body. He pulled back and thrust again, and then again, gaining in speed and power.

The wet sounds of thrusting flesh and the sharp sounds of his hips slapping against her ass filled the small cabin.

Rafael chuckled low and feral. "You are rocking the helicopter, my hearts."

Aramis loosed a rumbling growl. "Good."

Elaine twisted under him. She could feel his balls pounding her clit deliciously with every stroke. Fire mounted and burned in her core. She could feel her climax rising with maddening speed and vicious intent.

"Ah, you are close." Aramis's breath was harsh in her ear. "Come on my cock, my heart. Come on my cock and squeeze me tight." His thrusts suddenly increased in tempo. "Come now!"

Elaine tensed and her breath caught. Climax roared up in a hot, wet tidal wave and crashed in a glittering blaze of erotic fire. She shouted out her release and writhed in frenzy beneath him.

Aramis thrust his arm under her lips.

Elaine bit down and drank.

Against her back, Aramis choked out a cry. Within her, his cock pulsed.

A second orgasm, sharp-edged and burning hot, slammed into her, accompanied by the sound of a thousand black wings. . . .

Aramis stuffed the last of the soiled tissues into a small plastic garbage bag and shot a glare at Rafael. "Was it absolutely necessary to . . . expend all over my ass?"

Seated in his chair by the hatch, Rafael smiled smugly. "You have a lovely butt, how could I resist?"

Elaine looked up from where she was trying to button the fly of her fatigues. So far, she hadn't ripped any off. "He . . . what?"

Aramis stuffed the garbage bag into the small cabinet under the armrest. "While you were feeding"—he curled his lip in Rafael's direction—"our beloved prince positioned himself behind me."

Rafael writhed in his seat, and blatantly rubbed his crotch, looking thoroughly pleased with himself. "I came all over his delicious butt."

Elaine stared, wide-eyed. How the hell did she miss *that*?

Aramis's gaze narrowed. "You also came in my pants and underclothes."

Rafael's brows lifted in a far-too-innocent manner. "Perhaps you should have taken them off?"

Aramis rolled his eyes and flopped into the seat beside Rafael. "If you had told me what you had intended, I would have!"

Rafael grinned. "I thought you liked surprises?"

Electronic static signaled that the intercom was live. "My prince, the radar indicates that we are being followed."

Rafael sat straight up in his chair. "What kind of craft?"

"I . . . can't tell, sir. It's too small to be an airplane or a helicopter. I would venture it to be some sort of glider, but gliders don't fly at this speed—though it does move as though riding the updrafts."

Rafael's jaw tightened and his eyes brightened to electric blue. A thick and powerful vibration filled the very small cabin. "I see."

Elaine's heart slammed in her chest. She could barely breathe past it. Rafael was very, *very* angry. She knew he wasn't mad at her, but her pounding heart and the cold sweat forming on her spine weren't listening to logic.

Rafael turned to the speaker by his window. "Increase speed as much as possible. I do not wish to be caught on the ground when we must refuel."

"Yes, my prince!"

Rafael sighed and the threatening atmosphere dissipated. He rubbed his brow.

Elaine took a deep breath and slumped in her seat.

Aramis frowned. "Do you expect an attack?"

Elaine stiffened. *Attack . . . ?*

Rafael snorted and smiled sourly. "Against me? Highly doubtful." He leaned back in his chair and crossed one knee over the other. "My guess is that he will wait for us to land, then strike."

Aramis turned to Rafael. "He . . . ? Do you know who it is, or what they want?"

Rafael looked down at his hands and smiled sourly. "I have my suspicions." His gaze settled on Elaine, and a small but feral smile curved his lips. "However, I doubt they have any idea what they'd be taking on."

Elaine's heart began to pound in an altogether different fashion than before. This time it wasn't fear, but anticipation. "Why do I have the sudden feeling that I'm the target?"

Rafael's smile softened. "Because, my beloved *enfant*, you have excellent instincts."

Aramis's jaw tightened. "Do I know this . . . person?"

"After a fashion." Rafael turned to look hard at Aramis. "You encountered him shortly after your rebirth. He has a taste for a very specific kind of fledgling, if you recall?"

Aramis stiffened. "The Persian . . . ?"

Rafael shrugged. "I could be mistaken. He's not the only being that can fly as swiftly as a helicopter. However, anyone else would be sure to notify me before attempting to approach in a manner that could be . . . misinterpreted."

Elaine's mind latched onto one particular word, and wouldn't let go. " *'Fly'?* Are you saying this guy can *fly,* as in, without an airplane? Does he have wings or something?"

Rafael lifted his chin and held her gaze. "He does."

What... ? Elaine's brain came to a complete and utter halt for an entire indrawn breath. "This guy has *wings,* like an angel?"

Aramis snorted and folded his arms across his chest. "He may have wings, but he is far from angelic."

Elaine frowned. "But that's ... impossible, outside of fairy tales and myths."

Aramis shrugged. "Vampires are considered myths, are they not?"

Elaine closed her mouth with a snap. He had a point. She shook her head. "Okay, but we're talking *wings* here!"

Rafael chuckled. "My dear *enfant,* there are a great many things considered mythical that do, in fact, exist."

Elaine's mouth dropped open. *What... ?* That's what she meant to say; instead, Elaine was suddenly attacked by an enormous jaw-cracking yawn. She barely got her hand over her mouth in time. Then her eyes started to close on her, and her upright position started to wilt. Apparently, her body had decided that since it had fed, it was time to go back to sleep. *Stupid vampire instincts!* She stiffened her spine in an attempt to fight it off, but her body was determined.

"Elaine?" Rafael's voice was gentle.

She opened her eyes, only to realize that she hadn't even noticed that they'd closed. "Damn it!"

Rafael chuckled. "You may as well rest. We have several more hours before we land."

Elaine struggled to hold herself upright. "But I don't want to rest!" To her profound disgust, her voice came out in a whine.

Aramis snorted and didn't even bother to hide his smile. "I really don't see you having much of a choice."

Elaine shot him a glare, but with the way she could barely hold her eyes open, she doubted it even counted as one. "You are *not* helping."

Rafael lifted a hand to cover his mouth, but he failed miserably to hide his grin. "I don't believe he was *trying* to help."

Elaine could barely hear him through the sound of wind and midnight feathers.

18

She dreamed of warm waves flowing against her skin and lifting her up, and cool waves that became downward slides. Oddly, the waves didn't feel wet, and she could breathe just fine. She couldn't actually see anything beyond an undulating gray haze, but that didn't actually matter because sliding up and down was fun. It was a lot of fun, except . . .

Except that the waves were shifting as though something else was moving among the waves with her, and it was getting closer.

Suddenly she found floating among the waves wasn't so much fun. She opened her eyes wide, straining to see through the shifting gray haze.

A dark . . . something rose through the currents just below her. A something that wasn't friendly. A something that felt . . . hungry.

She jerked to the side, to change directions and discovered that it was harder to go against the current than she'd thought. Panic made her heart pound and her body clench tight. Cold sweat formed down her spine. She twisted hard, nosing up through the currents. A warm wave pressed up against her. She turned into it and rose higher very swiftly, almost as though she was falling, only upward.

Her heart began to pound for a different reason. What if she couldn't stop rising?

A slight bump against her head startled her so hard, her entire body jolted. She landed facedown, hard, and a gasp exploded from her lips. Her eyes snapped open to see that she was lying on a broad white floor. She frowned in confusion and set her palms under her to sit up. She appeared to be in a huge, but unfurnished, white-floored, white-walled room she'd never seen before. In addition, she was dressed in a sleeveless low-cut nightgown of creamy unbleached cotton, which was trimmed in pale pink ribbons and snowy tatted lace. She didn't recognize the nightgown any more than she did the room.

Her gaze fell on what looked like a standing lamp positioned in the very center of the floor, except that it looked to be upside-down. The long glass baubles on the edges of the glass globe appeared to be pointing straight up. She turned to look over at the row of dark-curtained windows. They were awfully high from the floor, and the curtain rod was resting on the bottom of the windowsill, as though the curtains were falling up, not down.

Her thoughts stilled and her heart began to pound, deafeningly loud. She sat up and leaned back, looking up at the ceiling.

Directly above her head was a wide bed with a rumpled black comforter and gold sheets sitting on what appeared to be a burgundy carpet. Against the left wall was a mirrored dresser and folding doors, which obviously led to a closet, and on the right was a door that appeared to lead to a bathroom. At the foot of the bed was what could only be the bedroom door, and it was all pinned to the ceiling.

Unless . . . *she* was on the ceiling?

Her eyes widened. *Oh, my God . . .* Vertigo slammed from the pit of her stomach all the way up to the top of her head, bringing an icy sweat and bone-shaking fear in its wake. She was on the ceiling very, *very* far away from the floor—and absolutely nothing was actually holding her there. *I'm going to fall!* She flattened herself against the white expanse and shrieked.

The door slammed open; Aramis came charging through it. He stared at the rumpled bed, then looked around sharply. "Elaine . . . ?"

Elaine stared at the man standing on the carpet far above her head. Absolute terror closed her throat too tight to speak. She *was* on the ceiling. The tiniest of whimpers escaped.

Aramis looked up to meet her gaze and his eyes widened. "Elaine, did something frighten you?"

Elaine stared at him in shock. Her fear was suddenly swamped by frustrated anger. "You mean *besides* being stuck to the ceiling for no apparent reason whatsoever?"

Rafael stepped into the room. "Aramis, what . . . ?"

Aramis pointed upward and his mouth curled upward in obvious amusement.

Rafael looked up and blinked. "Well, I guess we can say that she has definitely inherited my bloodline traits."

Elaine banged her fist on the so-called floor at her side. Were they missing the point on purpose? "Never mind that! Can someone tell me how I got up here?"

A smile lifted the corner of Rafael's mouth. "Elaine, my dear, you put yourself there."

Elaine's heart stuttered in her chest. "I . . . I did . . . ?"

Rafael shook his head. "It's an instinctive reaction to danger very particular to my bloodline."

Elaine frowned. Reversing gravity was an instinctive reaction? "I don't understand. . . ."

Aramis approached the bed. "Something must have frightened you, or this would not have happened. What was it?"

"Um . . ." Elaine scowled, trying to think past the pounding of her heart. "I had a nightmare?"

Both men stilled completely, the amusement draining from their expressions.

Rafael's eyes narrowed. "Describe it, please."

Elaine frowned and sucked on her bottom lip, carefully. She still wasn't quite used to having fangs and tended to nick herself every now and again. "I was swimming, I think. I couldn't see anything, it was all gray and misty. Something—I couldn't make out what it was—was coming after me. I kind of went . . . up to get away from it." She looked up at her two sires. "And then I woke up here."

Aramis turned to look back at Rafael. His brow lifted.

Rafael nodded and sighed.

"By the way"—Elaine looked around at the unfamiliar and rather plain room—"where is . . . *here?*"

Rafael stepped over to the bed, sat down at the foot, and pulled off his shoes. "We are at my main residence in the Carpathian Mountains." He leaned back to look up at her and smiled. "This is one of the guest bedrooms. You were sleeping so sweetly that I decided to leave you to continue your nap while our belongings were put in the master suite."

"Oh, that's nice." She clenched her fingers in her nightgown and tried very hard to smile. "Can I get down now? Please?"

Rafael nodded and rose to his feet. He held out his arms and rose slowly from the floor.

"Whoa . . ." Elaine's eyes opened very wide. "You can *fly?*"

Rafael smiled and continued to approach her. "I can, but in

this instance, I am merely floating." He held his hands out to her. "Stand up and take my hands."

Elaine rose to her hands and knees, but then her body froze. She couldn't make herself rise to her feet. "I . . . I can't stand up."

Rafael's smile broadened. "Reach for me, Elaine. Give me your hand."

Elaine lifted one shaking hand toward the descending Rafael.

He hovered close. "Go ahead, take my hand. Do not be afraid. I will not let you fall."

Elaine swallowed hard and grabbed onto his warm hand. The feeling of relief was so profound, she actually felt dizzy.

He held out his other hand. "Take both my hands and stand up slowly."

Elaine kept her gaze locked on Rafael's face and knelt up, setting one foot on the . . . floor. Her knees did not want to work at all, but somehow she got both her feet under her and stood.

"Good." Rafael smiled. "Do not close your eyes, and pay close attention to my heart. Can you hear it?"

Elaine strained to hear the soft and excruciatingly slow thump within Rafael's chest. It was odd, being able to hear a heartbeat when one wasn't actually pressed up against a chest, but she'd been able to do it ever since her . . . rebirth. His heartbeat was so much slower than hers. So was Aramis's, but Rafael's was even slower than his. "Yes, I hear it." But there was something else, too—a rushing sound.

Rafael's voice dropped to a soft whisper. "Can you hear the other sound, the softer one, like a wind?"

Elaine nodded. "Yeah, like a wind in the trees, or feathers." She felt her cheeks warming. "I dream of wind and feathers sometimes."

He nodded. "I thought you might." His gaze became intent. "I want you to listen to your own heart and find the wind there."

"Okay." She frowned in concentration, listening to her heartbeat. She almost couldn't hear it past the rushing sound, like a wind. It was almost louder than the sound of her beating heart. "Oh . . ."

Rafael smiled. "You hear the wind?"

She nodded. "Yeah." She frowned. "It's loud."

Rafael tightened his hands around hers. "I need you to make that wind soften, but do it slowly, gently. Begin by slowing your breathing. Take deeper, slower breaths."

Elaine took a deep breath, letting it out slowly, and then another. The rushing sound of the wind around her heart eased. She suddenly felt a little . . . lighter, like she was fading into a dream. Her eyes drifted closed.

"Good." Rafael tugged on her hands. "Don't close your eyes. Breathe deeper. . . ."

Elaine opened her eyes. Her long braid and her nightgown were floating around her. She tightened her hold on Rafael's hands, and took deeper and slower breaths. Her toes lifted off the white floor and she floated toward Rafael.

Rafael smiled. "Excellent. Continue exactly like that, no faster, no slower."

Elaine nodded and continued to breathe deeply and slowly. Abruptly something inside her head snapped, almost painfully, like a tendon suddenly loosening. Suddenly she really was facing the floor with her toes pointing at the ceiling. She stiffened in alarm.

Rafael squeezed her hands lightly. "Relax and breathe. Your sense of direction has merely corrected itself. Your body will adjust."

Elaine focused on her breathing and her toes drifted down

from the ceiling until she was lying flat in the air, floating—hand in hand—with Rafael. "Oh . . . I'm floating! *Really* floating." It was amazing. It was intoxicating.

Rafael smiled. "Yes, you are. And now we continue to take nice, calm breaths and let gravity draw us down to the nice, soft bed below us, yes?"

Elaine nodded and continued to drift downward, her feet slipping lower until she stood next to Rafael in midair, her skirts and braid floating around her. Her toes touched something slick and soft. She looked down. Her toes were brushing the surface of the bed. Gravity abruptly turned back on at full strength. She dropped like a stone to the bed and landed with a yelp, and with a small explosion of blankets and pillows.

Aramis leaned over the bed. "Are you all right?"

Elaine pushed to sit upright and rubbed her brow. "A little dizzy, but okay."

Rafael chuckled and drifted down like a feather to sit crosslegged at her side. "Not so frightening, after all, eh?"

Elaine shook her head. "Not now that I know how to get back down." She tilted her head back and stared up at the ceiling, at least fourteen feet above her. "Wow . . . I was really up there?" She pushed up onto her knees and looked over at Aramis. "Can you do it, too?"

Aramis's cheeks turned pink and he looked away. "I have not had the . . . need to do so in a long time." He lifted a red silk robe and held it open for Elaine to slip into.

Rafael leaned over to tie the belt around Elaine's waist. "Then you will not mind practicing with Elaine, yes?"

Aramis took a deep breath and sighed it back out. "I can see that it has become unavoidable."

Rafael chuckled. "I will have the ballroom prepared for you."

Aramis winced. "Good idea. We are going to need plenty of room."

Elaine slid off the bed. "Sounds like fun!"

Rafael caught Elaine under the chin and captured her gaze. "However, for your own safety, you must not step outside this house, not even into the gardens, until I have decided that you have mastered this talent."

Elaine frowned. "Why not?"

Aramis snorted. "Because we do not want to have to pluck you from the wing of a jet, should you suddenly shoot upward."

An ice-cold chill spilled down Elaine's spine. Suddenly she had absolutely no urge whatsoever to go anywhere that didn't have a firm ceiling. "No arguments there!"

Rafael nodded. "Excellent. Now, then . . ." He held out his hand. "Come along, Elaine, we have much to show you." He smiled and the tips of his fangs showed.

19

Elaine followed her sires out of the guestroom and up a vaulted hallway painted robin's-egg blue with white trim. The ceiling was painted the same blue, with fluffy white clouds. Graceful art nouveau wall lamps in brass, their frosted glass shaped like lilies, cast a soft golden glow on floor-to-ceiling gold-framed paintings of smiling, chubby women in sheer drapery. She blinked at them in passing. "Wow . . ." The scary part wasn't that she recognized more than a few of the paintings, but that they were all clearly originals.

Aramis patted her shoulder. "Wait until you see what's in the rest of the house."

Dull, throbbing pain spilled all the way across her. Elaine hissed and winced out from under his palm.

Rafael's eyes narrowed. "Elaine?"

"It's nothing." Elaine rolled her shoulders to ease the ache, but it triggered a pang that spilled all the way down to her tail-bone. "Ow . . ."

Aramis caught her by the wrist, stopping her. "Elaine, hold still." He swept his fingers lightly down her back. Small almost electrical jolts followed in the wake of his fingertips. "She is beginning to show signs."

Elaine twisted around to look at Aramis. "Signs of what?"

Rafael caught her chin and drew her gaze to his sky blue–colored eyes. "There is absolutely no need for concern. You are merely maturing."

Caught in Rafael's bright blue gaze, Elaine felt a surge of calm bloom in her heart and flood outward. Her entire body warmed and relaxed. She smiled. "Okay."

Rafael chuckled and turned to Aramis. "It appears that our Elaine is going to be a . . . What is that phrase? Oh yes, an early bloomer."

Aramis rolled his eyes. "Once again, Elaine proves surprising."

Rafael threw an arm over Aramis's shoulder and smiled. "Which only goes to show that you do indeed have very good taste in women."

Frowning, Elaine pressed her hand to her brow. "Huh . . . ?" One moment she'd been worried, and the next moment, it was gone. "What just happened . . . ?"

Rafael stepped ahead and turned back with a sweet smile. "Ready to see the rest of your new home?"

Still somewhat confused, Elaine forced a smile onto her lips. "Um, sure."

Aramis and Rafael exchanged glances, then led Elaine down the hallway, occasionally pointing out particular works of art.

Elaine followed her sires down a black marble staircase, then through hallway after hallway, with her eyes wide open in awe. She had thought that the *palazzo* outside of Prague had been huge. It was a cottage compared to the monstrous house that Rafael claimed as his main residence. The building seemed to go on for acres in every direction, and completely changed periods, styles, and number of floors, from wing to wing.

Rafael's entire private wing had clearly been neoclassical, but the main floor appeared to be medieval. The mortared stone walls were swathed with gigantic tapestries, with monstrous fireplaces that would comfortably house a love seat. The floors were black marble, covered in Ottoman carpets. The ornately carved black marble master staircase, and the life-size statues stationed at the very bottom, were distinctly Gothic in style. One wing over, and up a curving white marble stair, the décor became distinctly Italian Renaissance, but one room that they passed appeared to be an extremely Victorian gentleman's smoking room, complete with leather chairs and a pool table.

Elaine also couldn't help but notice that there seemed to be a clock in every hall and by every doorway, despite the period of the décor, and no two were alike.

Aramis mentioned in passing that there was even a clock tower on the house, though she wasn't about to step outside to see it.

Elaine began to wonder if Rafael was a clock collector of some sort.

The staff was rather interesting, too. Fully half the staff was dressed in nineteenth-century clothes, the women in long black dresses with petticoats, white ruffled aprons, and caps, and the men in tailed jackets and bow ties. The other half of the staff appeared to be guards in plain black fatigues and highly polished combat boots, but in addition to bulky-looking side arms, they also carried swords.

However, the most incredible thing about the house was the view out the windows. It was just as she'd been told. The house, as massive as it seemed to be, was perched on the side of a cliff in the hollow of a mountain, and it wasn't the only one. She couldn't see details through the night-dark windows, but she could definitely make out floodlit houses up and down the opposite cliff.

Elaine craned her neck to peer around corners and down halls, completely fascinated. "I am so totally going to get lost in a big hurry."

Rafael turned to glance back at her with a slight smile. "You will not get lost, as you will be accompanied at all times."

Elaine frowned up at him. "Are you saying that you're getting me a babysitter?"

Aramis turned to Rafael and shrugged. "I suppose that is accurate, yes?"

Rafael chuckled. "Indeed."

"Wait a minute!" Elaine stopped in her tracks. "I'm *not* a child!"

Both men turned to her and looped an arm through each of hers, sandwiching her between them. "Yes, you are," they chorused.

Elaine ground her teeth. It was absolutely no use arguing with them. "What's next? Are you sending me back to grammar school?"

Rafael nodded. "Tutors will come later, when you have matured enough."

Elaine looked up at him in openmouthed shock. "What . . . ?"

A monstrous *bong* echoed throughout the entire house, vibrating deep in Elaine's inner ears, as well as the floor under feet. A second *bong* sounded. Elaine winced and grabbed onto both her sires.

Aramis and Rafael stopped cold and looked up.

Elaine suddenly noticed that every staff member she could see—maid, footman, and guard—had stopped as well and also looked up.

The sound died away.

Both men exchanged narrow-eyed glances and started walking at a very rapid pace, towing Elaine between them.

Elaine trotted to keep up with both men. "What was that?"

Aramis tightened his grip on her arm, his mouth tight. "That was the clock tower."

Elaine would have rolled her eyes if she hadn't been so busy trying not to trip over her feet. "I kind of figured. . . . Big bells on that thing, by the way."

From the far end of the hall, four guards wearing black fatigues jogged toward them and then past them. They carried what looked like seriously high-tech machine guns. Another group of guards with machine guns came from down another hallway and passed them, and then another.

Her heart started pounding in alarm. "What's going on?"

Rafael led them up a short staircase. "The clock tower is part of our alarm system." He turned them toward a broad windowless hall with an arched high ceiling that had been painted deep burgundy. Art deco wall lamps were set above huge paintings of battle scenes. "The bell only sounds when someone of great power enters the environs."

"Enters the . . . *what*?" Elaine glanced up at Rafael. "And what's do you mean by 'great power'?"

Rafael turned the corner into a wide hall, with even larger and gorier war paintings. "Great metaphysical power—the strength of the sound and the number of rings indicate the level of force."

"Huh?" Elaine shook her head. "Wait—'metaphysical power,' as in . . . magic?"

Aramis nodded. "Among other forms."

Elaine very nearly tripped. "Magic is *real*?"

Aramis shot her a tight smile. "As real as vampires."

20

Elaine blinked. *Magic is real . . . ?* That was going to take some serious thought, when she wasn't trotting down a hall in her nightgown. Another thought suddenly came to mind. "Rafael, you're powerful. Do you set off the bells, too?"

Rafael glanced at her with a smile. "The tower sounds thrice for me."

Three times? This . . . whatever it was . . . only set it off twice. A good portion of Elaine's anxiety bled away. "Oh, okay."

Aramis tightened his hand on her arm. "There is no need for fear." He lifted his chin toward Rafael. "We are merely being cautious."

A pair of large wooden doors stained dark cherry and carved with elegantly curling leaves marked the very end of the hall. Four obscenely muscular guards stood at attention, two on each side, wearing black caps, and black military fatigues that were tucked into very shiny black boots. What appeared to be grenades hung on their equipment belts, and really big machine guns were held up against their shoulders. They also had swords strapped to their hips.

Elaine lifted her brow. *That's a lot of . . . artillery.* They looked like SWAT team members, only bigger. They also exuded a strange . . . aura, which was making her skin tingle. Elaine had the distinct impression that whatever these guys were, they definitely weren't human, but they weren't vampires, either.

Rafael slowed to a halt. "Elaine . . ." He turned to face Elaine and smiled down at her. "Your former life has ended. All that you were is gone."

Aramis moved to stand behind Elaine and his hands closed on her shoulders.

Elaine nodded. Her life as a college student, as a human being, was over. However, while staring up at Rafael, with the comforting warmth of Aramis's hands on her shoulders, what she had lost seemed so small in comparison to what she had gained.

Rafael took a deep breath. "Beyond those doors is the new world that you will walk in—my world, Aramis's world, where beings that you have been taught to believe are imaginary, in fact, exist."

Elaine snorted and cracked a smile. "I think the fact that you guys are vampires kind of gave away that some things are real, whether anyone believes them or not. It's magic I'm having problems believing in." *And people with wings.*

Rafael tilted his head to the side. "Yes, well, I am not quite a vampire."

Elaine's eyes widened. "You're . . . not?"

Rafael shook his head slowly. "I am . . . from many, many ages ago. Those more commonly known as vampires are my . . . descendants, one might say." He nodded to her. "As you are directly of my blood, my *enfant*, you are as I am."

"But what about . . . ?" Elaine glanced back at Aramis. He had been part of the whole "making" thing, too. Wouldn't that make her half vampire, or something?

Rafael's gaze moved past her to Aramis. "When Aramis came to me from Dimitri, he was still human." His lips curved into a smile; then he winked. "And far too lovely for any immortal to resist."

Aramis pressed his brow to Elaine's cheek. "I was also dying."

Elaine stiffened. *Dying?* "You made him, too?"

"I simply could not let him go." Rafael's gaze dropped back to Elaine and he nodded. "The rest you know."

Okay . . . Elaine frowned. Rafael made Aramis, who, in turn, made her with Rafael's help. The whole thing was beginning to sound vaguely . . . incestuous. She shook her head, deciding firmly to think about those ramifications some other time. "So, then, if we're not quite vampires, what are we?"

Aramis leaned over her shoulder and whispered, "That depends on what stories you read."

Elaine smiled as her own words echoed back once more. She pressed a quick kiss to his cheek. "Okay." She turned back to Rafael. "Are there differences between us and . . ." *True vampires . . . ? Actual vampires . . . ? Real vampires . . . ?* She cleared her throat. ". . . Vampires in general?"

Rafael nodded. "A few." He curled an arm around her shoulders. "All will be explained another time."

Elaine was swept through the huge doors and into a cavernous room that had to be at least two stories high, with a domed ceiling painted with a clouded night sky in deep blue and black. Wall sconces of amber glass shed soft golden light that barely pierced the shadows. The walls were painted in deep burgundy, like the hall, but the color seemed so much darker under the dim lighting. The entire left wall was floor-to-ceiling multipaned windows. The black velvet drapes had been drawn to the sides with tasseled gold cords, revealing a large night-dark formal garden enclosed by a high wall. A wide oval pool lay still and silent, reflecting the nearly full moon.

The right wall was commanded by a monstrous fireplace sculpted with chubby nymphs and leering satyrs. Within it, someone had lit a small bonfire, but the blaze looked tiny compared to the sheer size of the fireplace.

At the very back of the room was a gigantic painting, *The Fall of Troy*. Before it was a huge desk that consisted of a thick sheet of smoked black glass resting on the shoulders of two sculptures. Facing right was a kneeling fairy, with folded-down butterfly wings, and facing left was a bowing satyr, with goat's legs and stubby horns.

A huge and extremely modern red leather presidential office chair sat behind the desk, slightly off-center. On the right corner of the desktop, by a small decorative desk lamp, a slender silver laptop sat open. Beside it was a very ordinary black office telephone with several lights blinking. Before the desk and resting on a rectangular black-and-gold Ottoman carpet was an ultra-modern overstuffed black leather couch, with matching armchairs to either side.

Rafael took a seat in the red leather chair and began typing on the laptop at insane speed.

Aramis encouraged Elaine toward one of the plush chairs in front of the desk, then walked around the desk to stand at Rafael's shoulder.

Elaine sat down with the distinct impression that she was in some kind of high-level corporate office. The only thing missing was a secretary.

Rafael nodded at his laptop. "He has arrived at the palace and has been given guest quarters." He looked up at Aramis. "He has asked for a formal audience."

Aramis frowned. "How . . . unexpected."

Rafael peered at the information on his laptop. "Perhaps there is more to this than the obvious?"

A *click* sounded on Elaine's right. She turned to look.

A part of the wall on the far side of the fireplace had opened like a door. A man stepped through, carrying a black tray with a clearly antique silver coffee service. His sleek silver-blond hair was just beyond shoulder-length and looked a little overgrown. His bangs were brushing his jawline. In contrast, his clothes were almost painfully tidy. His knee-length black coat was severely cut, his gray trousers creased, and his snowy white shirt was starched. However, his royal blue cravat was loosely tied around his pointed collar. A thick black book, held closed with a heavy brass buckle, was carried on his hip by way of a crosswise shoulder strap of black leather.

Elaine blinked. *Don't tell me—the secretary?*

The blond nudged the wall door closed with his elbow and headed for the desk with brisk, long strides. "The senator from Venice is en route from the palace, and should be here in the next fifteen minutes, my prince." He set the coffee service on the corner of the desk and offered a gleaming data disc to Rafael. "I have your schedule ready for today, as well as the next week, since you are currently in residence."

Oh, my God . . . Elaine lifted a hand to cover her smile. *He really is the secretary.*

Rafael took the disc and leaned back in his chair. "Erik, you remember Aramis, yes?"

"Yes, of course." Erik turned to present a small bow. "Welcome back, Lord Aramis."

Aramis smiled. "Good to see you again, Erik."

Rafael nodded toward Elaine. "This is our *enfant*, Elaine."

"Your . . . ?" Erik turned and his gaze fell upon Elaine sitting in the far chair beyond the couch. His leaf-green eyes widened. "Ah . . ." Abruptly he clicked his heels together and offered a short bow toward Elaine. "Welcome, Lady Elaine."

Elaine stiffened. "Thank you, but I'm not a lady."

Erik turned away and began pouring coffee into cups. "I beg to differ. As the child of the prince of the Penumbral Realm, you most certainly are a lady." He glanced at her briefly. "Cream and sugar?"

Elaine sat up in her chair. "Yes, both please." Then the rest of what he'd said sank in. "Prince of *what* . . . ?"

Erik stiffened and lifted his brow at Rafael.

Rafael cleared his throat and wiped a hand down his jaw. "I hadn't quite gotten around to explaining the . . . details."

Erik rolled his eyes and turned to offer Elaine a cup of coffee on a saucer, with a spoon and a small napkin. "I suggest you do so, and quickly, my prince. The senator will take great delight in taking advantage of your lapse."

Elaine took the cup carefully, her eyes wide. Someone was actually scolding Rafael?

Aramis rolled his eyes and whispered something that sounded suspiciously like, "I told you so."

Rafael took a deep breath and looked over at Elaine. "As you have discovered, there are beings that the world considers to be legendary, or mythic, but do, in fact, exist."

Elaine nodded. "That's what you were saying before."

Aramis smiled. "To continue where we left off, vampires are only one of many different races of what are currently considered mythical beings."

Elaine paused in the act of sipping her coffee. "Many? How many?"

Rafael shrugged. "Just about every type of mythical creature you can recall does, in fact, exist, though hidden from the eyes of the human population. We call this hidden world 'the Penumbral Realm.' "

"Creatures too?" Elaine felt a smile lift her lips. "Like unicorns, and dragons, and elves?"

Aramis took the coffee cup Erik had offered and smiled at the young man. "Yes."

Elaine stiffened. "What . . . ? You're saying that unicorns and dragons really exist?"

Rafael's gaze drifted to Erik. "And elves."

Erik busily slid his book from his hip and opened it. His cheeks were a rosy pink.

Aramis cleared his throat and shot a quick narrow glance at Rafael. "And since you are Rafael's direct blood descendant, and he is currently the reigning prince over the entire realm—"

"What . . . ?" Elaine very nearly choked on her coffee.

Aramis continued without pause. "—This makes you not only a lady, but a viscountess."

"A . . . *viscountess*?" She stared at Aramis, her mouth open.

Rafael shot an equally narrowed glace at Aramis. "You are also a direct descendant, and therefore a viscount in your own right, my consort."

Aramis smiled. "Why, so I am, my prince."

Elaine waved her hand. "Wait a minute! You're not just the prince of vampires, you're the prince of . . . *everything*?"

Rafael snorted and turned in his red leather chair, behind his expansive smoked-glass desk, to face Elaine. "Being prince of the Penumbral Realm is not as impressive as it might sound. While I am the acknowledged sovereign of all vampires, I'm merely the chairman of the Penumbral Senate. The senate is the true ruling power in the realm."

Elaine blinked. "There's a senate . . . ?"

Rafael nodded. "The realm is world encompassing, and far too large for only one sovereign. Each race has their own sovereign, and each land their own senator to represent their concerns to all the other lands."

Elaine tilted her head and smiled. "Like a mythical United Nations?"

Aramis smiled. "Very much like that."

Elaine shook her head. "Wow, this is . . . complicated."

Rafael nodded. "Which is why you will be needing tutors."

Erik flipped a page in his book. "I have a list of six candidates currently in residence that would make excellent tutors in social studies, political science, and history."

Elaine groaned. "I never liked political science or social studies."

Aramis snorted. "A pity, as they will be extremely important for you to know."

Elaine's lips curled into a sour smile. "Well, with unicorns and dragons, it should be a lot more interesting this time around." She frowned. "By the way, are you guys part of the actual United Nations—the human one?"

Rafael shook his head. "The human populations of the world do not know we exist."

Elaine stiffened. "Not at all?" She frowned. "But if you're all over the world, how could anyone *not* know?"

Erik shrugged. "Well, for one thing, we have magic and humankind does not."

Elaine smiled sourly. "Okay, that could explain a lot, but—"

Rafael shook his head. "All knowledge of magic—of us—is forbidden to humankind."

"Forbidden . . . ?" Elaine eased forward on her chair. "But . . . why?"

Rafael sighed and turned to face his laptop. "Because of a petty squabble between two human princes, one poorly constructed curse decimated a full two-thirds of the human population."

Elaine's frowned deepened. "*Two-thirds* of the population? I never heard anything about a war that big."

Rafael looked over at her. "But you have heard of the Black Plague, yes?"

Elaine lifted her shoulder. "Well, yeah, but that was caused by rats, or rather their fleas."

Rafael gave her a sour smile. "One rat, actually. One cursed white rat that was created for a Turkish prince who was annoyed with a Frankish prince. The curse was indeed spread by way of fleas, though—to every rat on the ship that carried it. When the Turkish ship finally landed in Europe, it released a literal flood of cursed rats that spread the curse all across Europe, killing every creature in their wake before anyone realized what had happened. To keep such an . . . accident from ever happening again, the senate passed the Covenant of Shadows, an edict created with the intent to isolate the human race from magical influence and familiarity."

Erik nodded. "The sleepers shall remain undisturbed."

Elaine frowned. "And people just . . . forgot—that fast?"

Rafael shrugged. "With the human population so heavily decimated, it only took two generations for all knowledge of our existence to be considered little more than figments of a fevered imagination."

Elaine frowned. "But your staff is almost entirely human."

Rafael folded his hands together on his desk. "When we withdrew from human society, a few human families chose to come into exile with us."

Elaine looked over at Aramis. "But there are still legends and myths?"

Aramis nodded. "Which are considered make-believe."

"And will *remain* make-believe. Humankind is entirely too destructive to be allowed even the smallest knowledge of magic." The voice was richly accented, and very deep. It was also right behind them.

Elaine turned to look.

A clearly European man approached from the main doors. He had brilliant blue eyes and a mane of midnight curls that tumbled well past his shoulders. His floor-sweeping red velvet robe was lined in black fur and was closed at the throat, with his hands folded together and concealed by the voluminous sleeves. He looked perfectly human, except for the way he walked, gently swaying from side to side, as though he moved without feet.

Aramis's mouth thinned to a straight line.

Erik moved to Aramis's side of the desk.

The man stopped by the far corner of the desk next to the chair by the coffee service. He set his hand over his heart and bowed to Rafael. "My prince."

Rafael nodded in return. "Senator."

The senator turned to Aramis and lifted a brow. "Viscount Aramis, it's been a while."

Aramis presented a small, stiff bow. "So it has, Senator."

Rafael nodded toward Elaine. "Senator Belus of Venice, this is Elaine, our *enfant*. Mine and Aramis's."

Belus's straight black brows arched over ice-blue eyes in a manner that was clearly assessing. "Indeed?"

Suddenly Elaine wasn't quite so comfortable running around in nothing but a nightgown and silk bathrobe. While the senator was quite handsome, for some odd reason, he also gave her a serious case of the creeps. However, what concerned her far more was that Aramis clearly did not like the senator from Venice. Even so, she rose from her chair, set her cup on the edge of Rafael's desk, then turned to smile at the senator, but it took some effort. "Senator Belus."

Belus's deep scarlet Cupid's-bow lips curved up into a sweet smile, which gave his cheek a dimple. "Charmed, very charmed." The senator turned and eased back into the far chair. He had a boneless grace that simply couldn't be human. "So, my prince, how new exactly is your Elaine?"

Rafael peered at his laptop. "Sixteen days."

Belus tilted his head, his brows lifting. "She hasn't even been weaned?"

In the process of sitting back down in her chair, Elaine stiffened. *"Weaned?"* She dropped into the seat like a stone. "What am I, a puppy?"

Rafael shook his head and smiled. "More like a hatchling."

"A hatchling?" Was that supposed to be *better?* Elaine scowled, crossing her arms and legs in open annoyance.

Belus chuckled, then turned to face Rafael. "As to the other matter, it seems that your . . . *cousin* has asked for a formal audience, with the several ruling members of the senate." The senator's lush lips curved into a sly smile.

"The senate?" Rafael narrowed his eyes at the senator. "Do you happen to know what he wants?"

"As a matter of fact, I do." Belus's smile broadened, showing the points of needlelike fangs. "It seems that his mountain fortress was destroyed and he needs a new place to live."

21

"His fortress was destroyed . . . ?" Rafael's eyes widened. "How?"

Belus took the cup of coffee from Erik's hands. "According to my sources, the cliff caverns, where he made his home, were bombed. Apparently, he had to dig his way to the surface, and his sudden appearance from under the rubble during a battle set off a general panic among the combatants."

Rafael wiped his hands down his face and groaned. "His aura alone would incite a panic."

Aramis folded his arms across his chest. "At least his aura is strong enough to erase any photographs."

Elaine blinked. *An aura that erases photos . . . ?*

Belus shrugged and sipped his coffee. "The local civilian population was thrilled, as the fighting was stopped for several days, giving them time to evacuate."

Rafael leaned forward on one elbow, with his chin supported in his palm, while glaring at his laptop. The long nails of his other hand tapped lightly on the glass desktop. "Where can we possibly send him?"

Belus snorted, his lips curling into a nasty smile. "Good luck finding a senator that will allow *that* creature into their region. I certainly don't want him in mine."

Rafael focused intently on his laptop and started typing.

Elaine leaned back in the chair. "Is he really *that* bad?" She swept her fingertips along the side of the chair's arm.

Aramis scowled and curled his lip, showing one long fang. "Yes."

Belus turned to smile at Elaine. "Imagine someone with very nearly the same amount of power as our prince, only completely and utterly selfish, with no concern for anyone beyond himself."

Elaine winced. "Okay, I agree that's bad."

Aramis smiled sourly. "There are those that say similar things of you, Senator."

Belus leaned back and narrowed his gaze at Aramis. "Why, yes, there are, Viscount. However, while I am indeed narcissistic, I also care a great deal for the peaceful well-being of all the people within my region."

Aramis bowed slightly. "Point taken, Senator."

Elaine felt something moving lightly against the back of her hand. Startled, she snatched her hand into her lap and turned to look.

Nothing was there. The leather arm of the chair was sleek, shiny, and spotless under the bar of moonlight that fell from the tall window.

Elaine frowned and set her hand back on the chair's arm, her hand sliding under the silvery moonlight. A faint tingling erupted along her fingers. She stiffened. *What the . . . ? Am I feeling the moonlight?* She wiggled her fingers experimentally, moving them into and out of the beam of moonlight. It felt almost as though her fingers were moving through soda water.

Elaine blinked. She *could feel* moonlight. She rolled her

eyes. *I don't know why I'm so surprised. I can feel sunlight.* Not that she'd actually seen any sunlight since her ... rebirth. Curious, she leaned on the arm of the chair and cupped her hand in the silvery light. Only, it wasn't exactly silver, the light seemed to tint her pale fingers with subtle opalescent rainbows that moved like liquid. *Wow, if only I could bottle this for paint!* On a whim, she cupped her hand.

The tingling concentrated in her palm, and her hand seemed to hold a barely visible viscous liquid.

Elaine blinked, then pulled her palm from the moonlight and into her lap. The small amount of liquid remained in her palm. She dipped her finger into it. It was thick, smooth, and slightly cool ... like finger paint. An embroidered butterfly the size of her hand on the couch caught her eye. She brushed her finger along the outline of the butterfly, smearing the semi-liquid moonlight along it.

The butterfly shimmered where the paint had coated it.

Amazed, Elaine grabbed another scoop of moonlight to paint the rest of it. In the background, the conversation continued. Since it was about people she didn't know, Elaine ignored it, concentrating instead on the butterfly she was coating in moonlight.

When the entire butterfly was coated, it turned opaque, and shimmered.

Elaine ran her fingers around the edges. It felt thick enough to be a sheet of thin plastic. She gripped the edges and peeled the paint free and set it across her palm. She stared, fascinated. A whim struck her. She blew gently on it.

The butterfly began to glow softly, then twitched. Six small legs sprouted from it, then antennae. Suddenly the wings folded, and then unfolded, like a proper butterfly.

Elaine smiled. *Wow*... But could it actually fly? She blew on it again.

The gently glowing butterfly fluttered from her hand, leaving a trail of rainbow sparkles, and flew upward. It moved in drunken circles until it passed over Rafael's desk. The butterfly circled his head once, and fluttered past Aramis's nose, then over Erik's head, then back over to Elaine's chair.

She held out her hand, grinning. *Wow, it really can fly.*

The butterfly landed in her palm, opening and closing its iridescent wings.

All conversation stopped cold.

"Elaine . . . ?" Rafael's voice was calm, but completely devoid of emotion.

Elaine looked up from her creation and suddenly realized that four pairs of masculine eyes were watching the tiny glimmering creature in her palm. A cold spike of terror stabbed her through the heart.

The butterfly in her palm popped like a balloon, scattering shimmering dust motes that promptly dissolved.

Elaine hastily set her hands behind her. "Um, I was just . . . playing?"

Rafael blinked slowly. "Playing . . . ?"

Elaine felt heat flood her face and she hunched her shoulders. "Yeah, with the moonlight."

Aramis winced.

Belus's startled wide blue gaze dissolved into narrow-eyed amusement. "Well, you did mention that she was a talented artist, my prince."

Rafael rolled his eyes toward Aramis and lifted one brow. "She didn't get *that* from me."

Aramis lifted his chin, his expression as bland as his pink cheeks would allow. "Moonlight manipulation was something I discovered . . . later."

Rafael turned to face Aramis with a slight smile lifting the corner of his lips. "And you forgot to mention this little talent because . . . ?"

Aramis lowered his brows. "I did not think it would appear so soon!" He looked over at the painting on the back wall. "And it's not particularly useful. The effects are only temporary."

A stab of disappointment went through Elaine. "It's only temporary?"

Aramis lifted his shoulder. "What you create only lasts as long as the moon is above the horizon, or until dawn. Sunlight destroys it."

Elaine slumped in her chair. *Well, there goes that idea for a new paint.*

Belus stroked his chin thoughtfully, then narrowed his electric blue gaze toward Aramis. "Out of curiosity, can you manipulate any other forms of energy, such as"—he rolled his fingers in a lazy arc—"lightning or electricity?"

Rafael shot a cold, hard glare at the senator.

"No." Aramis stepped around Rafael's desk to Elaine's side and set his hand on her shoulder. "Electrical energy in any form is . . . painful."

Belus's brows lifted. "Is that so . . . ?"

Aramis leaned down to whisper against Elaine's ear. "Think in terms of sticking your finger in a light socket."

Elaine winced and whispered back, "No playing with electricity. Got'cha."

"Hmm . . ." Erik looked out the window and frowned. "In that case, I suspect that it is your aura that is actually being manipulated."

Aramis straightened and his brows lifted. "My aura?"

Erik nodded at Aramis. "If you are using your aura, which is an extension of your soul, then, of course, you will only be able to grasp and contain only that which you can naturally handle. High-energy sources, such as electricity or sunlight, are not things a vampire deals with well."

"That would be the most logical explanation." Belus sipped at his coffee. "As there was no trace of enchantment in Elaine's . . . creation."

Rafael straightened in his chair. "Oh?"

Elaine blinked. *If that* wasn't *magic, then what* was?

Erik lifted his book and held it propped open in one hand, while using the other to pull out a black-and-gold fountain pen. "I shall make some inquiries to find a tutor in aura manipulation." He made a quick notation in his book.

More classes? Elaine rolled her eyes. "Terrific."

Erik turned his hand over and peered at his wrist. He closed his book with a snap and turned to look over at Rafael. "It is time, my prince."

Rafael rose from his chair and looked over at Aramis. "I should be back in a few hours."

Aramis pressed on Elaine's shoulder, encouraging her to stand.

Elaine rose from her chair. "Are we going somewhere?"

Rafael turned back to smile at Elaine. "I am going to work, and you are going to our suite and back to bed."

"To bed . . . ?" Elaine's hands fisted at her sides. "I can't come with you?"

Aramis set his hand under Elaine's elbow, encouraging her to stand. "The senate is far too dangerous."

Elaine snorted. "I'm not helpless."

Aramis shook his head. "I am well aware of that. However, among the senate are those to whom even vampires are prey."

Elaine's eyes widened. "Vampires are . . . *prey*?" She turned to look sharply at Rafael. "Is that why there are so many soldiers here?"

Rafael smiled sourly at Elaine. "That, and I am something of a political figure who is not always popular in my policies."

Elaine stiffened, her mouth going dry. Rafael was clearly talking about assassination attempts.

Rafael stepped out from behind his desk with a smile. "Be at ease, I am quite difficult to kill." He dropped a kiss on her brow, then lifted his gaze to catch Aramis's eye. "This shouldn't take too long. I'll be back as soon as I can."

Aramis nodded.

Rafael turned on his heel and strode toward Erik. "The door, if you please?"

Erik nodded, then strode to the far side of the ornate marble fireplace. With a hand gesture, he opened the door in the wall.

Rafael strode through the open door.

Belus eyed Elaine and Aramis briefly, then swayed after Rafael, his robes rustling softly with his movements.

Erik followed the two of them beyond the door. The door closed seamlessly into a blank wall.

Elaine looked up at Aramis. "Is the senate really that dangerous?"

"Only a few come close to Rafael in raw power, and fewer still would think to challenge him directly." Aramis lifted his arm and gently guided Elaine toward the main doors. "However, a large number of the household staff are merely human." He smiled sourly. "The guards are for their protection."

Elaine accompanied Aramis past the massive doors into the hall and glanced back at the huge guards. "The staff . . . ?"

Aramis shrugged. "It is a common strategy." He turned left, leading her into a narrow mortared-stone hallway. "When an opponent is too strong to attack directly, it's fairly common to attack their subordinates, instead."

Elaine stared at him, horrified. "But the human staff? That's—that's horrible!"

A loud hissing *pop* sounded, and two small darts buried themselves in Aramis's back. The tall vampire gasped, his eyes widening. "What . . . ?" Electricity snapped and hissed between the darts. Aramis's body spasmed and shook hard, then dropped facedown on the cobblestoned floor, twitching.

Elaine froze, unsure of what just happened. "Aramis . . . ?"

"Now that he's out of the way . . ." The voice was masculine, smug, and very familiar.

Alarm jolted through Elaine, hard. In that instant, her body reacted—by throwing her straight up. Elaine's back slammed hard against the curved ceiling of the vaulted hallway. She winced and looked up, or rather down at the floor far below.

Standing just around the corner of the archway they'd stepped through, a man in black military fatigues scowled up at her. "Shit." In his hand was a square black handgun. There were bandages around his throat and a black billed hat on his head, but there was no mistaking Dimitri's familiar face.

"Dimitri . . . ?" Fury poured through Elaine. She lunged to her feet and shouted up at the floor above her. "What did you do to Aramis, you asshole?"

Dimitri smiled sourly. "Electroshock." He pulled a cartridge from the nose of the gun, letting it fall to the floor, and pulled a small box from his hip pocket. "Unfortunately, the Taser's charge isn't nearly high enough to kill him." He slammed the box into the nose of the gun and pointed it up at Elaine. "But it'll be more than enough to deal with you!" With a loud hissing *pop*, two darts raced toward Elaine.

22

Before Elaine had a chance to think, her instincts took over. She bolted down the hallway's curved ceiling as fast as her bare feet would carry her. She took the first turn available, jumping the archway into the hall beyond.

To her stunned dismay, the ceiling proved to be a good four feet higher or, to her, feet deeper than the hallway's. She landed on her hands and knees on a floor that was heavily coffered. She rose to her feet, only to realize that running flat out was impossible without breaking an ankle. The heavily decorated framed boxes were a good six inches deep and barely wide enough for her feet. "Shit!"

Dimitri shouted from the hall behind her. "You're not getting away from me, you bitch!"

Without bothering to look behind her, Elaine began stepping along the narrow frames. "Damn it, damn it, damn it! I've got to get off this ceiling!" An archway opened up on her right, but it was four feet up. She went for it, anyway. Hopefully, that ceiling would prove easier to navigate. Gripping the white-painted arch, she hauled herself up and threw one leg over. The ceiling beyond showed another arching hallway, but this time it was redbrick and ceramic smooth. "Yes!"

"There you are!"

Elaine glanced over her shoulder.

Dimitri was pointing the Taser straight at her.

Elaine dropped over the side and rolled.

Two darts hissed past her, *thunking* into the wooden archway. There was a short burst of electrical zapping.

Elaine hiked up her skirts, lunged to her feet, and bolted down the steeply arching hallway, her scarlet bathrobe and white nightgown flying behind her. Her bare feet slapping on the smooth brick, she dodged what appeared to be hanging light fixtures and headed for what appeared to be a pair of double doors at the very end. Best of all, at the bottom of those doors high above her head were a pair of guards armed with huge guns, as well as swords.

Elaine shouted for all she was worth. "Hey! You guys!"

The guards stiffened, their hands going to their weapons. They glanced sharply around.

Elaine waved. "Up here!"

Both guards looked up, their eyes widening.

One of them scowled. "Who are you?"

The other merely looked confused. "How'd you get up there?"

"Never mind that . . . !" Elaine skidded to a stop over their heads and gasped for breath. "Aramis was shot!"

"What?"

"Where?"

She pointed behind her. "The guy's right . . . !"

A pair of darts struck each guard in the chest. Electricity arched. Both guards gasped, shook hard, then slumped to the floor.

Elaine blinked at the fallen guards. "... Behind me." She turned to look behind her.

Dimitri trotted up the hall, with a snarl on his lips, while he set new cartridges in the Taser pistols he held in each hand.

Elaine fisted her hands and ground her teeth. *Damn it! He has two of those stupid things!*

Dimitri slowed to a walk and grinned, showing long fangs. "Dead end, bitch!"

Elaine looked back at the doors before her. Their handles were down near the floor—a long, long way from her reach. "Son of a bitch!" Furious at being trapped, and by someone whose ass she'd already kicked, Elaine whirled and threw out her heel in a flying axe kick. Her heel slammed into the doors' seam.

A sharp wooden crack sounded, and both doors flew open to smash against the walls.

To her shock, Elaine found herself tumbling through the open door and into darkness. She screamed.

Her back slammed against something that cracked ominously under her. She opened her eyes to discover moonlight spilling past her. She was sprawled in the deep bowl of a domed glass ceiling of a two-story-high rotunda ballroom—the glass dome she lay in added yet another story. A careful look to the side showed her that not only had the glass cracked from her impact, the frame under her, which was holding the glass, had cracked, too.

Abject terror gripped her, freezing her where she lay. She was only one careless move from being thrown into the sky.

Far above her, Dimitri strode across the floor his gaze and his Tasers pointed upward. It was obvious that he was looking for her.

Utterly terrified to make one move, she could only watch,

knowing that it was only a matter of time before he realized where she was.

A warm yet powerful voice whispered within her. *"Elaine . . ."*

Elaine blinked. That sounded like . . . She took in a slow breath, wary of the creaking wood under her back, and spoke in barely a whisper. "Rafael?"

"Yes."

Elaine blinked and glanced about, but she saw only Dimitri. "Where are you? I don't see you?"

"I'm on my way."

She frowned. "How . . . ? How are you talking to me?"

A chuckle sounded within her. *"I'm inside you, remember? In your heart, in your blood."*

She nibbled on her bottom lip. "Telepathy?"

"Of a kind. Elaine, do you trust me?"

Elaine trembled with the effort to hold perfectly still. "Dimitri . . . he—he shot Aramis with a Taser!"

"Aramis is fine. He's on his way, too. Do you trust me?"

Elaine blinked. "Trust you? Of course."

"First, can you hear the wind around your heart?"

The wind around my heart . . . ? She concentrated and suddenly realized that the rush of wind was actually quite loud. "Yes, yes, I hear it."

"Good. Now break the window under you and let yourself go into that wind."

For an instant, Elaine swore her heart stopped. "B-break the window?"

"Yes."

"Are you sure?"

"I thought you trusted me?" The distinct feeling of pique flared through her heart. It was strangely reassuring.

Elaine let out a soft breath. "Okay."

"Cover your eyes while you pass through the glass, but once

you're clear of it, keep your eyes open. Let the wind around your heart spread until it covers you. All right?"

Elaine licked her lips. "O-okay." She took in a deep breath and slowly raised both her feet. "Here I go." She slammed down on the frame with her heels.

Wood splintered and snapped. Glass cracked and gave way. Elaine fell through.

"Elaine! Open your eyes!"

Elaine opened her eyes to see the dome of glass and the house it was attached to falling away under her. A huge black pit yawned at least a mile wide directly below her.

Alarmed, she threw her arms wide. The wind around her heart exploded out of her with a deafening roar. There was a tearing sound. Pain lanced from the back of her skull, all the way down her spine. She screamed, high and piercing.

Black feathers were suddenly everywhere, surrounding her in a thick, shimmering cloud. The pain faded utterly.

For a long moment, she couldn't see past the cloud of feathers, and then she could. In fact, she actually could make out currents in the air around her. It had become almost like water. Somewhere in that moment, gravity had righted itself, but she wasn't falling—she *wasn't* falling either up or down. She was floating on one of the currents, exactly like in her dream, but this time it wasn't a dream.

Fear disappeared, replaced by wonder.

Something at the corner of her eye caught her attention. Wings—black, yet gleaming with midnight rainbows, and they were on her back. She could actually feel them, like a second pair of arms spread wide and holding her up on the current. They moved slowly, churning the air like huge oars. Something else was there, too, at the base of her spine. She could feel it shifting like a rudder, keeping her on a slow, steady course.

She twisted around to look, and her wings moved to keep

her steady on that current. She had a tail—a feathered tail. She had wings and a tail, like a bird.

It felt strange yet wonderful. Laughter exploded out of her. She was flying, just like a bird! Or rather, like a bird had somehow attached itself to her back and was carrying her. Her wings and tail were definitely attached to her, but they were moving by themselves. The wind on her face felt warm, but it wasn't all that strong.

"*Elaine,*" Rafael's voice whispered within her. "*Look up.*"

She turned her head to look up. The silhouette of a gigantic bird floated hundreds of yards above her. It looked to be about the same size as a passenger jet. She gasped in shock, yet it didn't seem dangerous. In fact, it seemed very familiar. "Rafael?"

"*Yes.*"

She shifted to get a better look, but her wings wouldn't allow her to move very far. "Wow, you're huge!"

"*Thank you. Look below and you will see your other sire, Aramis.*"

Elaine looked downward. Another birdlike silhouette floated below her. It wasn't quite as large as the one above her, but it was much bigger than she was.

Aramis's voice entered her thoughts. "*Are you all right?*"

Elaine grinned. "I'm great!" The memory of seeing him fall from the Taser shot slammed through her. "Are you okay?" Ice-cold shame spilled into her heart. "I'm sorry I left you like that."

Annoyance shimmered from Aramis. "*Do not be. I am glad you were wise enough to run, rather than try to fight him. I was out for only a few moments.*"

"Okay." His words didn't exactly make her feel better, but she was just a little too tired to wrestle with it. She eyed the houses on the cliff and the gigantic mile-wide darkness far, far below. "Um, this is lots of fun, but how do I get down from here, and which house is ours?"

Aramis chuckled in her thoughts. *"I will show you the way."*

Above her, Rafael's silhouette eased away. *"I will join you later. Unfortunately, my work is not yet done."*

Elaine was very nearly too tired to pout. "Okay, see you!"

Below her, Aramis arched over to the right. *"Follow me by leaning in the direction you want to go, nice and slow. Do not try to control your wings. They already know what to do."*

"Okay." Elaine leaned in Aramis's direction and her body obligingly went sliding down a current in the air after him, her wings open wide. "Um, what about Dimitri?"

Aramis released a spat of annoyance. *"The guards already have him in custody. He will not bother us again."*

Elaine bit back a yawn. The last thing she wanted was to catch a bug in her open mouth. "How did he get in, in the first place?"

Aramis glided over the turrets of a huge house, clearly aiming for the wide green lawn on the far side. *"It seems that he used one of the employee entrances. Two of the guards were discovered unconscious in the garden."*

"Oh." Elaine blinked hard to keep her eyes open.

"I simply cannot believe that man's audacity for even trying to attack you in Rafael's own house." Roughly in the center of the lawn, Aramis leaned back, setting his feet before him. His wings churned, bringing him to nearly a complete stop in midair. He eased down to stand on the grass. His wings and tail dissolved into a flurry of black feathers that floated away, and faded into shadowy mist.

Elaine blinked at the sight, then leaned back to bring her feet forward. Her wings began to churn, bringing her to a halt in midair. She eased slowly downward, until her toes touched the grass. Gravity abruptly slammed into her. She dropped to her feet. Her knees promptly gave way. Behind her, her wings and tail dissolved into a flurry of midnight feathers, then mist.

Gasping, Elaine rose to one knee, but she simply couldn't make herself stand. "Wow, that's tiring."

Chuckling, Aramis caught her under the elbow and helped her to stand, but he was clearly out of breath, too. "Yes, it is." He leaned down and scooped her up into his arms. "Which is why we will need to practice."

Elaine smiled up at him. "Good! I like flying."

Aramis shook his head and carried her toward the house. "I thought you might."

Ahead of them, the French doors were pushed open and held by a pair of maids in long dark dresses and white aprons. Light from inside spilled out onto the dark lawn.

Elaine frowned up at Aramis. "I've never heard of vampires with wings, though."

Aramis lifted her higher in his arms. "Well, we are not exactly vampires. As Rafael tells it, once upon a time in ancient Persia, our race was considered gods." He smiled down at her. "There are carvings of us, of Rafael, in fact, still embedded in the sides of certain mountains."

Elaine frowned up at him. "Ancient Persia? Like, during the time of Xerxes and the Greeks?"

Aramis shook his head. "Long before that, before Zoroaster."

Elaine's eyes widened. *Before Zoroaster? Wasn't that before even the Egyptians?* "That's—that's a hell of a long time ago."

Aramis sighed. "Yes. Yes, it is. Few beings walking this earth can claim such age."

Elaine frowned up at the night sky. "I can't imagine how many friends he's outlived."

Aramis sighed. "A great many. A *very* great many." He leaned down to press a kiss to her brow. "We will talk more of this later."

Elaine meant to nod in agreement, but she ended up yawning, instead. She hastily covered her mouth with her hand. "Sorry about that."

Aramis chuckled. "It is to be expected. You have had an adventurous evening."

Elaine rolled her eyes. "Now there's an understatement!"

Aramis's smile widened. "And to think, this is only the beginning of your new life."

Elaine groaned. "Is that a threat or a promise?"

Aramis tilted his head and pursed his lips. "Both."

Elaine snuggled deep into Aramis's embrace. "Somehow I have absolutely no doubt of that whatsoever." She looked up at him. "Can we go to bed now?"

Aramis nodded. "Absolutely. In fact, I think I'll join you."

Elaine grinned up at him. "Good!"

Laughing, Aramis stepped from the night into the brightly lit mansion.

The maids closed the French doors behind them.

If you enjoyed INSATIABLE
then please turn the page for a sneak peek of
Morgan Hawke's
KISS OF THE WOLF
now on sale at bookstores everywhere!

Prologue

It was so cold. . . .

Her breath steamed from her lips. Naked and shivering, she rose from her crouch. Her long pale brown hair that fell over her bare shoulders, and the tall white dog pressed against her side, were her only sources of warmth.

The windowless basement of the abandoned textile factory was thick with shadows. She couldn't see the walls or ceiling at all. The only light came from the circular design inscribed on the worn plank floor, blazing an eerie blue all the way around them.

She needed to get out of there.

Just beyond the edge of the glowing circle, her patched corduroys, sweater, boots, and squashed cap lay in a crumpled heap on top of her canvas shoulder bag still full of undelivered newspapers. Arms across her bare breasts, she padded across the icy planked floor toward the edge of the design, heading for her clothes.

Her dog, Whitethorn, followed her toward the circle's edge, her black claws clicking on the wood floor. The dog's head stayed low, though her tall pointed ears swiveled back and forth, her silver fur glowing like the moon in the odd light.

Two rings from the edge, she rammed face-first into—nothing. She stepped back and held out her palms. An invisible wall shivered and clung to her skin like spider webbing. She pressed against the shivery nothing. Current vibrated in her bones. She pressed harder against it. The buzzing current increased, vibrating up her arms, down her spine, and in her teeth. Her hair lifted from her back. Pain sparked sharply across her palms. "Ow!" She jerked back and rubbed her hands together. *Damnit!*

There had to be a way out of this.

Hands outstretched, she wandered the entire glowing inner circle, Whitethorn's claws clicking at her side. There was no opening in the nothingness, no way out, no escape.

Whitethorn shoved her head under her hand and rubbed, begging for a pet.

She knelt and swept her hand across the thick, silky ruff around Whitethorn's neck. Her silvery white fur was sleek, warm against her bare skin.

Whitethorn's yellow eyes looked into hers, and a long pink tongue swept out to lap along her jaw.

She smiled and kissed the dog's cheek. She didn't care that the men who had kidnapped them insisted that Whitethorn was their escaped wolf. She had found her. Wolf or not, Whitethorn was the sweetest, gentlest, and smartest animal she had ever known. *Finders, keepers . . .*

Whitethorn looked off to the side, laid her ears back, and growled. Her black lips curled back, revealing long curved fangs.

Together they hurried to the design's center. No one had touched them, other then to take Whitethorn's collar and her clothes, but that could change. She'd heard horror stories about what men did to naked girls.

A tall man stepped out of the darkness in a long black over-coat. Under the curving brim of his bowler hat, the circle's blue light reflected on his dark spectacles. His orange beard and handlebar mustache seemed to glow. "My apologies for keeping you waiting." He pulled his gloved hands from his pockets.

She hunched down and clutched her dog around the neck, pressing against Whitethorn's soft, furry side. She glared at their kidnapper, the man who had put them in this cage of light. "Are you going to let us go now?"

"Let you go? But I only just acquired you." He walked around the glowing circle's edge.

She turned her head to follow him and shouted. "Who are you people, and what do you want with us? I'm just a paper-boy, and she's just a dog!"

He stopped, and his red brows rose. "How many times do I have to tell you, young lady? That is not a dog." He peeled off his black leather gloves. "That is an arctic wolf, *canus lupus arctos,* from the Alaskan tundra."

Her fingers tightened in Whitethorn's fur. "Fine, whatever you say. What has that got to do with us?"

"I am the Doctor." He shoved his gloves into his coat pocket, and his smile turned cruel. "And you are my test subjects."

A chill shivered down her spine. "You're a scientist?"

"After a fashion. Allow me to show you." He lifted his hands and recited a string of words in a language she didn't know.

The design started to shift and move, rotating in counter circles. The light brightened from blue to white.

Every hair on her body stood up.

Whitethorn's fur ruffed out, and she snarled.

The light on the floor blazed to blinding brightness.

Pain exploded in her heart and ripped through her. She fell, screaming.

Whitethorn collapsed on top of her, yelping in obvious pain.

Consumed by fire, their terrified voices joined—and ended in a single long agonizing howl.

I

November 1876

The Fairwind, *American Line steamship*
En route to Constantza, Romania

Thorn gasped and jerked upright, knocking the pillows off the small brass bed and onto the floor. Her entire body shook. She pressed one palm over her slamming heart. "A dream . . . just a dream." She shoved the long pale brown strands of hair from her damp cheeks. It was long since over and done.

She jerked the white cotton sheets from her naked, sweat-soaked body and slid from the cot to stand. The waxed hard-wood deck of the steamship's tiny iron-walled cabin was cool and rocked gently under her feet. She turned to stare out the cabin's porthole. The moon floated among rags of cloud, and the sound of the sea rushed in her ears.

Once upon a time, she had been Kerry Fiddler, an ordinary girl, with an ordinary paper route, who had found an extraordinary white dog. And then the Doctor had found them.

But that was years ago.

She couldn't stop shaking. She moved to the corner and the small washstand. "It's over and done, over and done, damnit!" She had long since become used to being someone else, some-

thing else, something wilder, something fiercer, something feral. She splashed water on her face.

The moon's light silvered the mirror's glass. Beneath her dark slashing brows, her dark gold eyes caught the light, and the hearts caught fire, glowing like two green-gold coins—wolf eyes.

The night shadows within the ship's small cabin seemed to close in on her. Her sweat-slicked skin chilled in the cool air of the cabin. She shivered and gasped for breath. She couldn't get enough air. She shook her head and forced herself to take deep, slow breaths. It was over, it was done, and she had escaped. It was nothing but a memory.

Thorn turned to look back at the moon floating outside her small window. The damned nightmare came whenever she spent too much time in too small a space. She needed to get out of this tiny iron box. She needed to run.

She took three long steps to the cabin door and jerked it open. The wind from the ocean caressed her naked skin and swept through her waist-length hair. Moonlight tinted the fine straight strands with silver. She lifted her face to the moon and let her wolf rise from her soul in a tide of fur and joy. She dropped to four paws and shook her silvery fur into place. Ears forward and long tail lifted, she trotted down the deck, her black claws clicking on the slick wooden surface.

"A large white dog was seen running loose on the ship last night." Seated behind his elegant golden oak desk, carried on-board for his express use, Agent Hackett, fine, upstanding representative of the United States Secret Service, wrote with a hasty hand. His Parker fountain pen scratched busily across the very fine parchment. "What do you have to say for yourself?" He did not look up.

Thorn Ferrell's hand tightened on the brim of her charcoal-gray leather hat. "I needed some air."

Agent Hackett scowled at his writing while working the top back onto his fountain pen. "So you ran around the deck on four legs? You couldn't do it on two like a normal human?"

Thorn didn't bother to answer him. He wouldn't have liked the reply. Why should she act like something she wasn't?

In complete contrast to her farmboy appearance, he was fashionably dressed in the attire of most governmental associates. His restrained frock coat of midnight green was buttoned over a severely understated waistcoat of black damask, and a floridly knotted cravat of black silk was tied around the high collar of his white shirt. With his blond hair combed back into a ruthless wave, and neat mustache, he was considered handsome by many.

Thorn considered him a self-righteous prig.

Agent Hackett tucked the fountain pen inside his jacket's breast pocket. "This makes four times you've exposed yourself." He gently blew across the damp ink.

Thorn rolled her eyes. "They saw only a dog. . . ."

"That is not the point." Agent Hackett ruthlessly folded the paper and reached for his stick of sealing wax. "If you cannot be trusted to control your baser urges and at least act like a human, I do not see why you should be treated as one." He struck a lucifer match against the side of his desk.

The stench of sulfur burned in her nose. She winced back. The bastard knew damned well she hated the smell of those things.

A smile twitched at the corner of his mouth. "Perhaps your return trip should be done at the end of a leash." Melted wax dripped onto the folded paper. "Or better yet, in a cage."

A leash? A *cage?* Thorn's temper flared white-hot. Did he

honestly think she would allow either to happen? She swallowed to hold back the growl that wanted to boil up from her chest. His attitude clearly begged for a reminder of whom, and what, he was dealing with, but a show of temper would only work against her. She needed something far more subtle.

She dropped her white canvas pack and dark gray, black fleeced, sheepskin coat on the expensive carpet. Casually she stepped slightly to one side, choosing a spot by the corner of his desk very carefully. She adjusted her position to allow the light from the small oil lamp to shine directly into her highly reflective and inhuman eyes. It had taken ages to figure out the exact angle, but the results were always worth the effort. Pleased, she jammed her thumbs into the pockets of her faded dungarees, relaxing into her pose.

"Now then, Courier Ferrell . . ." Agent Hackett looked up from his desk and froze, staring into her gaze. The pupils of his eyes widened, and the acrid scent of his sweat perfumed the air, betraying his instinctive alarm.

Perfect. Thorn smiled. Yes, my dear Agent Hackett, your brain may be dense, but your body knows very well that it's in a small room with a dangerous predator.

Agent Hackett tore his gaze from her eyes and lunged to his feet. Scowling, he yanked open a desk drawer and pulled out a small brown-paper-wrapped parcel with a white card. He came around the desk to tower head and shoulders over her and offered it to them. "This is the package. You already know the route. The card has the address you are to deliver it to. It is vital that you arrive as swiftly as possible."

Thorn took the package and card from his hands and then knelt to tuck them into her small canvas pack. She knew the "preferred" route, all right. It hadn't taken much to memorize the map they had provided and to deduce that she would cover the territory a hell of a lot faster if she didn't bother with roads. But Agent Hackett didn't need to know that.

He held out a second card. "When you return to Constantza, I will be at this address." His blue eyes narrowed, and his painstakingly neat mustache twitched. "No delays on the return trip, either, you wanton little beast. I don't want to remain in this godforsaken country any longer than necessary."

Still kneeling, she looked up at him. He was standing so close her lips were but a kiss away from his crotch. Well aware of her suggestive position, she smiled. "Do I really look like a wanton to you?"

Agent Hackett's eyes widened, and the perfume of lust rolled off him. She could smell the evidence of an erection growing under his knee-length midnight-green coat. He jammed the card into her hand and jerked back a step. "You look like a street urchin." His voice dropped to a growl. "However, your reputation for shameless exploits precedes you."

"Dungarees are better suited than skirts for what I do, Agent Hackett." She rose to her feet and dragged on her fleeced coat. "And I'm not ashamed of my exploits." She shouldered her pack and smiled. "I like sex."

He jerked his chin up, refusing to look at her. "Why in God's name did they saddle me with you?"

Thorn snorted. "My guess is you pissed off somebody upstairs."

His cheeks flushed, and his jaw clenched. He pointed at the stateroom door. "Get out of my sight!"

Thorn headed for the door and jammed her hat on her head, chuckling softly. Agent Hackett simply could not accept his physical attraction to her. His morals wouldn't let him. Too bad. He obviously was in dire need of a good fuck.

She stepped out onto the steamship's crowded deck and

blinked against the late-afternoon winter brightness. The icy wind from the dark Romanian port city smelled bitterly of coal smoke. The Black Sea, behind her, smelled just as strong, but far cleaner. Damp chill crept down past the collar of her sheepskin coat and up the legs of her faded dungarees. She'd thought to bring her good boots and flannel shirts, but she should have brought a heavy sweater, too.

Among good-natured farewell shouts and horrific blasts from the steamship's horns, she eased in among the ship's debarking third-class passengers and marched toward the narrow roped walkway leading down from the steamship to the dock. Setting her hand on top of her battered hat to keep the wind from blowing it away, she tromped down the gangplank into a maelstrom of humanity.

Keeping her head down, she jogged across the busy docks, dodging drays hauling freight and coaches with passengers. The occasional steam carriage chugged by, disturbing the horses with their whistling pops and loud, grumbling hisses. The train at the far end loosed a long, high whistle that raised the hair on her neck.

She entered the city proper and jogged swiftly through the wasteland of crumbling buildings, garbage heaps, and casual violence. She dodged gazes as she hurried by, just another kid in a battered sheepskin coat and faded dungarees. She snorted. The illusion would have been a lot more effective if she'd been a little more flat-chested and narrow-hipped.

Thorn reached the city's limit just at nightfall. Farmland stretched before her, and, beyond that, clean forest. Strands of her hair escaped her braid and flitted around her cheeks. Snow scented the wind.

The next leg of her journey was the easy part. Run. A lot.

* * *

The snowstorm finally ended, and moonlight bathed the snow-covered mountains and forest, creating near-daylight brilliance.

The she-wolf ghosted out from under the snow-heavy, ground-sweeping conifer, her silvery winter coat blending perfectly with the fresh snow. The chill hadn't been a problem, not with her thick arctic coat, and the long nap under the draping tree had given her a much-needed rest. She gave herself a firm shake to settle the white pack strapped to her long slender back and then launched into a gliding lope.

Her long strides and wide paws carried her atop the snow and through the moon-bright forest with blinding haste. Her sensitive nose caught occasional traces of the far smaller, and darker, red-coated European wolves that lived in the small mountain range she was passing through. They weren't too difficult to avoid. They stank from eating human garbage. She smelled them long before they could scent her.

A trace scent of human drifted on the breeze.

She stilled and lifted her nose to sift the wind. What the hell was a human doing all the way out here? Along with wool and sweat, there was something odd about the scent, something subtly wrong. . . . Her tail switched in annoyance. She figured out where the scent was coming from and moved away, deeper into the trees. She preferred avoiding humans as much as possible. She had no interest in their noisy, cramped spaces, their stinking food, and their lies about what they wanted and didn't want.

Her loping pace ate distance, and the moon drifted across the sky, marking the passage of hours. Her long strides carried her out of the forest and higher, into the mountains. The pass she was headed for was impassable for humans in winter but not for a wolf.

She moved swiftly upward over rock and snow. Her muscles

burned with the effort. Her time on the ship had held far too much inactivity. She was going to need to rest again. Dawn was only a few hours away, so finding a safe place to sleep through the day was probably a good idea. She could start out again at sunset.

Halfway up the mountain, among the cliff heights, she found a small opening in the rocks. The opening proved to be the mouth of a small tunnel. She squeezed into it and wove her way into the back, where she found a rather roomy cave. There wasn't one speck of light, but her nose told her that a tiny runnel of water slid down one wall and a crack offered a draft for a small fire.

Perfect.

She shivered into her human form. Her breath steamed out and chill bumps washed across her naked skin. It was way too cold to play human, even with a fire. She hastily dragged her pack off her back and pulled out her sheepskin coat. Throwing it on the rocky floor, she slid back into her wolf form. Warm and comfy in her thick fur, she curled up, nose to tail, on the black fleece lining of the gray coat and promptly drifted into sleep.

Scrabbling among the rocks at the mouth of the cave's tunnel jolted her out of a sound sleep and onto her paws. The fur along her back rose, and she snarled loudly. Whatever was trying to enter needed to get the hell back out or she would kill it and eat it.

Shifting stones betrayed that whatever had entered was moving deeper into the tunnel.

Her tall ears flicked forward, and her tail switched in annoyance. Just how stupid was this creature? Other than a bear, she was the biggest predator on the mountain. Her snarl should have given that away. She snarled again and gave it some serious volume.

It progressed closer.

She jolted, dancing back on her paws, thoroughly alarmed. Whatever it was, it wasn't heeding her warnings. That meant it thought it could take her in a fight. What the hell thought it could take out a wolf? It couldn't be a bear; a bear was too big to fit in the cave. It had to be her size or smaller. Was it insane?

Scent drifted into her section of the cave: wool, leather, dust, earth, old blood, and cold human.

A human? She sifted through the more subtle scents. The human was male, with silk, oil, steel, and gunpowder. A gun. She snarled in pure reaction. A stinking hunter? This high in the mountains in winter? The scent of oiled steel smelled small, like a pistol. What kind of idiot went into a wolf's cave carrying only a pistol?

She crouched, her muscles bunching tight, in preparation for a lunge. If he wanted to kill her, he was in for a nasty shock. It took a hell of a lot more than a mere pistol shot to kill her. Her voice dropped to a deep, rumbling growl. *Last chance to escape death, moron.*

Light flared in the inky blackness of the cave.

She blinked and flinched back, but her growl remained.

A man with long straight silver-white hair, swathed in a bulky black wool coat, knelt at the tunnel's exit with one gloved hand held palm up. A tiny ball of light floated above his hand—a ball of light that did not smell like fire.

Her ears flicked forward briefly. Light without heat?

He spoke in a language she didn't know, but there was no mistaking his meaning. "Wolf."

She curled back her lips and flattened her ears to her skull. Stupid human. What else did he think was growling, a bunny rabbit?

His eyes opened wide and reflected the light above his hand with an emerald-green shimmer.

Every hair on her body rose. This might look human, but it wasn't human. Human eyes reflected red, like a rat's, and they did not reflect easily.

The light rose from his palm, floating toward the cave's low ceiling.

Her gaze followed the curious floating light.

The man smiled, showing long upper incisors and shorter lower ones, the teeth of a hunting predator.

Her gaze locked on the creature's bared fangs. A deliberate challenge? Snarling in anger, she dropped to a crouch. *Fine, die.* She lunged, teeth bared to rip out his throat.

He caught her by the fur of her throat and was bowled over backward by the momentum of her charge. He snarled, baring his long teeth in her face.

She snarled right back, writhing in his grasp, snapping for his arms, his face, his throat, anything she could reach.

Twisting with incredible dexterity, he kept her fangs from his skin while holding her with ferocious strength.

She writhed and stretched her neck. Twisting suddenly, she sank long teeth into his forearm, tearing through the wool of his coat to reach flesh and blood. *Got you!*

He threw back his head and shouted in pain.

His blood filled her mouth, thick and hot—and nasty. It burned in her throat like whiskey. She pulled her fangs free but couldn't escape the taste.

His black eyes wide, he stared straight into her eyes and shouted.

A black spike slammed into her mind and sizzled down her spine. She yelped in surprise and pulled back.

His fingers closed tight in her neck fur, holding her gaze locked to his. He spoke. She didn't know his language, but the meaning was crystal clear. "Be still."

Black pressure smothered her anger. Her growls stilled in her throat, and she froze, trembling.

He spoke again, his words an indistinguishable waterfall of liquid syllables, and yet she knew their meaning. "Your bite is deep, but my blood is strong, yes?" He sat up slowly, easing her back and off him while holding eye contact. Gripping her neck fur with one gloved hand, he stroked his other gloved hand down the silver fur of her shoulder. His voice dropped to a low croon. "Yes, wolf, be stilled. Be at ease."

Languid ease infiltrated her mind and spread, making it hard to think, making it hard to stand upright. Off balance, she rocked on her paws.

"Yes, very good, you are a brave wolf." He stroked her neck and shoulders with both hands. "Rest. Lie down, and sleep."

Pressure increased on her mind. She wanted to rest. She wanted to lie down and sleep, just like he said. She stilled. Like he'd *said*? It was him; he was in her head! She jerked back.

"Wolf?" He caught her by the neck fur. "What disturbs you?" His narrowed gaze pierced into her mind, probing her thoughts with smoky black fingers.

She twisted sharply, fighting to break away, and a frightened whine escaped her throat. *Get out! Get out of my head!*

"What?" His silver brows rose and then dropped. "A wolf should not have such thoughts."

She froze. He could hear her? He was listening to her thoughts?

His gaze focused. "Human intelligence? How is this?" His curiosity drove fingers of darkness deeper into her mind, questions looking for answers.

Panicked, she twisted her head to break eye contact. *No, no, no! My secret!*

"A secret!" He gripped her neck fur and fought to keep eye contact. "Tell me your secret!"

No! She reared up and back, dragging him with her.

"Yes!" He wrestled her to the cave floor and pinned her on her side, holding her down with his greater weight. He caught her long muzzle and forced her gaze to his. "Tell me now!"

A steel spike of power slammed through the center of her skull. She howled in agony—and changed.

Thorn snapped aware, naked and curled up on the icy stone floor. She shivered and opened her eyes.

The silver-haired man poised above her on his palms, framing her naked body with his. His expression was one of complete astonishment. His eyes narrowed, and his long teeth appeared. "Who has done this sorcery?"

She wrapped her arms about herself and trembled with cold and fear. He had forced her to change into her human form. Would he kill her now?